I0630787

# ONE
# OF
# FEW

## TERRI DOTY

PERPETUALLY OFFBEAT, LLC

To those that pushed, pulled, and endured me.
You went through hell and all you got was this lousy dedication.

... And maybe pizza.

# 1

*LET'S DO THIS AND BE DONE WITH IT.*

Her muted senses caught the uproar. Keeping both eyes shut, she willed choice curses and taunts away. Leather gloves covered her whitening knuckles. After three deep breaths, she opened her eyes.

Two before her, one on the right side, another on the left, and two behind. The convoy was never fewer than this. They sat, weapons at the ready, stern expressions in place. Soldiers' uniforms, head-to-toe ebony, clashed against muted blues and grays of her own attire.

*Doing what few can. How fortunate I am.*

The work did little to make Eleven feel accomplished. Not that she complained. Unlike the so-called guardians surrounding her, Eleven lacked a sense of duty and drive.

She recoiled when a brick hit the windshield.

*Wonder what new regulation spawned this turnout. Had to be something big. Maybe a new health service mandate?*

Millions flocked to third-kind facilities each year. Their

health services provided what many viewed as miracles. Advanced technologies and knowledge couldn't be matched by anything humanity referred to as "modern medicine." The blind could see, the deaf could hear, cancers were cured, and the infertile turned fruitful. All with outpatient procedures. Though their methodologies remained need-to-know, one couldn't argue with the results. But nothing was without cost.

*Another reason for the public to hate third-kinders. To hate those that work with them.*

Eleven chewed on the inside of her right cheek.

*To hate me.*

Words from the left tickled her eardrum. Still, she kept her gaze forward. Eleven brushed back a lock of dark brown curls. She went through the trouble of adjusting the plugs wedged in both ears. Her gloved fingers made the task challenging.

People continued to approach. The swarm outside the vehicle posed no real threat. That's what those in power told Eleven and her comrades on more than one occasion. Her emotionless façade slipped ever so slightly with the growing crowd. Eleven's frustrations often fell on deaf ears. So she kept her opinions to herself as best she could.

*They have only themselves to blame.*

A heavy hand gripped Eleven's knee. Noticing her scowl, the soldier responsible released his hold.

"Are you ready, Princess?"

*How many times must I remind them about the stoppers?*

Eleven motioned to her visibly plugged ear. Her state-of-the-art stoppers were designed specifically for those with evolved auditory systems. Though it helped in the work itself, Eleven, and others like her, found it difficult to function when in public or surrounded by various unknowns.

The soldier on her left rolled his eyes. He mumbled something indecipherable. Quite a feat considering Eleven read lips. But he didn't need to know that. None of them did.

"Ready?" he signed with fingers concealed in leather.

*The gallows would be more welcoming.*

Eleven nodded. Double-checking her ears, she sighed through her nostrils. A female soldier in the front passenger seat, Designation SB47, turned away from the action. Eleven strained to focus as SB47 spouted off words, unbothered by the secured plugs.

"Fuckers are getting restless," SB47 joked to her comrades.

*It bothers her to sign. Likely because it's a skill involving zero bloodshed.*

A flash to the communicator on SB47's left shoulder stopped her mid-chuckle. She responded while motioning with a series of nods and gestures to the others in the cramped vehicle. Glancing at Eleven, SB47 signed, "We're all set, Princess."

*Her Majesty, My Lady, My Liege, Your Highness, Princess... When a guardian finds something amusing, how they love to drive it into the ground.*

Eleven wasn't a soldier like them. The jabs made light of their requirement to constantly supervise her. This, paired with preferential treatment from higher-ups, irked those like SB47.

*Prattle on.* I'm *not interchangeable.*

Doors opened from all sides. Eleven held her breath as others vacated the vehicle. However fleeting, she appreciated the illusion of being alone as the doors slammed shut in disjointed harmony.

*Best part of my day. How pathetic.*

Eleven fiddled with the strap of her worn leather messenger bag. She dug a gloved thumbnail into thick grooves of the knitted fabric. Subjecting herself to the cretinous public unnerved her. Anything a guardian said, whether in front of her or not, paled in comparison to what onlookers served up. As the right passenger door opened, Eleven drew the hood of her ash-colored long coat up before braving the less-than-adoring public.

*Here we go.*

Daylight stung her sensitive eyes. Her fair complexion brightened, reflecting rays of sunlight. Despite her stoppers, the outcries distracted her.

"You're monsters!"

"Abominations!"

One shout of "No third-kinders" turned into a chant.

*They could at least be creative.*

SB47 led the way with AM23, second-in-command, by her side. One guardian on Eleven's right, another to the left, and two followed at the rear. Peering down, Eleven kept in line with the military detail. She got a sense of the crowd through peripheral glances. Her accomplices had not overstated the present situation. Hordes of people surrounded fenced-off areas near a dilapidated parking garage. They headed toward the concrete structure.

A boy no older than twelve caught Eleven's attention. He fervidly waved a sign with language beyond his comprehension.

*How do these zealots keep finding us?*

Chain-linked barriers created a clear path to the concrete entrance. Additional guardian forces, though meant to ease tension, intensified matters. Civilians pushed against the tall fences. Eleven caught herself moments before colliding into SB47's rigid form. Calls and curses from the horde dwindled as her detail came to a halt. The faint sound of sirens penetrated her ears.

*Perfect.*

Rumblings from below cracked the already fractured ground. As seismic activity grew, many civilians fell to the splintered gravel. Others covered their heads as they scattered for shelter. Eleven's detail gave no indication of concern. As they'd done several times before, the group widened their stances. Guardians near the fences protected the barriers from potential breaks.

Aside from fisting both gloved hands and straightening her arms, Eleven stood still amidst the chaotic tremors. She watched as loved ones scurried to find one another, running to safety.

*They act as though this is something new.*

In less than two minutes, the sirens stopped, as did the shaking. SB47 took advantage of the distraction. She motioned to continue through multiple plastic-like sheets at the garage's main entrance. Holes in upper levels still ached from the quakes. The center of the forgotten lot's lowest level swarmed with bustling soldiers and temporary monitors. Many hurried to recover the space from the prying public and unconfined access points.

SB47's crew evaluated the area. A couple of guardians paused when noticing their arrival, several eyes landing on the woman at the center of the detail. Eleven drew back her hood as all but SB47 dispersed. She winced as she removed the stoppers, failing to adjust quickly to the strange environment.

"Five by five, My Liege?" asked SB47.

Eleven thought better of a verbal response. Her words had a tendency of being misinterpreted. Using her index finger, middle finger, and thumb, Eleven signed that she was okay.

"Yeah, I'll bet."

SB47's sneer waned as an unfamiliar guardian approached. The tall muscular man with caramel skin and hair buzzed to the scalp carried an eagerness never seen in the experienced. The soldier tried desperately to fit in, making him stand out all the more.

*They sent unseasoned recruits on a daytime mission? This just keeps getting better.*

"Designation?" SB47 prompted.

"HD62, ma'am."

"You can drop the *ma'am* shit," she replied. SB47 scrutinized him from head to toe. "Perimeter sweep?"

"Nearly complete," he answered. "The quake slowed progress, so we're just—"

"Local law enforcement?" SB47 interrupted.

"Limited. We're attempting to pull from neighboring counties."

"By the time they get here, we'll have packed up."

Before HD62 could answer, the commander disregarded him. He closed his mouth fast as she moved farther into the garage's center and spoke with others.

*I'm his first locator.*

His awed glance at Eleven proved her theory.

*Bully for me.*

Turning away from him, Eleven grazed teeth against her lower lip. The removal of her thin gloves put the graphite-like etchings near each nail's cuticle on full display. Widening her fingers, she closed her eyes. She waited for just the right note to present itself.

*Where is it?*

The hard clearing of a throat broke her concentration. HD62 continued to stand behind her. Eleven said nothing as she glared at him.

"Don't mean to wreck your zen, but just wanted you to know that we're almost set."

Without acknowledging the guardian, Eleven stalked about the concrete environment. Her fingers wiggled as she paced, feeling out the area and tuning out external factors. In spite of HD62's wide proximity, his presence still unsettled Eleven.

"Something else?" Eleven asked over her shoulder.

"No, ma'am."

Eleven took two steps, as did HD62. She faced him. "While I understand this is your first field assignment—"

"That obvious, huh?" A corner of HD62's mouth turned up.

Exhaling, Eleven looked past him. Her crew, as well as the other guardians, were less than amused. Still, they did nothing to stop the new recruit. Interruptions increased the likelihood of unwanted attention.

"Quite," she replied. HD62 opened his mouth to speak again when Eleven stepped forward. She sustained eye contact until her point was clear. The new recruit eventually withdrew.

Guardians understood intimidation more than anything else. Their mutual abhorrence left casual chatter to a minimum. HD62 would be better served learning this sooner rather than later.

"Problem, Duchess?" SB47 asked from afar.

Shaking off distractions, Eleven returned to the task at hand. She raised her arms until they ran parallel with the floor, resuming her earlier pacing. The closer she got to what remained of an elevator, the stronger the sensation. Fingertips ached and a hum vibrated her earlobes. She stretched her right hand forward as both eyelids fell.

*No—Not quite.*

When Eleven's hand aligned with her abdomen, she paused. Dropping her left hand altogether, the locator opened her eyes.

*There you are.*

She extended her right middle finger until she hit resistance. Eleven moved her hand clockwise in a spiral motion. Her steady wrist made another turn. And another.

*Okay. Let's see what we've got.*

Taking a deep breath, Eleven thrust her hand into the void. From HD62's perspective, part of her limb vanished. Seconds later, she retracted a box glowing like embers.

"What's the verdict, Locator Eleven?"

The locator examined the object. "Nanbo in origin."

"Dangerous?" SB47 asked.

"Not likely."

Eleven pulled her satchel forward. She placed the unusual container in the bag's deepest pocket. The locator found a bewildered HD62 staring at her.

"Pack it up, boys and girls," SB47 commanded. "We got what we came for."

Soldiers tore down makeshift barriers in an instant. Members of Eleven's crew contributed. She stood in place, busying herself with retrieving stoppers from her coat. Another guardian forced HD62 to assist in the tear down.

Tumbling rubble from above made everyone look up. A large crack allowed a peek to the upper level. Booted strides resonated as a slender shadow ran out of view.

"Fuck me." SB47 hit her communicator. "Possible unfriendlies. Second floor. Proceed with caution."

The communicator beeped. "Ready EMP?"

"Unclear on device capabilities," SB47 responded.

"Got nothing topside," another radioed.

"Find them," SB47 replied. The guardian surveyed her numbers. "Four at the entrance, two at the vehicle." She paced as she schemed. SB47 slowed in front of HD62. "How many are you?"

"There are six of us, ma'am."

SB47 motioned to AM23. "Suggestions?"

"Securing the locator and chamber contents is top priority."

"Think newbie's got a chance at tracking down whoever or whatever the hell was up there?" SB47 asked.

"We can do it," HD62 said as he stepped toward SB47.

AM23 groaned. "If sweeps had been carried out properly, we wouldn't be in this bind. Gonna tell me that's not on you?"

Another beep from SB47's communicator. "Two down. No fatalities."

"Unfriendlies?" SB47 pressed.

"Ghosts, ma'am."

"They could be using the crowd as cover," AM23 said.

SB47 cursed to herself before hitting the com on her shoulder. "EMP at the ready. Weapons too. Conceal arms unless engaged."

"Formation," AM23 ordered. Guardians surrounded Eleven.

HD62 frowned. "You're gonna take her out there without any confirmation as to numbers or intent?"

"They're gone, all right?" SB47 snapped. "And so are we. Clean up your own goddamn mess."

Eleven re-secured her stoppers and thin leather gloves. She took one last glimpse at the disheartened recruit as she pulled up her hood.

SB47 ignored HD62's further inquiries, motioning the detail to move. The guardians and their locator proceeded back to the fenced pathway.

Innumerable factors at play gave the locator pause. On occasion, SB47's ineptitude in acclimatizing to unforeseen complications resulted in bloody consequences. Much had changed since the group entered the broken-down concrete cube. With guards no longer present, the trail appeared more grueling than the original trek. Pressure from the masses sagged and warped their chain-link barricade. Numerous people snapped photos with handheld portables, while others hurled insults, threats, and questionable liquids.

*Just get me back.*

Gunshots rang out. The guardians around Eleven searched for a source, to no avail. SB47 motioned for her people to stop entirely, but the ensuing pandemonium proved the order difficult. Panic along the perimeter reached a breaking point. Eleven ducked as her guardians warded off the bulk of a falling fence.

"Get to the transport!" SB47 said.

The weight of panicked civilians exacerbated the guardians' attempt to remove the fencing. All seven of them were pushed to the ground. AM23 broke formation to reach for a nearby post. The gamble paid off, giving them much needed leverage. Keeping their backs to Eleven, her detail hurried to the transport.

People crashed against the guardian circle. Their go-to configuration was no match for the chaotic current of bodies. As the circle disintegrated, Eleven lost her balance and fell hard. The six guardians rushed back into formation with someone dressed like her at the center.

"Wait!"

The madness muted her cry. Scurrying legs made it tough to keep eyes on her retreating detail. A toothed piece of aluminum caught her leather boot.

*I will not be left behind.*

Willing herself to keep breathing, Eleven tore at the fencing. Her gloved hands didn't help in her efforts. Finally, she yanked her foot free of its constraints.

In spite of her limited view, she attempted the original trajectory. Bodies bumped against Eleven. Frenzied swaying threw her in every direction but the one she desired.

*North. Remember north. We parked north of the garage—unless they moved the convoy while we were inside.*

The locator hugged her messenger bag.

*Stay calm. If they leave, someone else will come. Someone better. Maybe even—just remember protocol. Don't engage civilians. Don't attack unless provoked... What else? Think.*

Rough hands gripped her. With no time to react, Eleven was lifted to face a filthy man with bloodshot eyes. He tugged on her coat and messenger bag.

*Protect chamber contents at all costs.*

Eleven moved to the side to throw her attacker off balance. The ploy gave her enough momentum and opportunity to push the crazed man into an opposing flow of the swarm surrounding them.

A hard knock to her right temple from a stray elbow brought Eleven back to the ground.

*Remember... protocol.*

An audible assault signaled the loss of a stopper. Eleven hastily covered her right ear to block the now half-impeded wild noise. Her frustration and pain blended into the crowd's panic.

*There's too much—why are they so loud?*

The locator clutched the bag while keeping her eyes shut. She allowed herself to be trampled as she curled into a ball.

*Why haven't they come back? Would guardians risk losing me? I'm lost without them.*

The onslaught of sounds became too much. "Shut up!"

A calloused hand grabbed her wrist. An aged brute of a woman sneered at Eleven's ensemble. She jerked the locator upright.

"I've got one of them!" the old woman said as she revealed a gun.

An arm wrapped around Eleven's collarbones. "Pretty one, ain't she?"

"Seen better." The woman gestured to Eleven with a wave of her pistol. "What do you think?"

Eleven cringed at the man's proximity and, most notably, his stench. "Think we got a good pay day with this one. Imagine what third-kinders would dish out to get a lab rat back."

*Talk about adding insult to injury. They think I'm a guardian?*

The man's body stilled as a low voice said, "Remove yourself from her."

He released Eleven immediately. She turned to find HD62 pressing a short blade against her attacker's spine.

"Let him go," ordered the woman.

When HD62 didn't respond, Eleven said, "Violence is prohibited."

The guardian smiled. "Not when acting in self-defense."

Aiming at Eleven's head, the female assailant added, "I'm not asking again."

"Drop the gun." HD62 pulled the man closer to him. Both the woman and Eleven tensed. "You might get a shot off. But not before I paralyze your boy here. That's one of the happier outcomes."

The woman tossed her weapon to Eleven's feet. HD62 shoved the man away. The would-be kidnappers fled the scene, disappearing into the crowd.

Eleven tilted her head at the guardian's display of machismo. HD62 kicked aside the archaic revolver. Without a word, he took her by the hand.

After minor scrapes and throws, the two made their final approach toward the transport. Eleven's detail showed no relief upon seeing her or HD62. Her earlier stand-in was nowhere to be found. They hurried to Eleven's side.

A distinct click slowed Eleven's run.

*No.*

Eleven's eyes widened as fire and force ripped apart the convoy vehicle. Energy from another wave of explosions threw everyone to the ground. Flying back, Eleven brought the messenger bag to the front of her.

*When will it end?*

A shard of glass slid across her forehead. Eleven's lungs emptied in a rush as she landed hard on her back. Her sight doubled as a deafening ring muted the disaster around her. She ignored a dull pain in her stomach.

Near Eleven, HD62 rolled to his side, muttering curses. At least, that's what the locator assumed. In her present state, Eleven could barely make out the lines of his face. Cries of pain and loss became clearer.

*Get me out of here.*

"We have to—Christ!" HD62 crawled to her. "You're gonna be okay. Don't move."

"What?" Eleven followed his eye line.

*That explains a few things.*

A slickened fencepost jutted out of her abdomen. Irritated, Eleven tugged at the post with little to show for her effort. She stopped when sensing eyes, electronic and otherwise, watching her.

*Protocol.*

Hitting his communicator, the guardian said, "Designation HD62 requesting cleanup to Locator coordinates. Authorization: Juliet Foxtrot Delta Alpha." He took in the crowd. "Immediate EMP surge. I repeat, EMP, ASAP."

*No witnesses.*

Within seconds of HD62's request, all documenting the incident crinkled their brows. Sirens followed.

"Cavalry's coming." HD62 leaned down to Eleven's ear. His breath warmed her lobe. "Better play dead until then." She relaxed in his delicate embrace. He lowered her to the ground and closed her eyes with a brush of his fingers.

•••••••••••

A CRUDE TWIST AT ELEVEN'S TORSO ROUSED HER. Medics yanked at the post firmly lodged in her side. "Sorry to disturb your slumber, Princess."

The locator surveyed the tight space she found herself in. Her vision narrowed at the fluorescent lighting and off-white surfaces. Incessant swaying from the bumpy ambulance ride didn't help her unease. Two medics towering over Eleven pulled again at the object in her abdomen.

"We need you to hold her down," one said.

HD62 hovered over Eleven with reservation. "Shouldn't you dose her first?"

"You must be new," the medic replied.

Chuckling, the other added, "We got you covered, don't worry. Just do us a solid and keep her steady."

The guardian disregarded the dirty looks from the two men.

He put his weight onto Eleven's shoulders. Studying the metal fragment, HD62 asked, "This gonna hurt?"

"No more than a bee sting," joked the first medic.

Eleven bit her lip.

*Keep it together.*

Against her will, she let out a guttural sound when they tried again. As the rough cylindrical item left her body, Eleven went limp. HD62 pushed aside her frizzed hair while wiping her sweaty forehead.

"Come on, Princess. Not like you haven't had worse," said the first medic. "Probably."

HD62 glowered at the chuckling pair, though neither considered him. The guardian moved to Eleven's side and took her drooping hand.

The locator intertwined her fingers with HD62's as the familiar process began. Minor gashes on her neck and face had already vanished. Eleven winced as the tissue at her torso reassembled itself.

She ignored the guardian's eyes. Instead, Eleven focused on the stinging sensation which accompanied healing. New skin soon became indistinguishable from older bordering skin.

"Amazing," HD62 stammered.

"If only we were all so lucky," added the second medic as he approached the guardian. Without warning, he injected a substance into HD62's jugular. "Has a bit of a kick. You'll want to rest up after eating something."

*Dilated pupils… inflamed eyes.*

Unlike a locator, a guardian's ability to heal stemmed from a vialed concoction—the contents of which remained secret to all but a select few.

Eleven freed herself from his hold. Slowly easing upright, she inspected her bloodied and torn apparel.

*Damn. I liked this coat.*

Remembering the purpose of today's excursion, Eleven

scoured every viewable surface. She sighed in relief when her eyes landed on the worn satchel behind HD62.

"Think I'd let you forget?" the guardian asked through a weak smile.

"I seldom give guardians the benefit of the doubt."

"Well, that's just common sense. Especially after—"

The driver interjected. "Your presence has been requested, Locator Eleven."

"Am I expected upon arrival?" The silence that followed served just as well as a verbal response.

Eleven slid down to her back. She covered both eyes with a heavy arm. A summons meant a visit to the home office. The calls were anything but social.

*Hope she's in a good mood.*

# 2

ELEVEN'S TRANSPORT TOOK THE LONGER, LESS scenic route back to Region 5 headquarters. Her view of the outside was limited, most windows being blacked out or covered. Gazing out the windshield, she kept her eyes on the barren streets. Few vehicles busied the roadways. Concrete tunnels underground made the journey bleaker than Eleven's morning trip.

HD62's cheery disposition waned in his short time with her. He ended attempts at small talk after his third failure to get a laugh out of Eleven. The jittery guardian scrutinized her in stolen glances, as did she.

Just under the three-hour mark, they arrived. The sharp lines at corners and scale-like exterior of the cluttered buildings always took her breath away. Her eyes fixed on the tallest structure at the core.

*How long before I can lock myself up for the night?*

After passing checkpoint after checkpoint, her convoy entered a hanger in the fringes of the complex. The building disappeared from view moments later.

Eleven sat stock-still as others around her scurried else-where. Guardians, including those in her detail, went their respective ways. HD62 hesitated before leaving Eleven's side. After taking a deep breath, Eleven exited the vehicle. Two stoic soldiers waited for her straight ahead.

*Onsite chaperones. At least they're not Banaedrut.*

The armor-coated men said nothing as she walked between them. Bulbs overhead lit her skin in an unflattering alabaster hue.

Eleven's stomach growled. She put a hand to her bloodied blouse in an effort to cease the hunger pangs.

*Took more to heal than I thought. I should've eaten more this morning.*

All three came to the end of a hallway. The soldiers each went to a side of the door while Eleven stood at its threshold. Nothing gave an indication as to what loomed on the other side. Due to past experiences, Eleven had more than an inkling as to the room's hazardous potential.

*Can't be worse than anything the good doctor cooks up... unless her plan involves him. Stop acting like you have a choice in the matter.*

Eleven twisted the doorknob, allowing herself a small breath as she entered. Four white, unaccented walls with a comparable ceiling and floor lay before her. Save for a minimalistic desk and two chairs, no furniture inhabited the space.

A tall, reserved being sat behind the desk. To the left of the seated female entity stood her trusted advisor. Curious alien eyes analyzed holographic images and texts that hovered above the desk. The two didn't acknowledge Eleven's presence. Trah-Ul of the once-great Ceruleman Empire sat across from the tattered locator. Dyssae, part of an order of Ceruleman knights called Banaedrut, seldom left her side.

Nicknamed a Blue Blood by human advocates, the alien

royal differed from that of an average third-kinder. Similar to humans, a common Ceruleman or Banaedrut had the capacity to blend in a public setting until closer inspection. They carried their lanky frames and moved with an exotic ease. Oval-shaped cobalt irises disturbed the astute observer. All but the area surrounding their eyes had a naturally sallow hue, varying from pale pink to deep purple. More third-kind in appearance, Trah-Ul and her brethren had crystalline-like flesh and elongated skulls.

*Speak only when addressed. How long will she make me stand here?*

Trah-Ul acknowledged the disheveled locator after completing her analysis. The Blue Blood took in Eleven's grave appearance. Trah-Ul made no indication of dissatisfaction or irritability. She turned to Dyssae and nodded. He gestured to the empty seat across the desk.

*Great. She wants me to sit. Sitting implies I should get comfortable, as if that were possible in these circumstances.*

Clearing her throat, Eleven approached the two. Her stomach rumbled. She curbed her discomposure as she reached the metal side chair and sat.

Trah-Ul intertwined her thin, lengthy fingers on bare counter space. "Why have I called for you?" The colorless voice conveyed not a single tone Eleven could categorize. Leaning against the seat's cool backing, she forcibly relaxed fingers and palms in her lap.

*Oh, let's see… my crew abandoned me while on mission, resulting in my almost being taken by crazed, weapon-wielding—no. Somehow I doubt that's the way to begin.*

"Today's assignment," Eleven answered.

Dyssae's eyes flicked to her grisly attire. Unlike Trah-Ul, he was easy to read. His apathy for locators, guardians, and sympathizers suggested a mere tolerance. Dyssae never contradicted his beloved master in her dealings with those outside their race. Few questioned a Blue Blood's actions and lived.

"Civilian interaction is strictly prohibited," Dyssae said. "You are aware of this."

*Ah. I see reports were filled out in record time today.*

"I didn't deliberately engage, sir."

Referencing the hologram, Dyssae continued. "You separated from your unit during extrication."

"Again, sir, I didn't—"

Dyssae interrupted. "Multiple accounts state otherwise."

*Multiple accounts that likely make no mention of my stand-in or how easily they were manipulated.*

Eleven's eyes fell from Trah-Ul's council to the documents floating between them. She could read backwards and out of sequence, so she scanned the reports. Each guardian account, save for one, listed her responsible for the disorder that followed their mission.

"Locator Eleven, what do you have to say?" Trah-Ul asked.

"Nothing."

"Nothing?" Dyssae pressed.

Tilting her chin up, Eleven said, "Nothing that wouldn't contradict the statements before you."

Trah-Ul deterred Dyssae with a raised hand. "By all means," she started. The elegant extraterrestrial pushed away from the table. Trah-Ul circled the desk and moved past the locator. Stopping directly behind Eleven, Trah-Ul rested palms on the top corners of her chair's backing. "Negate."

*This ought to do wonders for my popularity.*

"Though I believe it unintentional," Eleven began, glancing at Dyssae, "my extraction was sloppy at best. Ill planning, namely on the part of lead Designation SB47, resulted in numerous uncertainties. Lack of forethought culminated in my protectors unknowingly deserting me."

Trah-Ul clasped her hands. Dyssae's changing gaze hinted at his master's agitation. Eleven stared at the wall behind the

Banaedrut soldier.

"What do you make of the undetected emissary?" asked Trah-Ul.

"Little."

The Blue Blood turned back around to Eleven. Trah-Ul leaned against the edge of her desk and peered down at the locator. "Haven't the slightest notion?"

"That isn't what I meant, ma'am."

"Rather than hint, elaborate," Dyssae said.

Eleven looked up to her superior, straining her neck in doing so. The two locked eyes. "Whoever they were, they're highly organized. Our methodologies are familiar to them. The transport's destruction is clearly connected. Maybe even the frenzied state of local citizens."

Dyssae tilted his head. "And?"

"And someone posing as me in great detail," Eleven finished.

"Reports make no mention of a doppelgänger."

"Yet surveillance picked up nothing near the convoy. You don't find this suspicious?"

*Snapping at a superior? Brava, Eleven. I'll end up in observation within the hour at this rate.*

"Are you suggesting Designation SB47 intentionally omitted this from official record?" Dyssae asked.

"No. She's loyal." Eleven sighed. "Just misled in this case, sir."

"Such a summation is anything but little." Trah-Ul's eyes fell to Eleven's feet. The locator's satchel rested against her right boot. "Despite your difficulties, the assignment was still successful."

"Yes."

Trah-Ul bowed her head. "You do us proud."

"Thank you, ma'am. Would you like to see?"

"A trinket from Nanbo carries no importance," Dyssae

scoffed.

Trah-Ul's mouth turned up. "A locator's efforts are appreciated all the same." She returned to her seat behind the desk with Dyssae pulling out her chair.

Dyssae shut off the hologram. "In a scenario where the electromagnetic pulse had not been a viable option, what would you have done, Locator Eleven?"

*Continued to cower in the fetal position.*

An alternative didn't present itself. The most probable outcome would have been the decimation of every observer in the immediate vicinity.

*Who says they stopped at the EMP? No. They wouldn't kill that many people in broad daylight.*

Eleven's aversion to the masses notwithstanding, genocide had never been a welcome thought. Yet it happened. Civilians could only see so much of Ceruleman dealings, only what they wanted the public to know. Neither mining fourth dimensional pockets nor witnessing an impaled woman heal herself fell under this heading.

"I'd have continued to rely on guardian intervention." Eleven adjusted in her seat. "Their purpose is to protect and serve. It is not for me to question."

"And Designation HD62?" Dyssae asked. "What do you make of the guardian?"

*Strange. Unsettling.*

Eleven exhaled. "If not for him, I am unsure of what my current state would be."

"A troubling thought," Trah-Ul replied.

Dyssae glared at Eleven. "Agreed."

"Has your confidence in Designation SB47 wavered?" Trah-Ul asked.

*Trust is a funny thing.*

"I remain confident in the abilities of all my guardian brothers and sisters."

"Very well." Trah-Ul forced a smile.

"You are dismissed," Dyssae told Eleven.

Throwing a strap over her shoulder, she left the confines of Trah-Ul's uninviting office without another word or glance. The soldiers at the door did not follow.

Eleven relaxed as she turned the corner but kept her pace steady.

*That could have gone worse.*

· · · · · · · · · · ·

*I SHOULD'VE JUST BRAVED THE PLEBEIANS BLOOD-spattered and begrimed.*

The impromptu debrief hindered Eleven's normal dine and dash practice. As the freshly showered locator entered the headquarters' cafeteria, she groaned at the long line to her left. The commissary held hundreds, capacity never being a factor. Its smooth, matted walls devoid of color tricked the untrained eye to make it appear larger.

Glancing side to side, Eleven approached the somewhat stationary line. Opening chambers and healing did wonders for the metabolism. Eleven debated eating there or retreating to her room.

*Peace and quiet be damned. I'm starving.*

Row after row of rectangular tables hinted at camaraderie. Living in close quarters led one to believe that locators, guardians, sympathizers, and Cerulemans got along. Most stuck to their own. Some strictly ate. Others used the space as an alternative workstation.

Catching snippets about today's mission, Eleven's pace turned brisk. She willed away the frustrations of the day. Instead, the locator fixated on the slow traffic of the food line. Every delay worsened both hunger and attitude.

Less than an hour later, she exited the opposite end of the

line with two overflowing trays, the majority of food being carbohydrates or questionably processed. Laughter carried from numerous tables. Most soldiers occupied the corner nearest the kitchens. As Eleven passed one of many guardian-filled tables, conversations cut off.

"Duchess!"

Hollow from starvation, Eleven continued to search for a free table. Determined footsteps followed the unpleasant scraping of metal against stone. The locator came to a stop.

"Turn around."

*What I wouldn't give for another EMP surge.*

"I know you heard me."

"Leave me be," Eleven said over her shoulder.

"Or what? I'll get into deeper shit?"

*That isn't a rhetorical question, is it?*

The area fell quiet. Eyes became glued to the developing scene. Eleven placed the two food trays on a neighboring bench. She snatched a fry before facing SB47.

"Disciplinary leave for the lot of us. Now why do I feel like you had something to do with that?"

Far from her first confrontation, the sheer gall of SB47 in that moment amused Eleven. "The decision was not mine."

"Right."

The very public assertion went monitored by onlookers and cameras throughout. In defiance of protocol, the guardian chose hostility over better judgment. SB47 closed the distance between them with mere centimeters separating the two.

"Is that all?" Eleven asked.

SB47 slapped her. Whispers rose from the crowd circling them. With hands on her hips, Eleven tested her jaw, moving it from left to right. Her vacant expression further frustrated SB47.

"They wouldn't have done shit to you. Why couldn't you just leave it alone?"

"What would you have me do, SB47? Apologize? I owe you nothing. Best we leave it at that."

As Eleven returned to her trays, SB47 pounced onto her back. The locator landed chest-first onto cold flooring. Her attacker's weight knocked the air from her lungs. Eleven was forced to lie on her stomach.

An unseen bystander spoke up. "Designation SB—"

"This doesn't fucking concern you, pencil pusher."

The guardian ran fingers through Eleven's hair, yanking a section. SB47's breath warmed Eleven's cheek. "Do you have any idea what you've done?"

Eleven winced as chairs scratched the floor and silverware fell to trays. Many had risen for a better view of the altercation.

*Not a Ceruleman in sight. Typical.*

SB47's incessant pulling caused Eleven's scalp to throb. The locator licked her lips, debating on whether or not to reply. She twisted her neck as best she could to face SB47.

"How is this bettering your situation?"

"Designation SB47," said an unmistakable voice.

*Damn it. Anyone but him.*

Though the grip on her hair loosened, Eleven's muscles constricted further. SB47 peered upward to a clean-shaven man with a crisp lab coat standing amidst a gap in the crowd. He nudged his glasses into place.

"Isaac, I—"

"Dr. Kepler," he corrected. The doctor adjusted his tie as he took a step in their direction. "And don't waste your breath in backpedaling."

SB47 hurried to her feet. She adjusted her clothing and wild hair as Isaac approached. Meanwhile, Eleven remained on the floor.

"Locator Eleven?"

*He's nothing.*

Eleven sucked in a breath before standing. She avoided

Isaac's gaze—instead she stared at her neglected food. Silence grew through the grand hall. The locator rubbed a temple with the back of her dominant thumb, only allowing a peripheral view of the doctor.

"To your quarters."

"Who?" SB47 asked Dr. Kepler.

Isaac frowned at the guardian. "That question isn't worthy of a response, Designation SB47. This outburst suggests an adjustment to your dosage may be required. We'll discuss it at length later."

*That's going to be a one-sided discussion.*

Peering over in the direction of her comrades, SB47 found her table empty. She lowered her head as she shuffled to the exit. Not even a breath accompanied her departure.

"As you were," Isaac said to the crowd.

Sounds picked up and strengthened. Eleven eventually allowed herself a glance at Dr. Kepler. She found him watching her with great interest. His face softened as their eyes met.

"We have an appointment, correct?"

"Yes."

Isaac pushed up his glasses. "I'll be expecting you shortly."

As Eleven watched Dr. Kepler leave, another man stole her focus. Freckles above the cheek, unruly dirty blonde hair, and a tan complexion caused his grey irises to stand out. He leaned broad shoulders against the entrance's doorframe. Armed with a smirk, the man raised an eyebrow at Isaac as he exited. Neither acknowledged the other further.

The right corner of Eleven's mouth twitched. Ignoring the glares, she picked up the food trays. Eleven sauntered over to the sly individual.

His smirk deepened as she advanced. "Do you consider this a dull moment?"

"In comparison," Eleven replied.

"Tad dramatic." Stepping away from the entrance, he picked

at the food on her trays. She didn't protest in the slightest. "Even for you."

"Considering the day I've had—"

"Tell me about it."

The locator entertained the idea. "If only."

"Skip your assessment."

*You can't dodge another appointment.*

"It's not that simple. You, of all people, should know this."

"What's Kepler gonna do?"

"Another time," Eleven said.

"Come on. They need us a hell of a lot more than we need them. Don't forget that." The man laid on a wicked grin. He always had a way of soothing her just with his mere presence. Leaning forward, he added, "Catch me up."

*The good doctor isn't going to like this—to hell with him.*

The locator smiled. "You're incorrigible."

"You love it." Eleven turned to the nearest table. The man took a tray from her. "Not here."

He walked out of the mess hall. Eleven considered her remaining tray. The food had cooled. "Ten."

"Better keep up," he called. "You know poorly prepared penne vodka is my favorite."

• • • • • • • • • •

SITTING ATOP THE TALLEST BUILDING ONSITE, Eleven and Ten enjoyed the solitude. Or, at least, the veneer of it. No one on the complex was ever truly alone, though a vacant rooftop often tricked one into thinking otherwise. Minimal external force counterbalanced the stunning views it lacked. Miles away, the nearest metropolis's lights were barely visible.

"All the good stuff happens to you."

Eleven rolled her eyes. "That isn't remotely accurate."

Ten picked at stray bits of abandoned cuisine, waiting for her to open up. Eleven chewed on a now stale biscuit. She'd made quick work of the first tray of food and was relishing her second helping.

Undeterred by his friend's trademark standoffishness, the tenth locator pressed on. "Felt tremors coming in. Honestly, I don't know how you stand it."

He moaned in mock frustration when Eleven shrugged. Ten brushed away crumbs and reached for his bag. The pack was identical to Eleven's, aside from the crude etchings branded into the leather.

"Ah ha!" Ten revealed a worn, blue book. When Eleven didn't take the offered gift, he waved it in front of her. "More for my favorite brooding bibliophile."

Staring at the book, Eleven forced down a half-chewed piece of biscuit. She smeared stray flour onto the sides of her trousers before snatching the dancing book from Ten.

"Finding hard copies of anything decent is getting harder and harder."

Eleven skimmed the pages. With care, she searched the contents. A hasty flip through would cause irreparable damage.

Eleven frowned. "A diary?"

"In French," Ten added. "Amazing what's for sale these days, isn't it?"

"Bit gauche."

He tipped his head to the side. "Like it matters to you."

Eleven jumped to the inside of the back cover. A blurry red stamp read *Literal Lee's*. She beamed as her fingers slid over the worn words.

"Hope your linguistic skills are sharp."

"Where did you get this?"

Ten leaned back on his hands. "A friend told me about a shop in the outskirts of Region 4. Taking an alternate route let me happen upon the place."

*A "friend" meaning Region 4's static locator.*

Eleven clamped the book shut and placed it in her lap. "How'd you manage a detour?"

"Animal magnetism and bribery," Ten said, gazing up. "Mostly bribery." Leaning toward Eleven, he wiped at a corner of her mouth. "Screw risk-free dealings. It's pretty much a tradition at this point. I bring you books. In exchange, you're compelled to hang out with the likes of lowly ol' me."

"Ten."

"Accept the damn present, Eleven. You do this every time. Save us both the effort of the go-to bickering and bitching."

"Fine. This is very thoughtful. Thank you."

"Don't thank me yet." Scooting closer to Eleven, Ten rested his back against the rooftop gravel. He placed his hands underneath his head for a makeshift cushion and crossed an ankle to the opposing knee. "Translate away, mademoiselle."

Eleven masked an eye roll with fluttering lids. "Since when does Locator Ten require a bedtime story?"

"You're not the only person that's had a long day," Ten replied. He adjusted, true comfort escaping him. "No accents, okay? Think you've suffered enough embarrassment."

Twisting to face him, Eleven sat cross-legged and relaxed an elbow on her inner thigh. She reopened the book, hoping the French cursive wouldn't get the better of her.

# 3

"GOT LESS THAN AN HOUR BEFORE CURFEW, LOCA-tor Ten."

Four soldiers stood near the rooftop entrance. Their unwel-come presence stopped Eleven mid-sentence.

"We're well within our allotted time," Ten said to the guard-ians. He glanced at the diary in Eleven's lap, scooting closer to help her conceal it. "By my estimate, we have twenty min-utes."

Off-duty interactions with one of the eleven were limited and done on a case-by-case basis. Communications between locators had the harshest restriction of no more than one hun-dred twenty minutes.

The bulkiest of the group stepped forward. "That doesn't factor in curfew. The barracks aren't accessible after lights out, Locator Ten."

"The barracks," Ten repeated. "Oh, my dear Eleven, how jealous you must be of me in this moment."

"Painfully so," she replied. Grateful for its small size, Eleven secured the diary underneath her shirt.

"Statics get all the perks."

Eleven nudged Ten in his ribs. "Actives get to travel."

"Anytime you want to switch places, you just say the word."

*Like we have a say in anything that happens to us.*

"We'll escort you," said the lone female guardian.

Ten grimaced. "That won't be necessary."

"We insist."

Eleven chewed on her lip, waiting for Ten to make a move. When he didn't, she said, "Protocol dictates—"

"Don't even start reciting protocol to me, Eleven."

Throwing his arms up, Ten made a show of getting to his feet. He offered Eleven a hand. She took it, but tensed to keep the diary in place.

"How long are you in 5?"

*Say weeks. I'll even take days.*

"Heading out before sunrise," Ten answered. He looked down when noticing Eleven's disappointment. "I'm at the mercy of the chambers. Just like you."

Eleven sighed. "That's one way of putting it."

"Until next time." He raised his arms.

"We are not hugging."

Ignoring her protests, Ten drew Eleven into an embrace, squeezing her tight. "Watch out for flying aluminum."

Eleven shoved him. "Go before you get sent to the home office."

"Wouldn't want that," Ten said as he tucked a lock of curls behind her ear.

The eleventh locator watched her colleague strut away with his guardian entourage. Her smile dwindled as Ten's distance increased. Eleven took one last glimpse at the dark skyline before descending to the lower levels alone.

As a static locator, she kept permanent accommodations. The single constant for actives like Ten was travel. Posts and headquarters provided little aside from a bed in the guardians' barracks.

This particular level of living quarters housed those in notable positions. Corridors shared the appearance of countless others. Surrounding sounds were difficult, if not impossible, to distinguish. Eleven relished the quiet.

Approaching her room, Eleven tucked Ten's gift under her left arm. She waved her right hand over a steel cover plate where a doorknob normally rested. When the door closed and locks met latches, her tension eased. The locator tossed her newest read on a neighboring office chair. Eleven kicked both shoes off to an opposite corner of the room.

Stacks of literature accented two walls from top to bottom with not much else in the way of décor. Her books, along with discarded clothing and accessories splayed throughout, offered sparse bits of color in the sterile-white space.

Tripping over bloodied clothes, Eleven flicked on the bathroom light. The day's earlier apparel laid crumpled below her stainless steel sink. Her meticulously put-together outfit could not be salvaged. She chucked it all into a bin opposite the toilet.

*No use crying over spilled blood.*

Eleven snatched the book from her chair and fell backward onto the bed. Her partial interpretations on the roof had given insight to the life of a woman named Angelique. The mother of two had written in the journal often.

"It's as close to God as I'll ever see," Eleven interpreted.

The locator submersed herself in Angelique's journal. Cerulemans had just made themselves known to the public.

*Ils souhaitent avoir notre confiance.*
*Avoir un accueil chaleureux.*
*Nous avons entierement confiance sans aucun doute. Ils le méritent?*

"They wish to be trusted. Welcomed." Eleven continued to translate. "We trust so easily. Do they deserve it...? One can hope."

She moved to her stomach, kicking both feet up in an effort to get comfortable, while keeping eyes fixed on the wrinkled pages.

*How fast things change.*

A knock on the door broke her concentration. Eleven forced an exhale as she slid off the bed. "Just a moment."

Eleven stopped halfway to the door. Returning to Angelique's journal, she hid the diary behind volumes of outdated encyclopedias on one of the lower bookshelves. Possessing the journal didn't violate any rules, but Eleven worried as to what someone might think of the book. And, more importantly, to the significance of who gave it to her.

Another knock. "Be right there."

The locator hurried to the door, not bothering to see who awaited her. Eleven's hand hovered just out of reach as she mentally prepared herself. She leaned against the door's edge after opening it.

"Good evening." Dr. Kepler kept both hands behind him.

"Evening."

Isaac peered from side to side. "May I come in?"

The locator dug half-moons in her palms, threatening to break the skin. Pushing off the door, she retreated backward into the room. Dr. Kepler followed her inside.

"Making a habit of missing assessments." Isaac kept his eyes on Eleven. He forced the door shut. "An unscheduled visit shouldn't come as much of a surprise at this point."

*Don't let him affect you.*

"Something came up."

Eleven's speedy delivery confirmed something for him.

Isaac nodded as he stepped toward her. "Need I remind you of procedure? Particularly when complications arise?"

*"Examination for all parties involved is required within the first forty-eight hours of an incident."*

*How could I possibly forget?*

Returning to bed, Eleven kept her expression blank. She busied herself with a book from her nightstand, thumbing through the pages.

"I'll make an appointment first thing—"

"Not only were you scheduled, you confirmed." Isaac cleared the room's lone chair of dirty clothes. He sat facing the locator. "Therefore, you had an obligation to meet me."

*Are there no other physicians qualified to examine me?*

"I'm sorry, Dr. Kepler. I'll be more mindful in the future and do my best to adhere to all arrangements. Medical or otherwise."

A thick silence fell, lasting for what felt like minutes. Eleven pretended to read while Isaac kept still. The quick turn of a page was the sole sound.

*I really am testing the limits today, aren't I?*

Isaac softened his tone. "You must've been frightened."

"I wasn't."

*Liar.*

"I suppose getting pierced through the gut could be considered relatively uneventful to your kind." Isaac stood. Approaching the bed, he said, "I've taken the liberty of rescheduling you for tomorrow morning."

Eleven's fingers stiffened at his nearing proximity. She loosened her hold on the pages when noticing her whitening fingertips.

"Eleven?"

She kept her eyes on a paragraph. "Assessment tomorrow morning. Thank you. I'll be there. You have my word, Dr. Ke-

33

pler."

Isaac tilted his head. "Why do you keep calling me that?"

"It's your preference."

"Not in private. Never with you."

*Just go.*

"Have I done something to upset you?"

*Where should I start?*

The doctor sat on the mattress corner nearest Eleven. She stared at the page. She absorbed none of the text, but moved her eyes back and forth all the same.

"No. No, you haven't done anything."

Isaac caressed her neck. Eleven jerked away from the contact. Dropping his hand, he asked, "What's wrong?"

"Nothing."

*If only that were true.*

"Look at me." He snagged the book from her and tossed it to the floor.

"Isaac—"

The doctor lifted Eleven's chin. Hooking his index finger, Isaac forced her to meet his scrutiny. Wariness mixed with mild ambiguity etched deep lines on his forehead.

"Should I be worried?"

Eleven shook her head. "I'm just tired."

"Is that why you've been avoiding me?" Isaac brushed his thumb over Eleven's lower lip. "I've missed you."

"It's late." Eleven angled her head down. She fixed her eyes on the ruffled comforter resting between them.

"That it is." Isaac took off his glasses. Folding the temples, he placed them on the nightstand.

*He never makes it simple.*

Gripping the back of Eleven's head at the nape, Isaac pulled her against him. He breathed her in as he forced her eyes to lock with his.

"Poor lost girl nearly of heaven, surrounded by dangers unknown."

*So tired.*

Isaac smirked. Cupping Eleven's cheek, he continued. "One of few, never of many."

Eleven's vision blurred. Lightheadedness threatened to overtake her. She closed her eyes to regain composure.

"Seldom would she be alone... Eleven?"

When she didn't respond, Isaac took her face in both his hands. Eleven secured trembling fingers over them. She leaned her forehead against his.

"Are you all right?"

Eleven nodded. After several deep breaths, she opened her eyes.

"Would you like me to leave?"

She answered with a rough kiss. The doctor chuckled against her lips. His five o'clock shadow scuffed her supple skin.

Isaac drew back. "Tell me, Eleven. I want to hear you say it."

"Don't go."

• • • • • • • • • • •

A BOISTEROUS ALARM JOLTED ELEVEN UP AMIDST chaotic bedding. She glared at the analog clock to her left. Her fist landed heavily on the retro timepiece responsible for her rude awakening.

It silenced and, much to her surprise, remained operational. Eleven unfurled on the mattress, struggling to keep her eyes open. Shades turned then withdrew to reveal unforgiving sunlight. The harsh rays stung. Eleven hid her face with an adjacent pillow.

*Ugh, it smells like him.*

She braved the ultraviolet beams, chucking the pillow toward the window. An unimpeded, full-bodied stretch gave Eleven just enough energy to bring herself upright. Eleven looked to the right side of the bed. Isaac never stayed long after carnal activities.

Wiping away sleep, Eleven saw a note underneath the clock. She scowled. In horrible penmanship read:

DON'T FORGET.

*He set my alarm? Overbearing blowhard.*

Eleven crushed the note into a ball, tossing it at the clock. She groaned while kicking her comforter aside. A thud brought her attention to the window.

*Cardinalis cardinalis? A red cardinal in Region 5. Imagine that.*

She dashed to the rarity poised on the window ledge. The winged creature adjusted. Eleven knelt down.

"There are better places to be, my friend."

Rapid knocks managed to scare both locator and bird. Eleven smiled as the cardinal flew out of sight. Animals were rarely seen outside laboratories. Cerulemans viewed birds as nothing more than bringers of pestilence.

"Got other orders to deliver, Your Highness," said a voice through the door.

• • • • • • • • • • •

DISTANCE BETWEEN ELEVEN'S QUARTERS AND THE laboratory of Dr. Kepler left much to be desired. Still, Eleven dismissed the transport Isaac had reserved for her in favor of walking. She took any opportunity to postpone further interaction with the good doctor.

*"Your health and safety are my top priority, Eleven."*

*Didn't seem that way last night.*

Several kilometers later, Eleven reached one of many medicinal workshops that filled the floor. Judgmental glances fueled her anxiety.

Text floated next to her:

- REGULAR EXAMINATIONS REQUIRED.
- ASSESSMENTS DETERMINE WHETHER ONE IS ABLE TO PERFORM THEIR ROLE.
- PRESENCE OF ANY PHYSICAL, MENTAL, AND/OR EMOTIONAL ISSUE(S) MAY PREVENT ONE FROM ACTIVE DUTY.

*Unless you're one of eleven people qualified for your coveted role.*

For those not of Ceruleman lineage, assessments were a regular occurrence. Examinations didn't stop at the average physical. Most testing went unexplained. Not that Eleven inquired anymore.

*It's not my place to question.*

Stepping toward the threshold, both wide doors slid open. Eleven blinked to adjust to the intense void of color. Her silver and periwinkle shirt with black pants contrasted against the stark white interior.

One of Dr. Kepler's assistants sat at a grand reception desk. Eleven sighed as she approached the woman working behind the counter.

"Locator Eleven," said the assistant. Her tight hair bun tugged at her artificial smile. "Running a little late this morning, aren't we?"

*It appears we are.*

"Trouble with my alarm," Eleven lied.

Isaac's assistant typed away on several keyboards set in front her. Gesturing to her right, she said, "He's ready for you."

Another set of doors opened. Eleven entered the belly of the beast. Sterility and indifference drenched every corner. Nothing gave any indication to preference or personality. Though that was likely the point. Cerulemans cherished uniformity. No better example than the medical facilities.

"Dr. Kepler?"

No one answered.

Taking advantage of being left unattended, Eleven perused the shelves above the nearest workstation. Unlabeled binders filled both rows. She rubbed her fingertips together. The temptation to have a peek had crossed her mind more than a few times.

"An hour behind schedule. I must be losing my touch."

Eleven turned to Isaac. He made notes on a portable as he approached her. "We have a lot to do in a short amount of time, Locator Eleven. If you please."

Knowing the routine, Eleven walked to the center of the room. She hopped onto the padded examination table.

Isaac's eyes stayed on the portable. "How are we feeling?"

"Does it matter?" Eleven replied.

The doctor looked up from his busywork. "I'm sorry?"

*Oh, hell. You choose* now *to be bold?*

"We're the picture of health, Dr. Kepler."

"Very good."

Unseen machinery activated around the pair. Buzzes and clicks from concealed apparatuses perked Eleven's ears. Isaac continued preparations on the device resting in his widened hand. "How are the headaches?"

*Looming any time you're near.*

"Manageable."

Isaac stepped to her side. "And the stoppers are helping in the field?"

"Just as you predicted they would."

"Yes or no?"

*Speaking of headaches.*

"Yes."

Catching a faux leather stool with his pointed shoe, Isaac sat in front of her. Eleven's neck muscles strained at the close proximity.

"Anything I should be made aware of?"

*The cologne you wear is repulsive.*

"No."

Impervious to Eleven's apprehension, Isaac remained diligent in his note taking. "We'll need to run another work up on blood."

"All right."

"But that will be included in your post-engagement."

Eleven frowned. "Not now?"

"Tomorrow."

*Then why am I here?*

"What's today?"

Kepler pushed up his glasses. "You really must keep up with morning memorandums, Locator Eleven." He met her narrowed glare. "Standard preparations today."

"A new assignment?" Eleven asked. "I just returned."

"I advised against it. Apparently, this chamber is high priority. My documentation doesn't go into specifics. You'll know more than I do once you review the particulars. If I had to guess, I'd say the details are likely strewn about your bedroom floor at this very moment."

Eleven fell back as the table reclined. With a few more presses on Isaac's portable, he locked down the room and dimmed all unnecessary lighting. A circle of blue light faded in around the two.

The stronger the hum, the brighter the light.

"Still the picture of health?"

Eleven closed her eyes. "Yes, Dr. Kepler."

Bright blue intensified after the press of a button under her headrest. Light encapsulated Eleven's cranium like a halo. The buzz grew to the point of pain.

Eleven peeked up to see Isaac place a thick pair of dark-colored glasses over his existing framework. She snapped her lids shut before he could notice her stolen glance.

*Keep them closed until he says. Don't give him a reason to keep you any longer than necessary.*

Eleven gripped the edges of the table. Her skin warmed from the glow. She kept facing forward despite the painful blinding light.

*Don't flinch. Phase 1 is nothing.*

"3, 2 . . ."

The locator opened her eyes after the unspoken 1.

"What do you see?" Isaac flipped another switch. Moments later, sand-like particles floated above her.

Squinting, Eleven said, "An arrow."

"And now?"

"Lightning."

Isaac waited. "Be specific."

"A lightning bolt." Eleven licked sweat pooling above her lip.

"One more."

*My head is killing me.*

"A lion?"

"You're not sure?"

"A lion."

The room went black. Eleven's ragged breaths filled the space as the table brought her upright. Hands trembled at her sides. She batted her eyelids, still seeing the images when she closed her eyes.

*Phase 2.*

A ceiling tile glowed the palest of yellows. The slab barely contained the light behind it. Sliding open, a yellow sphere the size of Eleven's palm drifted downward. It stopped when it reached eye level. Discombobulated from Phase 1, Eleven grumbled at the bit of machinery.

"Dr. Kepler—Isaac?"

"Just a little more, Locator Eleven."

"I—can I have a moment to collect myself?"

"Focus on the center," Isaac said, ignoring her plea. He gestured between Eleven and the sphere. It brightened as it began to turn. "No blinking."

Eleven hurried to expel tears as she fixated on the strange orb. As its rotation sped up, all but the core became translucent. Harsh flashes hit her in waves, filling her head with images and sounds. She failed to make sense of anything the device exhibited.

Her eyes singed. Eleven healed in time with shimmered breaks.

*This won't break you. It can't.*

Pain lessened as the orb's speed diminished. When the glowing sphere stopped turning completely, the light dimmed to its original state. The orb floated back to its canopy compartment with a wave from Isaac. He showed no sign of concern or worry. Taking off his dark-colored glasses, he placed them in his coat pocket.

Returning to his portable, the normal overhead bulbs flickered on. Eleven trapped her eyes in their respective palm. Tears puddled where her hands met her face.

"Well done." Isaac moved to a stationary console. Typing away, he ignored the disoriented woman in front of him.

Eleven wiped a sleeve at her tears. The locator slid off the table. She swayed toward the exit, her first few steps uneven.

Isaac continued to type. "I'd arrange you a transport, but it seems you prefer walking."

The snide comment brought Eleven back to the here and now. She righted herself as she approached the double doors.

"Eleven?"

Both doors opened. Eleven stopped at the threshold. "Yes?"

"Be prompt post-engagement. Do we understand each

other?"

"Yes, Dr. Kepler."

"I'm pleased you and I are on the same page," Isaac replied. Adjusting his glasses, though there wasn't call to, he added, "I trust you wouldn't relish being reprimanded."

• • • • • • • • • • •

*DAMN MY PRIDE. I SHOULD'VE FOUGHT FOR TRANS-port.*

With lunch time in full swing, crowds around medical were at their heaviest. Eleven wobbled into opposing traffic patterns. A thick check to the shoulder pushed her against a wall.

The "necessary" procedure bewildered her more than usual today. Every blink brought images Eleven couldn't make sense of. A resonate hum troubled her ears.

*Arrow, lightning bolt, lion. Arrow, lightning bolt, lion. Arrow, light—*

"Hey, Eleven!"

Eleven didn't acknowledge the hail as she continued to her quarters. The path suffered a gridlock. Slowing traffic came to an almost immediate stop.

"Locator Eleven!"

Complaints and shouts accompanied a voice drawing closer. Eleven squinted, peering over those ahead. Many cursed at the idiot driving a transport in the middle of the hall. An idiot the locator soon recognized.

"Make some room," HD62 said as he honked.

Several had colorful responses, but they squeezed past the guardian. Not all rushed out of his transporter's trajectory. He parked in front of a stagnant Eleven.

"Was hoping to run into you."

"Literally?"

HD62 smiled. "Girl's got jokes. Aren't you full of surprises?"

Eleven flinched at a sharp pain near the center of her brow. She spoke low. "Another time." With the path now free, she resumed her journey.

"Where ya headed?"

"My room," Eleven said.

*"I'd arrange you a transport, but it seems you prefer walking."*

*I* prefer *to remain upright, you malcontent, sadistic—*

"Hold up!"

A hefty slam against the wall forced Eleven to turn around. The guardian grappled with the steering wheel. HD62 awkwardly maneuvered the transport, hurrying to reverse it. Eleven appeared to be the lone observer amused by the spectacle.

"Can I offer you a ride?" HD62 asked pulling up next to her.

*Yes!*

"No."

HD62 accelerated past Eleven. Looking back, he said, "Reconsider. A lot to discuss seeing as how we're working together now and all."

"No, thank y—wait. Say that again."

This revelation served better than a slap to the face.

"Thought that might get ya." HD62 leaned a forearm over the steering wheel. He motioned to the passenger side. "You could use a break."

"Is that a fact?" she asked.

"More of an observation."

Curiosity as to what HD62 meant urged her to get in. "My room is—"

"I know where it is," HD62 interrupted. He watched his new passenger settle in next to him. "Everyone does. I mean—not to say that *everyone* does. It's just—shit. I'm off to a killer start, aren't I?"

*Still better than walking?*

The first few minutes were quiet. HD62 stole the occasional glance but said nothing. His twitching lips started and stopped.

"Used to drive one of these babies daily," the guardian said. The surrounding crowds thinned out. He made a hard right turn. Eleven jerked toward HD62. "Shit, sorry."

Eleven buckled her seatbelt. "It's fine."

"Not as fun as it seems. The driving, I mean. Trust me on this."

"In what way are we working together?"

"It was in today's directives." HD62 turned to her. He chuckled. "But your face is telling me you haven't read it just yet."

*Am I the only one without a memorandum pinned to my chest?*

"In what way?" Eleven pressed.

"You're talking to the new head of your detail." Her new commander carried on. "Suppose I've got you to thank for the promotion."

"I'd never have endorsed you."

"Oh."

*This makes SB47's reaction seem positively tame.*

"What of the others?"

"Everybody is new." HD62 shrugged. He took the next turn slowly. "Might've worked with a couple here and there, but your main guys had been together for a while, right?"

*Years.*

HD62 concentrated on the path ahead. "The briefing's after lunch. Sure you got time to drop by your place?"

"I don't go to the briefings."

"Why not?"

*I've never been asked.*

Eleven kept her eyes forward. "They don't concern me."

"That's not true. Seems like a wasted opportunity. We're

supposed to be a team."

"The detail itself is a team, perhaps. I'm something else."

HD62 smirked. "What if I wanted your take on things before making anything concrete?"

*I'd say you're doomed.*

"It isn't for me to debate strategy."

"Been here longer than I have," the guardian replied. He steadied the wheel with his knees. "You know more about all this stuff than I do."

*That's putting it lightly.*

Reaching behind him, the guardian searched for something. The transport swerved hard to the right. Eleven clasped her hands together. HD62 returned forward, bringing a pack with him. His steering suffered as he searched the pack resting in his lap. Giving up, he threw the sack to Eleven.

"Take a look at my portable. See what I've got so far."

Eleven crossed her arms. "I'm confident whatever course of action you choose will be adequate."

"Did you feel confident with the last commander? The one that allowed you to get left behind, manhandled, and skewered?"

Resistant to HD62's charismatic nature, Eleven found herself wondering. She was rarely afforded such an opportunity.

As instructed, Eleven ransacked HD62's belongings. Weightier items fell while others made a swift exit from Eleven's open window. The locator pulled the portable out and dropped the bag.

"First file on the starter."

*No encryption code or passkey? Laughable. Let's see... military experience... law enforcement... all guardians volunteered... no mention of Designation HD62's background.*

Scrolling over schematics and plans, Eleven finished her read-through in no time. She leaned back in her less than comfortable seat after tucking away the device.

"Everything seems to be in order." Seeing HD62 waiting, Eleven inhaled. "A more tactical option would be to go at first light. Chambers in fluctuation tend to be unstable. The longer we wait, the higher the likelihood of it phasing out of sync."

Smiling, HD62 asked, "What else?"

"There's no mention of seismic activity. That should always be addressed, especially in this region. Switching from day to night means more civilians. Add at least two additional convoys for crowd control."

"See? You're not half-bad at this."

"Most of your subordinates aren't—" Eleven stopped. She thought how best to describe it. "As *well-read* as one might surmise."

HD62 laughed. "Dumb it down, got it."

Another sharp pain to the center of her forehead blinded her. Eleven clenched her eyes shut and waited out the discomfort.

*Damn it.*

"As promised."

Eleven opened her eyes. Meters from her quarters, she tensed. The locator hopped out of the vehicle as HD62 put it into park. Without a word, she headed to her door.

"Guess I'll see you tomorrow." HD62 honked as he sped off.

*He still smiles. And people think I'm strange.*

# 4

THICK POLLUTED FOG BLOCKED THE LUSTER OF moonlight. The dense, inert clouds accompanied nightfall. Debris trailed sidewalks and roads, while some wreckage huddled together in corners amidst forgotten buildings.

*I sincerely hope that stench is coming from outside.*

The interior of the guardian vehicle resembled Eleven's former conveyance with upgraded defenses. HD62 took the front passenger seat with DR21, his second-in-command, playing driver. One guardian to the right of her, another to the left, and two behind with Eleven in her usual middle spot. An auxiliary crew had parked behind them.

*I say first light; he chooses the dead of night. What a waste of breath.*

Stoppers in place, the locator kept her gaze on the world just outside. Sleek Ceruleman instruments and clean-cut soldiers clashed against their decrepit surroundings.

"How we feelin'?" HD62 asked.

The lead guardian looked behind him. He signed the

question to Eleven. Avoiding his curious eyes, she answered "fine" with a gloved hand.

"Great." HD62 pulled down his sun visor. He adjusted the small interior mirror. Eleven now had a perfect view of his lips.

"Everybody else?" HD62 peered over to the driver's seat. DR21, as well as the other four guardians, didn't react. The new commander deflated. "Right."

Electricity buzzed through adjacent power lines. The locator noted the absence of artificial light. That, paired with murky air, left little of the neighborhood visible.

Tilting his head down, HD62 sought Eleven. She caught this attempt in her peripheral. Her mouth flattened into a straight line as she focused on his reflection. The talkative guardian prattled on about the briefing she'd missed and particulars as to the mission itself.

"Quite the neighborhood back in the day. Funny how much can change."

Eleven strained to keep up with him. She sighed in relief at the minimal aberrations as she removed her stoppers.

DR21 scratched the back of his head. "Signing to Locator Eleven during field operations is preferred."

"Even when it's just us?" HD62 asked.

"Procedure, sir."

The lead guardian shrugged at DR21. "Just making small talk."

"Customarily one should reserve conversation for off hours," Eleven replied.

"Jokes and schooled in etiquette. Learning all sorts of new things about you, Locator Eleven."

A guardian behind Eleven grumbled. HD62 glanced through the rear windshield. The backup unit was still scanning the area for potential threats. Keeping his eyes on them, HD62 hit the communicator on his shoulder. "How we lookin', Designation

RP56?"

"This round's nearing completion," answered a static-ridden voice. "Floor to floor coming up, sir."

"Chamber in this sort of flux is on the delicate side, from what I hear. Make it snappy."

*Now he listens.*

A minute later, headlights flashed. "We're clear," RP56 responded. "Heading in now."

Eleven watched as the backup unit left their lustrous ebony transport. The six guardians scattered. Search lights flashed here and there as they infiltrated a steel-framed building to her right.

"Stationed at access points. Awaiting further instruction."

HD62 hit the com. "We're headed your way."

"Understood," RP56 replied.

Without a word from HD62, the others did a final weapons check. Eleven returned the stoppers to her ears. She raised her coat hood when sensing HD62's stare.

Even through stoppers, faint droning teased her ears upon exiting. Foul odors forced Eleven to breathe through her mouth. She hurried her steps to keep pace.

Gazing skyward, HD62 signed and said, "Light her up."

DR21 pulled a gadget from his side. After inputting key commands, electricity throughout the entire block was restored. Aged bulbs painted the neighborhood in nostalgic tones. Magnetic murmurs tickled the hair on Eleven's arms. The structure had to be over fifty meters high with twelve stories total.

*Out of all the places for a chamber to present itself.*

"Well," HD62 said. "We're not getting any younger."

Crunches of shattered glass and cracked tile echoed through the first floor as the detail made their entrance. A decorative carriage on its side blocked a row of workstations. Now a den for drifters, the former finance building had evidently seen better days.

A spray-painted symbol on a thick marble column caught Eleven's eye. The Roman numeral for 3 was deep blue with a crimson circle and a backlash overlay.

*No third-kinders. Points for originality.*

"First drug den?"

Ignoring HD62's question, Eleven walked past the column. She halted near broken-down stone slabs. The dim noise from earlier became more prominent. A glimpse to the others confirmed they had noticed as well.

"The hell is that?" DR21 asked.

HD62 strained his ears. "Transformers?"

*I can sense it even with the stoppers. Can't he hear it?*

"Not bloody likely. Sir—" DR21 began.

"Time sensitive, right?" HD62 asked Eleven.

Eleven glanced at DR21. "Yes."

"Let's get the show on."

"Sir," DR21 started again. "We should run another sweep."

"A prior perimeter check turned up nothing, soldier." Unsatisfied with his commander's plan, DR21 stayed in place. "To your post."

Eleven fumbled with her gloves as DR21 and the others took their positions surrounding her. She pocketed her stoppers and drew back her hood to survey the lobby. Expanding both hands at her sides, Eleven closed her eyes. All ten digits kept steady. Unlike most chamber encounters, nothing begged for a reaction.

*The initial survey said ground level.*

"Problem?"

*Even if it'd faded, I'd still feel... something.*

"Locator Eleven?" HD62 pressed.

"Yes?"

"Is there a problem?"

Eleven considered HD62. "I don't know."

"Another joke?"

"I can't sense it," Eleven said. Her admission bounced off the walls. "The chamber, can you hear it?"

HD62 looked to his fellow guardians. "Not really in our wheelhouse."

*Novices.*

Eleven advanced toward the lobby's center. Still unable to discern the alleged fluctuating chamber, she raised her arms.

*Nothing.*

The remote resonance now mimicked roaring thunder. HD62's gaze shot to the revolving entrance. "Okay. Definitely heard that."

"Sound like a transformer to you, sir?" DR21 asked.

"Maybe a quake?"

DR21 snickered. "We followed your orders to the letter. Seismic activity isn't common this far north, sir."

"Something isn't adding up," HD62 said.

"Ah!" An invisible grip pressed against Eleven's temples. The intense sensation traveled to the base of her eardrums. She cupped a hand over her left ear, tilting her right onto her shoulder.

The unrelenting compression threatened her consciousness. A quick survey confirmed Eleven wasn't alone in discomfort. Guardians squirmed and fidgeted.

All but HD62. He appeared immune to this auditory assault. Hitting his communicator, he asked, "Anyone else getting a funky frequency?"

*Why isn't this affecting him?*

No one replied.

"Designation RP56, come in."

Then the signal went completely dead, as did surrounding power. Eleven and the others panted in slouched stances.

"Are you okay?" HD62 asked Eleven.

She nodded. DR21 took his standard issue blade from its

sheath. Through gritted teeth, he asked, "EMP?"

"Not ours." The lead guardian studied DR21's drawn weapon. Nodding, HD62 said, "Everyone, arms at the ready."

"This is a trap," Eleven whispered to herself.

"We don't know that," HD62 snapped. "Now put those plugs back in. That's an order."

Eleven expanded her arms. "There isn't a chamber here."

"We should retreat," DR21 said.

Charging toward Eleven, HD62 searched her pockets. The guardian pulled out the stoppers. He forced them into her palm. "Stoppers in now."

The severity in his tone jolted her. It was atypical of the man Eleven knew him to be. She didn't test her boundaries with this new side of him. She fumbled with the waxy buds, hurrying to put them in place. The growing pressure distracted her.

*None of this is right.*

Eleven fell to her knees, dropping the stoppers in the process. Still unaffected, HD62 knelt to retrieve them. Guardians, save for him, struggled against the new, stronger frequency. He cupped Eleven's ears with his gloved hands.

"What is this?" Eleven asked. Clattering corners stopped her from prying further.

"It'll be—get down!" HD62 pushed Eleven to the ground as shards of metal and glass scattered across the lobby.

Remnants flew at them from every direction. Designations WA76 and IR66 aimlessly fell, while others merely sustained mild injuries. Guardians rushed to their commander.

"We can put out a distress call from the car," DR21 said. He motioned to the exit. "Sir, we have to get her to safety."

"And what about the other team, soldier?"

"They've got transport."

HD62 continued to hover over Eleven. "Are you okay?"

A deafening explosion destroyed all surviving glass

throughout the revolving entrance doors. The commander covered Eleven's body with his own, covering her skull more than anything else. Guardians flew off in several directions.

Flames flickered amongst the strewn detail. Crackles and splinters tormented Eleven's senses.

"Shit," the commander grunted. He took a mental inventory of Eleven. "You still with me?"

She nodded. Noticing a scrap of metal lodged in HD62's shoulder, Eleven removed it without second thought. The guardian stifled the bulk of his outcry by remaining tight-lipped.

HD62 hobbled to standing. Helping Eleven to her feet, he said, "Locator Eleven active. Designation HD62 active. Sound off."

DR21 wheezed in his approach. "Designation DR21 active."

"Designation CF37 active," called the stoic, female guardian.

A soldier lying at the farthest corner pushed rubble aside. He wiped a thick coat of blood from his brow. "Designation OK50. Still active, sir."

"Sound off, soldier." HD62 leaned down to WA76 less than a meter away from them. As he turned him, the commander's face fell.

"IR66 is also down." DR21 closed IR66's eyes. He, as well as the other surviving guardians, rejoined HD62.

CF37 checked her com. "Still got nothing."

"Recollector should be on its way," HD62 said.

*Recollector?*

DR21's eyes widened. "Sir."

"What? It's standard procedure, isn't that right?" OK50 asked DR21.

*There's no mention of recollector in my protocols.*

HD62 answered for DR21. "With Banaedrut backup not far behind."

Steps from above stopped everyone's movements. Squeaks from the ceiling and floorboards hinted at deliberate pacing. HD62 signaled to the stairwell behind him. OK50 wasted no time hustling up the stairs. CF37 accompanied him.

"What are we dealing with, sir?" DR21 asked.

"RP56's crew?"

"I have my doubts." The second-in-command peered outside. "Sir, we need a rough count on potential unfriendlies. It isn't wise to send anyone—"

HD62 interrupted DR21. "Evaluate, I get it. Thinking a loner. Two guardians should be more than enough, don't you think?"

*Tell that to Designations WA76 and IR66.*

Grabbing the underside of Eleven's arm, DR21 led her to the thickest shadows without so much as a glance to his commanding officer. Stunned at the situation, Eleven allowed him to guide her. He motioned to an alcove opposite a line of lackluster elevators.

HD62 unsheathed the blade at his side as he followed the pair. "Good idea."

"Thank you, sir."

"We're getting out of here," HD62 told Eleven. He stepped toward her. "Don't worry."

*I'm less than reassured.*

"Why haven't we heard anything?" DR21 whispered.

"Coms are still down."

"That's not what I meant and you know it," DR21 said.

HD62 kept his eyes on the door to the stairwell. "Reinforcements are en route."

"Banaedrut or not, nearest support is at least half an hour out. You think they give two shits about *us* making it out of this?"

*How many will die because of you?*

Eleven had seen it more times than she cared to remember.

Guardians often lost their lives in the field.

"Guessing you glossed over the part where it's your fucking duty," HD62 replied. "Stay on task."

A loud thud from the middle elevator caused the three to jump. Motioning for DR21 to take point, HD62 hurried to the doors. Using his baton, the guardian jimmied the elevator open to reveal a dead body.

"One of ours?" DR21 asked.

HD62 nodded. "CF37."

"Shit."

A shrill blare pierced Eleven ears as a bullet shot passed HD62's head. The guardian used CF37's body as a shield. He peered up when additional firing ceased. "They must be out."

"Or they're headed straight to us," DR21 ventured. He snapped his thumbs on both sides of his head, testing his hearing.

*He heard it too. Who are we dealing with? What are we dealing with?*

The commander stepped away from the elevator. "We're not dealing with a marksman."

DR21 grimaced at Eleven. "That's it. I'm getting you out of here."

"She's not going anywhere until the cavalry arrives. We'll neutralize the threat ourselves if we have to. It's just one guy."

Shaking his head, DR21 said, "How can you know that for certain?"

"They needed shadows and us separated to pull this much off."

*DR21 is right. There's no way to be sure.*

"Eleven?"

*Kill or capture, I can't let them take me.*

HD62 pressed. "Stay with me, Eleven."

Any sort of response was halted by a swing of the staircase door. HD62 motioned for Eleven to tuck herself in the corner parallel from the elevators. DR21 raised his blade as boots stomped into the lobby.

"Unger?" called the assailant, a female voice.

The two guardians regarded one another, forming a plan with a series of gestures and nods. Eleven found herself grateful for the small comfort the darkness provided.

*This woman and Unger make two. What if there are more?*

"Don't know how many are with you, but we're running out of time here." The adversary grew closer. "Get it done already."

HD62 exhaled. "Damn it."

His second-in-command quirked his head. Eleven saw a question arise. She trailed DR21's eyes to HD62's forehead, then to his shaking fingers.

"I think I can take her out," HD62 whispered.

DR21 inched backward but tilted down his weapon. He moved in front of Eleven while tightening the hold on his blade.

"Unger?" called the voice again. "We don't have all night."

DR21 raised his blade toward HD62. "Gonna answer her?"

"Stand down, Designation DR21."

"He's a conspirator," DR21 told Eleven.

Taking advantage of the shadows, DR21 handed a dull pocket knife that didn't meet regulation to Eleven with his free hand. Their commander ignored the looming menace, turning toward the cornered pair. His nerves became evident as he fiddled with his own blade.

"Please don't make me do this," HD62 said to DR21.

"Lower your weapo—"

A thick mist warmed Eleven's face, painting her features in deep crimson. Her ears rang as DR21's body crumbled to the floor. She kept silent while tucking DR21's knife into her coat's interior pouch.

HD62 sucked in his bottom lip. "I had that."

*It's true.*

"Bullshit." The mysterious shooter lowered her smoking gun as she approached his backside. Her silhouette left much to the imagination. She wore black from head to toe. Relieving herself of a knit facemask, she added, "Got what we need?"

"Rest is on its way."

*What do I do?*

"Better be. Got major kink potential making a beeline."

*What's the protocol?*

Any semblance of amusement fell from HD62's face. "How many?"

"Not including Banaedrut, still more than I can handle." The dark-haired beauty with high cheekbones and chestnut eyes set her sights on Eleven. "She's a hot third-kind commodity."

"Unger," Eleven said.

HD62 turned to her. She hadn't intended to vocalize the realization. She withdrew from the treacherous man as he motioned to her. Marble cooled her back. She pressed against the wall.

He scratched at his neck. "I prefer Felix."

*His candor and caring.*

"You're a fool," Eleven said to herself.

*Even his smile.*

"They're coming for me. For the both of you," Eleven said.

The guardian licked his lips. "You don't sound sure about that, Eleven."

*It was all an act.*

"Look," he continued, "I'm sure you've got a load of questions, but there will be time later."

"Wouldn't bother anyway," said the woman. "We'll just have to repeat it all with the big man."

"Vera," Felix scolded. "Ease up on the hard shtick."

She shrugged. "You're the boss, commander."

No scenario in training covered this type of situation. Attempting to sway these people seemed most appropriate, but Eleven's ineptitude in deception stopped the numerous pleas before they started.

"Incoming," Felix said.

A glowing sphere floated into the building. The device headed straight toward Eleven. It halted less than a meter from her, staying at eye level. She couldn't recall ever having seen it outside Isaac's laboratory.

*What's it doing here?*

"Catch," said Vera as she chucked a small bit of metal at the orb. When it made contact, the sphere went dark and fell. Felix lunged forward, catching it before it could hit the tiled floor. "They're playing our song."

Felix threw the orb to his partner. "Cutting it kind of close, don't you think?"

*I don't have to get far. I just have to hide until Banaedrut get here. If they're anything like Dyssae, these two will be dead before dawn.*

Just as Felix looked up, Eleven kicked him in the face. With the shooter blocking the path outside, she bolted to the open elevator. Felix caught her ankle, yanking her down. Eleven buried DR21's blade deep between his collarbones. She veered to the sliding doors.

"V, don't!" Felix shouted.

"Bitch hasn't left me with a lot of options."

A spray of blood hit the wall in front of Eleven. She clutched at a seeping wound near her stomach. Unable to feel her legs, she willed her feet to continue.

*It's just a bullet. You've had wor—*

Another gunshot forced her to drop. Blood rushed down Eleven's face and neck. She collapsed into the elevator, CF37's corpse cushioning her descent.

Consciousness was fading fast. The locator's heart slowed. Her eyelids grew heavy as her body cooled. No motor functions were possible.

"God damn it, Vera!"

*He made you trust him.*

"Calm down. It's easier this way, trust me."

"Eleven?"

*You* are *a fool.*

"End her outright, Vera. This in-between shit is cruel."

And then the world went dark.

# 5

*NOISE.*

Alloyed snaps and clicks ricocheted off walls. Tinkering partnered with approaching footsteps. The audible pairing of gears and unmeasured paces roused her. She kept her eyes closed and her breathing steady.

*It's all noise.*

"Gonna keep ogling or planning to actually help?" a woman asked.

Parallel to the inquirer, a deliberate stride stopped. A heavy shadow fell upon her face.

*Too loud.*

The shadow darkened above her. A man's voice. "Where is he?"

"Said he had instructions," answered the woman. "Knowing him, he's tearing apart one of his office's searching for them."

*Everything is too loud.*

"This is bullshit."

"He'll be here, okay, Unger?"

"She could wake up at any second."

"Felix," said the woman. The work stopped. "Take it easy. Crux keeps his word."

Felix resumed his pacing. "Deaden the room like I asked?"

"No."

He turned on his heel. "What?"

"His call."

"She needs things done in a certain way, Vera."

"I'm sure you know all about what she needs. Luckily, I don't give a shit. Better she get used to it now anyway."

*Who is* she?

The trailing silence increased an unspoken tension. Keeping still was becoming uncomfortable.

*Who am* I?

Felix stayed in place. "Guessing I missed a lot," he said. Vera picked up the pace of her work, full tinkering back in play. "Maybe when all this dies down, you can catch me up?"

"Maybe," Vera responded. A short energy burst coincided with a hard turn of gears. "Fuck me!"

"You okay?" Felix asked as he walked toward her.

"Fan-fucking-tastic."

"Thought you said you could figure it out."

Vera groaned. "I wasn't expecting to ride solo on this."

"What can I do?"

"I don't know, Unger. How schooled are you on third-kind technologies that make us look like goonfucks trying to create fire?"

Felix chuckled. "About as much as you are."

"Cute." Vera picked up her tools and resumed the task at hand. "Alien components aren't my forte. Ask me to put together a bomb using only pantry products, I'm your girl, but this? This is Crux territory. Fucker should've—"

"Language," said a new voice. The two of them jumped at the unexpected appearance.

"Jesus, Crux!"

"Good to see you again, Mr. Unger."

"Yeah, likewise."

Crux's somehow familiar scent filled Eleven's olfactory senses as he approached. His hand lingered over hers, centimeters from touching. Her fingers twitched at his warmth. Unlike Felix and Vera, Crux calmed her. For the first time since she'd awoken, she felt safe.

*Quiet.*

"Any trouble?" Crux asked.

"Nothing I couldn't handle."

"We," Felix corrected. "Nothing *we* couldn't handle, V."

"I stand by my previous statement."

Leaning down, Crux whispered into Eleven's ear. "No need to maintain this illusion. Sit upright. Allow me to greet you properly."

Eleven's eyes met thick lilac ones with crimson borders itching for attention. Doing as instructed, her pupils remained fixed on Crux's. The surrounding world and its inhabitants paled in comparison to the stocky figure standing before her. His square-jawline and prominent brow painted his unwrinkled face several cardinal shades.

"You were supposed to be keeping an eye on her," Vera said to Felix.

"I was."

"Do not worry," Crux said. "She is harmless in this state."

"Sure about that?" Vera asked.

"Quite."

Crux maintained eye contact as he backed toward Vera. He broke the connection when the tech savvy female placed a dim sphere in his hand.

Felix kept his gaze on Eleven. "Do you remember me?"

*More noise.*

"Of course she doesn't," Vera said. "Told you it'd work."

Felix frowned. "Even a legacy can't come back from a shot to the head. What makes her different?"

"Give it time, Mr. Unger." Crux took over Vera's work, fidgeting with delicate cogs inside the sphere. The alien exhibited no distress when another surge emitted. Vera took papers from Crux's side pocket. She simultaneously reviewed the documents while tracking his progress.

"Why isn't she saying anything?" Felix asked.

She *is me?*

"While she is suggestible, easy to influence, her true self is—" Crux stopped working. He searched for the proper words. "Think of her as a blank canvas. Something devoid of meaning without talent delineated across the intricate threading."

"Lights are on, but nobody's home?"

"Yes, Vera. Though your phraseology is objectionable." Crux put the finishing touches on the orb. It blazed like concentrated sunlight as he lowered his tools. "I am ready to begin."

"Don't you mean *we're* ready?" Felix asked.

"I do not," Crux replied. Carrying the radiating globe in his red clutches, he advanced toward Eleven. Felix blocked his path. "Mr. Unger."

Felix popped his knuckles. "Might need some help."

"Mr. Unger, should that be the case, I will summon you."

Vera snatched Felix by the bicep. He stiffened as she tugged on his sleeve. Crux waited for the door's latch to catch.

"Care to speak now that it is just the two of us?"

Eleven released the slab's edge. She watched as the color returned to her knuckles.

*So quiet.*

"I know what it is to be lost." Crux displayed his empty hand. Like hers, it was free of wrinkles and lifelines. When she tried to make sense of it, not a thought came to mind. "Would you like me to help you?"

Eleven's throat was scratchy from disuse. "Do I need help?"

"Oh yes," Crux answered.

"Are you wrong too?"

His eyes flickered as he thought how to answer. "Think us monstrous?" Crux took the hand parallel with his and held it tight. Eleven didn't reciprocate nor did she refuse his touch. "I am familiar, yes?"

"The others are too loud," Eleven answered. "But not you. You're quiet."

"Yet the two of us have never met." Inching forward, Crux added, "Would you like to know why I am quiet?"

"Yes."

"No matter the cost?"

"Yes."

"Do you trust me?"

"Yes."

Crux firmed his lips to contest a knowing grin. "You say that now, child." Keeping his hold on Eleven, he presented the glowing orb. "Skepticism is an admirable trait, one I am told you are quite fond of. If you will allow me, I wish to earn your confidence fully."

"With this?" Eleven motioned to the sphere.

"Its creators refer to it as a 'recollector,'" Crux said. He studied the object. "Origins aside, we are not unflawed. This restores memory should damage occur. Fabrications can also be implanted. Subdue, delude, call it what you like… the current application keeps the subject docile." Eleven's fingers twitched in Crux's. He surveyed her free hand. "It calls to you?"

"Yes."

The strange man gestured for Eleven to take the recollector. With reservation, her fingers idled underneath it. When close to touching, Eleven's hand retreated. She stared wide-eyed at the contraption.

"Answers await you." Crux turned the sphere downward, dangling it above Eleven's open palm. "No lies or half-truths. You will remember all."

*Remember anything.*

"Do I want to?"

"Want is irrelevant."

Eleven shifted. "Should I decline?"

Crux's rebuttal came in the form of a falling recollector. On impulse, Eleven caught the orb. Multiple perforations bit her fingertips, but not a drop of blood could be seen.

Whispers teased the hairs at her ears. Eleven's bottom lip quivered. When words failed her, Eleven stretched her arm forward. Crux had no intention of relieving her of the recollector's burden. He returned her back to the cool slab. "This will pass."

*Will it?*

"Eleven," a voice lacking identity called. In full force, it multiplied. "***Eleven***."

"The noise. It's too much. Please." The pressurized plea came out like a prayer.

Crux's face contorted. "I promise, it will—"

Eleven cut off his false comfort with an animalistic cry. She brought her hands to her chest. Goose bumps rose throughout as pain receptors were put on high alert.

*Is this what I need to remember?*

Fire traveled in her veins. The heat spread from her arms to her neck. Crux's words muted as warmth hit her temples.

*"Do you know what you are?"*

The familiarity in the question and the voice forced her eyes open. Now standing outside, Eleven looked to a tall silhouette before her. She stumbled to the ground. Focusing on the shaky limbs supporting her, Eleven watched tears soak into dirt.

*"Open it!"*

Night transformed into day. Planked walls now lay strewn about. Eleven's now splintered palms were covered in ash. The sight and smell of burning flesh overwhelmed her. Once tall barriers had turned to embers.

*"They've got us both now. I'm sorry."*

"No," Eleven responded.

She was restrained in a sterile room. Eleven fought against her restraints to no avail. Cold hands brushed across her cheekbones. She rejected the offered solace and lurched in the opposite direction.

*"Poor girl. You look so lost."*

Eleven's vision spun from black to white to crimson. Agony came in waves with short-lived bursts of relief.

*Stop.*

*"Come on, Princess!"*

*Make it stop.*

*"Two against the world."*

*Please.*

*"You belong to us."*

*No.*

Eleven choked on a gasp. Closing her mouth, she regulated her breathing through her nostrils. In less than a minute, the pounding of her chest dissipated to a lighter beat.

"Eleven?"

*No more.*

"Did it work?"

*Wait.*

The coolness of metal against Eleven's spine brought her back to the present. A heavy pulsing in both ears diminished. Two steady heartbeats and one erratic one circled her.

"Eleven, can you hear me?" Crux asked.

"Maybe it was too much," Felix said.

"She's fine."

"Because you're such an expert, V?"

Exhaling, Vera said, "She's responsive."

"Crux, did you follow the instructions?"

"Get the sand out of your vagina, Unger. She's just taking her sweet ass time."

"Vera," Crux interjected.

"Sorry."

"Shut up!" Eleven shouted.

The demand silenced the three. Her outburst surprised them all, Eleven included. She opened her eyes to find Felix, Vera, and Crux hovering over her.

Felix motioned to Crux and Vera. "Give her some room."

Eleven wiped at dark droplets hanging from her lashes. Red smeared her fingertips.

*Blood?*

Answering Eleven's unspoken inquiry, Vera said, "Subconjunctival hemorrhaging... I think."

"Dangerous?" Crux asked.

"You tell me."

*The beacon.*

Eleven pinched the back of her neck. She inched her fingers along every crease and bump, searching for the beacon with ferocity. Vera chuckled. "Plucked and destroyed during transfer. Coating it in your own tissue was all kinds of clever. Well, clever for third-kinders."

*They won't find me.*

Steadying herself, Eleven sat up. Remnants of the recollector lay to the side of her. She found the rest of it lying below her feet. Welcoming the distraction of the broken device, she ignored the three onlookers.

"She is quite changed when intact," Crux observed.

"How can you tell?" Vera asked.

"Difficult to explain."

*That voice… speech pattern and accent are unlike anything I've ever come across. Diction suggests his native language requires more elocution. Purple eyes, red skin… he couldn't be.*

Agony pierced the center of Eleven's forehead. Trying to recall anything after her full reset proved too much.

Felix reached for her. "Are you okay?"

"Don't touch me." She shrank away from him.

*"Have I done something to upset you?"*

*He's gone now. He can't touch you again.*

"Fair warning," Crux said to Eleven. "You may be… *reminiscent* over the next few hours. I am told the experience can be quite trying."

"We're sure it worked?" Vera asked.

Keeping his eyes on Eleven, Crux addressed Felix. "Mr. Unger?"

"I don't know." Scratching his head, Felix examined all that could be seen of his former comrade. Eleven's vision returned to the recollector. "All things considered, looks that way."

Vera rolled her eyes. "Is it her or not?"

*I have to leave. This isn't where I need to be.*

"Locator Eleven?"

*How long has it been since they took us?*

"Respond, Princess." Eleven immediately locked eyes with Felix. Smirking at her indignation, he said, "It's her."

"How can you know for sure?" Vera asked.

"Just am."

Eleven cut off the beginning of Vera's acerbic reply. "Where are the rest?"

*I have to see Ten now.*

The three shared a charged look.

Crux pursed his lips. "You are the first."

"When do the others arrive?"

"All good things to those who wait. We should all get some rest."

"I'm plenty rested."

Crux met Eleven's cold stare. The eccentricity of the crimson being's gaze likely intimidated most he encountered, but Eleven remained unbothered. "I am certain you are." He strode toward her. "However, you are in the minority." Crux considered Felix and Vera. "Much trouble went into your liberation."

*He's still there. He's still there with no one to protect him.*

"That's putting it fucking lightly," Vera added. She crossed her arms when noticing Crux's disapproval. "Sorry."

"I can show her around," Felix proposed.

"You're running on fumes," Vera said. "I think she can stand one night before being brought up to speed."

"Stop talking like she isn't right in front of you, V." Felix extended a hand to Eleven. "You game?"

*I can't go anywhere like this… and I could use the distraction.*

Eleven reluctantly took Felix's hand.

"The fuck ever." Patting Eleven on the back, Vera said, "Enjoy suppressing all the shit you're about to relive."

"She has a way about her," Crux told Eleven as Vera stomped out of the room.

*Then there's also the matter of him.*

"I shall leave you to it," Crux added. "Breakfast in the morning?"

"I can't stay here."

"You have nowhere else to be, Eleven. No place to call your own. Consider this a safe haven. At least for the time being."

As Crux exited, Eleven released Felix's hand. She wiped sweat onto a grungy pant leg. The two tensed, unsure of how to proceed.

*What I wouldn't give for a bullet to the brain right about now.*

# 6

*FAMILY... I THOUGHT I HAD ONE.*

*"Your parents must be proud."*

*They gave me parents. Sometimes siblings. All of them lies.*

Flickered images caused Eleven to stumble. Most recollections involved blood—a mere fraction of which belonged to her. Cerulemans countered acts of defiance with pain. "Good behavior" went unrewarded.

*"This stops when I say it does."*

Eleven willed one foot in front of the other. Neurons fired on all cylinders, making the simple task of walking nearly impossible.

*"You are the first."*

*How long before the closest thing I have to a blood tie is at my side again?*

"I wasn't here for the construction," Felix continued. Eleven hadn't latched onto anything he'd said in the last several minutes.

She blinked. "What?"

"Your 'safe haven' is something else, isn't it?"

"That's one way to describe it."

*He said something about ships and chemicals. When did the subject change?*

*"How did I get so lucky?"*

Eleven clenched one hand at her side while rubbing her neck with the other. Isaac Kepler had never been welcomed. Luck had nothing to do with their encounters, private or otherwise. Quick to speak of love, he often showed it in nefarious ways.

*If I ever see that man again—stop thinking about him. Or anything else for that matter.*

Her teeth chattered despite the warm surroundings. Each new level of the windowless, steel complex showcased ingenuity.

*They repurposed train cars. Used things no one would miss.*

*"We don't have to go it alone. You and me, we're cut from the same cloth. Why not combine forces?"*

*Ten and I were so naïve.*

A hand fell onto Eleven's shoulder. A concerned Felix knelt in front of her. She had slumped against the nearest ridged metal wall. Felix swept a calloused thumb across Eleven's temple.

Eleven slapped his hand away. "I don't need your pity."

"Obviously," he replied. Felix chuckled as the locator breezed past him. "Where ya headed?"

"Outside."

"Then you're going the wrong way."

"Designation—"

"*Designation?*" Eleven's slip up amused him.

*Felix. His name is Felix Unger. Names are important. That's something I've never forgotten.*

"If you'd been listening, you might recall there's only one exit. Hint? It's not on the third floor."

"Show me, Felix."

"With pleasure." The guardian offered his hand to her again. Eleven raised a disinterested eyebrow. "Don't overthink it," he added.

"I'm in no mood to be coddled."

"Good," Felix said. "Because I'm not your boy. The air is pretty toxic. Sure you're up for outdoor time?"

"My body can more than withstand noxious fumes."

"Nice to see you haven't lost your sunny disposition in all the tweaks and turnarounds." Felix took in the sight of her. Eleven's body constricted further with each passing moment. His skeptical gaze dropped to the floor. Shaking his head, Felix said, "Come on then."

The rush came again. Eleven stared at the base of her cuticles. Memories forced her eyes shut.

*"She hasn't done anything! We're not a threat to you! Leave her—"*

*When will it end?*

Recollections flooded over Felix's words. Pixelated specks burned the backs of her eyes.

*"The modifications are quite simple. I can get her where she needs to be."*

"Eleven?"

Isaac towered over her. She clutched her throat.

*No.*

Eleven pleaded for a reality where Dr. Kepler didn't occupy the same space as her. She refused to open her eyes. The simple act of breathing became taxing. She began to hyperventilate.

"Eleven?"

Rough hands cupped her face. When she didn't respond, the palms held tighter. She locked eyes with Felix. Her apparent relief mirrored his. Each new breath came easier than the last.

"Having fun yet?"

Exhausted, Eleven pulled at one of Felix's thumbs, peeling it away from her clammy cheek. "I'm fine."

"Telling me or yourself that?"

*No more cages.*

Felix's musky scent soothed her. Eleven couldn't think as to why. At that moment, the locator chose not to care. Unwanted reminiscence had been halted. For now, that'd be enough.

"Hope you're not expecting a lot," Felix said as he helped Eleven to her feet. "This ain't the view you're used to."

"I wasn't on holiday."

"Right. Sorry."

After passing through numerous heavy doors and two other levels accessible by rusted ladders, they reached the top of the peculiar complex. Felix helped Eleven up, securing the rooftop entrance afterward.

*I don't recognize anything.*

Amber hues accompanying putrid odors moved at an almost glacial pace. Towered rectangular blocks surrounded them with small pathways riddled throughout. Acres upon acres of forgotten freights and containers.

*An actual shipyard.*

"Ain't doing wonders for that head trauma you're sporting."

Eleven ignored the concern. "We're still in Region 5?"

"Yep." Felix circled the locator with his hands in his pockets. "Outskirts of District 4."

She had hoped for a horizon. Anything to hint at some hidden gem, preferably a gorgeous view of untouched nature.

"Like I was saying earlier, a chemical manufacturer nearby made this place uninhabitable."

*Where would Ten be right now?*

"You know better than I do how much third-kinders can't stand pollution," Felix continued. "Makes this prime real estate for people wanting to stay under the radar."

*Hiding in tramp trailers. How far I've fallen.*

"Trick is to stay small and thin. Hard to pin down a locale or a leader if we're spread out."

Eleven covered her nose and mouth with her shirt and coat. She looked to Felix, who fought back a cough. He played it off by chuckling. "Just because we can breathe out here doesn't mean we should. Let's get back in."

*"Answer the question! Do as you're told and the pain stops!"*

"No."

Felix turned his back to her. "If you want to brave this alone, be my guest."

The locator inched closer to the tall structure's edge. Lost in thought, an agonizing highlight from her past overwhelmed her.

*"Tell me!"*

Eleven hit her temples, begging the memory to cease.

"Okay," Felix announced. He steadied Eleven as she lost her footing. "That settles it. I'm taking you in."

Eleven allowed him to help her inside. When they reached the fifth level, Felix opened the door and motioned for Eleven to enter. The smell of food had more sway than the guardian's chivalry.

*Don't you dare make a sound, stomach.*

"What's it like having all that stuff sifting around in there? Sort've like a reboot type of thing?"

Eleven's focus drifted from food to the disharmonious symphony happening throughout the welded shipping containers. The refrigerator crooned in the kitchen. Above and below vibrated heavily, hinting at major machinery on each respective floor. Eleven couldn't recall the last time she'd been out in the open without some kind of audible protection.

Felix waved his hands in front of her. "And I've lost you again."

"The room opposite here is meant for me?"

"Correct-a-mundo," Felix answered. His eyes grew heavy. "Two levels actually. Kind of cool from the little I've seen. Come on, I'll show you."

*He's exhausted.*

"That won't be necessary. I can manage without your assistance." Eleven exited the kitchen, not granting Felix a passing glance as she scurried across the hall.

*At least I hope I can manage without his assistance.*

Every centimeter of her room fell victim to scrutiny. At first glance, the cold space paled in comparison to that of her Ceruleman quarters. Closer inspection revealed that everything carried purpose or reason.

A tall wooden armoire almost matched the height of the room itself. Its contents were clothes, shoes, and accessories, all in Eleven's size. The cot carried more appeal than that of Eleven's former overly sterile housing. A stand to the side of the bed held a rusted lamp.

A ladder peaked through a hole in the room's far corner. In no time at all, Eleven found herself in a lower level library. Bound pages shielded all four walls of the first floor. The eclectic mix of fictional and factual muffled surrounding sounds. She strained to hear anything outside her immediate vicinity.

*"Alone at last."*

The extent of the eleventh locator's recollections proved to be more or less consistent in nastiness. There could be no better example than Dr. Isaac Kepler. Soon after falling into

Ceruleman hands, Eleven had developed a reputation for being difficult. She reveled in her disregard for rules and regulations. Alterations aside, her behavior made her impossible to control. Rebellious acts included attempting to escape, murder, and destruction.

Two years into her capture, a new physician was eager to please. Isaac hoped to gain favor by showcasing his capabilities. Eleven gave him such an opportunity. His first endeavors failed, causing the slightest bit of glee for his defiant patient. A locator's immunity to mind altering substances further complicated matters. He deduced early on that one's psyche could be persuaded through external force.

"What is your name?" The question started each of their appointments. "Eleven" proved to be the one and only correct response. Any other answer appeared inadequate.

Isaac wouldn't just slice or hit—he'd take a souvenir. He seemed obsessed with Eleven's "captivating" hazel irises. Kepler favored them over any other organ or extremity. In a short amount of time, he'd filled several containers with just her eyes alone.

"Where do you originate?"

The go-to reply ran along the lines of, "I come from nothing."

When Eleven answered otherwise, Isaac changed course. Favoring the archaic, his method for correcting the eleventh locator's brand of insolence came in the form of voltage.

"What is your purpose?" The finale.

Eleven often replied with, "To be."

Isaac chuckled at that or anything else remotely idealistic. He'd then follow by wrapping his hands around Eleven's neck. Before she'd lose consciousness, he'd release her. As she'd gasp for air, he'd circle her like predator.

"Poor lost girl nearly of heaven, surrounded by dangers unknown. One of few, never of many. Seldom would she be alone." Isaac painted himself something of a poet. Misery stirred his excitement. Any reaction heightened Dr. Kepler's resolve.

Determined not to cooperate, Eleven refused to be vocal during one particular encounter. She allowed not a single whimper as Isaac drew blood. The locator kept her composure when electricity came into play. Then they reached the final question, the inquiry accompanied by asphyxiation. Isaac grew so aggravated that he didn't stop. Even as the world around her fell, Eleven didn't break. Isaac squeezed tight enough to crush her larynx and fracture two vertebrae.

*However temporary, death is a sweet release.*

Snapping back from the memory, Eleven took a deep inhale. She'd stopped breathing without realizing it.

*Distraction. You need to distract yourself.*

Eleven charged at the shelves. She jostled the publications, occasionally flipping through pages. When finding nothing of immediate interest, she chucked books to the floor.

What began as curiosity turned into frenzy. Her breathing became heavy and uneven as she continued throwing books. Welts and bruises came and went, as did paper-cuts and gashes.

*"What's the eleventh locator without a little bloodshed?"*

Eleven's feet hid under layers of books, some heavier than others. She knelt down.

*The luxury of being fervidly raw—I'm not sure I care for it any more. He'd handle it better, wouldn't he?*

Pulling at the follicles near her temples, Eleven stopped short of ripping her hair out. She welcomed the fleeting pain. Anything to divert her from thinking about the man Cerulemans called "Ten." Her scalp throbbed, as did her hands. The locator released clumps of fisted hair and looked at the meat of her palms.

*I'm getting you out, brother. That's a promise.*

Eleven dropped her hands to see the edge of a red book with a dented gold font. The umlaut suggested the book was German in origin. Curiosity got the better of her.

## Märchen

The inside of the German fairy tale publication had been overwritten in an off-world language with bright green ink. Resting Märchen in her lap, Eleven scanned the pages of other books surrounding her. Some stayed open, albeit inelegantly given their earlier harsh landings.

*Chronicles.*

All manner of panic had fallen by the wayside in the presence of knowledge. The language changed here and there, seldom being in anything resembling a human tongue.

*What have I gotten myself into?*

• • • • • • • • • • •

*MORNING PEOPLE.*

Warmth from the walls indicated the sun had risen some time ago. Eleven lay in the fetal position amidst her investigative chaos. Lazy scrapes of silverware against ceramics grated the locator's ears.

*Why did they have to be morning people?*

Eleven had slept no more than a collective hour. Between debilitating episodes, she had lost herself in recounts from distant and not-so-distant worlds. Somehow the stories had calmed her.

A light knock resonated from above. "Eleven, you up?" Felix asked through the upper level door. "If you're hungry, you better get over here."

Being no closer to determining whether or not she'd stay frustrated Eleven. She didn't know how to engage without having an answer at the ready. Eleven weighed pros and cons until a loud rumble reminded her that it'd been at least half a day since she'd eaten. Healing exacerbated matters.

She spoke to her stomach. "Fine. You win."

Felix was gone by the time Eleven opened the door. Her mouth watered as a surge of smells from the kitchen reached her.

"Look who decided to join us," Vera said as Eleven entered the cramped space.

With a nudge courtesy of Crux, Vera turned her glare to her half-eaten plate. The two sat next to one another at a flimsy dinner table. Felix worked at cleaning countertops.

Crux kept his eyes on the portable device in his hand. He picked rotted fruits and vegetables, eating them as if it were the norm. "Good morning," he said between chews.

Pulling out a chair, Felix said, "I'll make you a plate."

"I can—"

"No," Felix interrupted. "I insist."

Vera loudly sipped her coffee as Felix piled all he could onto a worn, chipped plate. With a wave of his hand, Felix presented breakfast to Eleven.

*Am I so desperate for sustenance?*

Eleven took the food and hurried to the offered chair. Starved as she was, she curbed the urge to shovel down the artificial scrambled yolks and soy protein.

As Eleven made herself comfortable, Vera pushed away from the table without a word. She took her plate to the sink and began cleaning up. The silence made the clanging of dishes intolerable.

"Did you sleep well?" Crux inquired.

When Eleven didn't respond, Vera filled in the blanks. "Tantrum last night kind of spells it out, doesn't it?"

Felix sighed. "V."

"What? Even I heard it, which ain't an easy thing."

"Might we have some privacy?" Crux asked Vera and Felix.

Vera reeked of incredulity as she tossed a sponge so hard into the sink it ricocheted to the left side of the counter. She snatched a full mug of thick liquid posing as coffee near Crux, choking it down as she stomped out of the room. Felix dried his hands with the bottom of his shirt. He nodded as he left.

"I trust your accommodations are more than sufficient?"

"Does it matter?" Eleven asked Crux.

"I would not ask otherwise."

Hunger far from appeased, Eleven shoved her plate aside. She leaned her elbows onto the table and worked fingers through her hair. Crux placed his portable down. He then toyed with the traces of spoiled goods stuck on his bowl.

"Shall I continue to dispense pleasantries or just delve into the heart of the matter?" Eleven showed no indication of replying. "Very well. I assume you have deduced a great deal."

*He knows what I truly am. Maybe Vera as well. Felix is a different story. The three of them are part of a larger group. A movement wanting my help. Needs it. And they're not afraid to get their hands dirty.*

Taking her silence as acquiescence, Crux continued. "Locators, as they call them, are a treasured asset to Ceruleman kind. These fourth dimensional pockets, the chambers, call to a locator."

"Everyone knows this."

"No. Not *everyone*, Eleven." Crux dipped his head down. "Billions upon billions throughout the world, and only eleven individuals can access these chambers. You cannot die, nor do you age. This information is unknown to the public. In fact, it is a guarded secret."

*People think we're nothing more than bastards of science when guardians alone carry that burden.*

"Chambers are not theirs to control."

*Nor are they yours.*

"Naturally," Crux added. "It makes sense to minimize their leverage."

"To what end?" When Crux didn't elaborate, Eleven asked, "And what of the other locators?"

"Understand," Crux started as he crossed his arms, "that liberating you was by no means easy. Mr. Unger alone researched your life for months before spending the last two years climbing guardian ranks. Vera worked with—"

"Spare me the particulars. Are you saving him or not?" Eleven cringed at her slip of the tongue. It left her exposed. "*Them.*"

"Answer me this," Crux replied. "Why were you our first attempt?"

*Isaac hasn't aged more than a decade since my initial capture, which means Cerulemans haven't had me for long... I'm the youngest.*

Eleven grimaced at her conclusion. Dropping her gaze, she zeroed in on the misaligned linoleum under Crux's boot. "I was the easiest to get to."

*The weakest.*

"I would not have put it so crudely." Crux wiped the corners of his mouth with a thumb and forefinger. "We all have our assignments. Some are the remaining locators."

"They'll be free when your people are ready. Is that what you're telling me?"

Crux smirked. "To put it simply, yes."

"What about any of this falls under simplicity?" Unaccustomed to conveying such harsh articulation, Eleven's eyelids fluttered. The pounding of her heart also gave her pause.

*What will they do to him in my absence?*

"With your help, plans may excel. Unforeseen opportunities could present themselves. Having a locator of actual use may prove quite beneficial in all respects."

Eleven's eyes darted to the ends of Crux's fingers. They

varied from hers as far as width and shape, but one similarity could not be discounted. Thick, dark etchings identical to hers lay just beneath the surface of his nails.

"You think of yourself as a sort of glorified locksmith, but that is not your circumstance." Crux took Eleven's nearest hand. His presence did not elicit anxiety. "My word is one of the few things I have left. When I say the others will be freed, you should be inclined to believe it."

"I think I'll remain apprehensive."

Crux held back a smile while tightening his grip. "My goal is not to reason with you, Eleven. If you stay, it is because you decided to do so."

"And should I leave?"

"You will not be followed," Crux said. "Whatever path you choose, know that it does not get easier."

"Nothing is ever easy."

"In my experience, the best things rarely come without sacrifice. Mull it over for the day." Crux gathered his belongings.

*Don't speak to me of sacrifice.*

# 7

ELEVEN SAT ATOP THE MAKESHIFT STRUCTURE FOR the better part of the afternoon. Harsh sunrays made the steel hot to the touch. Despite sweltering heat and the pungent aroma, the lack of walls appeased Eleven.

*"Even the tiniest creature knows something about sacrifice."*

She winced at the memory. It had been one of the last things Ten said to her before the Cerulemans captured them.

*"The best things rarely come without sacrifice."*

*Sacrifice or pain? Pain is something else. Elusive yet fixed.*

Settling and creaks were deadened by dense gases. Eleven kept her eyes on the subdued sunset in the filmy distance.

*Where were we before? What did the locals call it? He'd remember.*

The locator distractedly ground flakes of rust and grime in her clammy palms. Her eyes flickered to the stack of new-to-her books towering nearby. She fought the urge to scan the pages.

*Are the chronicles his doing? Even if they're accurate, staying is how I get real answers.*

*Revolution was not our intention at first.*

*How many others are involved besides Felix, Crux, and Vera? Dozens? Hundreds? More?*

*We wished to not only survive, but live.*

*These people aren't my responsibility.*

*"Who cares how they got here or why they chose us? What matters is what we do with this."*

*You'd disagree, wouldn't you? Would you trust this? Trust them?*

Boots climbing a ladder pulled Eleven away from her thoughts. She rose to her feet and peered over the nearest edge. Growing darkness paired with pollution made the ground difficult to see. She chewed on her bottom lip.

*Twelve meters, maybe more.*

Inhaling sharply, Eleven aligned her toes to the edge. With the climber's footsteps drawing closer, Eleven clenched both arms at her sides and descended into the darkness below with a single leap. Landing on unsteady gravel inverted her right ankle and caused her to fall. Repressing a grunt, she caught herself.

"Give you a 7.5 for the landing." Felix's voice bounced off neighboring containers. The former guardian emerged from the mephitic mist. "Maybe a full eight since you didn't break through the skin."

"Were you waiting for me?"

"Right. Because I don't have my own stuff to do." Lowering two duffels, Felix wiped his palms as he approached. Eleven stiffened when he offered his assistance. He retracted his hand as she pushed herself up. Noticing her now-healed injuries, he said, "Never gonna get used to that."

*He's too close.*

Picking the path opposite Felix, she turned on her heels to evade him.

"Figured you'd have made a break for mainland sooner. Though I didn't think it'd involve any actual breaking." Eleven's pacing slowed. "Kind of pointless if you don't know where you're headed, isn't it?"

She stopped. "I can manage on my own."

Felix laughed. He swaggered as he caught up to Eleven. "Up for an adventure?" Eleven looked every direction but his. Felix blocked her when she tried to continue down the path. "Come on. I could use a break just as much as you."

"I don't need a chaperone, Felix."

"No offense, but every inch of you reads saturated lapdog."

*Not offensive in the slightest.*

"Sorry," Felix said as if reading Eleven's thoughts. "Let's not forget, you've never been in the outskirts, or anywhere for that matter, without an armed posse."

*What this man doesn't know could flood the five regions.*

Felix continued. "A roguish couplet out on the town would be a hint less bizarre, don't you think?"

*This world is a changed one. My unfamiliarity with it could be my downfall. They're looking for me. I can't make it easy for them.*

"In or out?" Felix asked. He crossed his right index and middle fingers over his heart. "Strictly platonic."

"That goes without saying."

Felix laughed hard enough for his whole body to shake. When he regained his composure, he created distance between them. Smiling as he walked backwards, Felix said, "I'm in the mood for some good bad food and something with a kick."

"I didn't say I'd go."

"Might as well have. Get the lead out, Eleven. We gotta make you presentable."

*I'm going to regret this.*

• • • • • • • • • • •

ELEVEN LEANED AGAINST A WALL WHILE WATCHING Felix rummage through box after box of clothing in a container presumably meant for storage. He seemed determined not to give any hint as to what he was searching for. Grumbling with each failure to locate this questionably pivotal item, Felix visibly relaxed as he pulled out a military green wool bomber jacket.

"Finally," Felix said. Shaking off aged mothballs and bits of dust, he picked off frayed seams and presented it to Eleven. "Okay, so I don't know shit about fashion, but this should fit you."

"I have a jacket," Eleven said.

Felix tossed the heavy outerwear to her. "Not like this one, you don't."

*Not synthetic wool, at least not completely. No label. Tight stitching. This isn't factory made.*

Eleven explored the intricacies of the curious hood. Squinting, she tried to make sense of three clumps along the brim.

"Play on some Ceruleman tech. My dad was kind of a tinkerer. Vera improved on it but refuses to tell me how." Felix motioned for Eleven to try it on. Though still uncertain as to his reasoning, she removed the shambled scraps of her pea coat. Both were surprised at the perfect fit, hugging the locator in all the right places. Felix threw up the hood. "And voilà."

"I can't see anything."

Felix grumbled as he drew back the hood. Eleven scowled as she met his gaze. "You're lucky I like you, Eleven." He appraised Eleven's overall appearance. Remembering something, Felix went to a nearby drawer. "Guessing you don't want people to see those," he said, indicating Eleven's fingertips. Felix chucked a pair of worn driving gloves at her. "Keep the hood up and they won't see you. Surveillance-wise anyway."

"How?"

"Scrambles frequencies or some shit. Vera explained it to me on three separate occasions and I just stopped asking after that. Point is, you want to stay hidden in plain sight. Especially now that bounties are posted."

*Bounties… like a common criminal. Of course.*

"Want to know how much they're offering for your 'safe return'?" Felix smirked.

"No," Eleven said quietly. She stared at her hands. "Maybe this is a mistake."

"Less doubt, more follow-through."

*Cerulemans and their bounties… they know what desperation breeds.*

"Still with me?"

Eleven nodded as she slipped on the gloves. She inspected the clothing Felix had gone through.

"Who did these belong to?"

Ignoring her question, Felix asked, "Ready to head out?"

"Where are we going?"

"The best place." Felix took a small device from his pocket. He tossed it without regard. "Okay, maybe not the *best* place, but... never mind. You'll get what I mean when you see the joint."

Eleven couldn't look away from the object Felix held. Every facet clear, the material was similar to quartz. Five circular guards secured Felix's left hand. Extending his fingers wide, a slight hum tickled the hairs on Eleven's earlobes.

"No time like the present," Felix said.

"Is tha—? We're going to teleport?"

"And you thought Cerulemans had all the perks."

A smiling Felix proved that Eleven's befuddlement was obvious. He pulled her close to him. Curiosity prevented Eleven from objecting to the guardian's bold gesture. Folding his digits over the teleporter one at a time, the frequency intensified when his left hand clenched.

"This should be fun."

Eleven gulped. "What's to be expected?"

"No idea," Felix responded. "Never done this before."

With a flash of burning white light, the two went from a dank shipping container to an alleyway amidst a grand city. Both rattled from the experience, they managed to keep their breaths even. Eleven remained transfixed on Felix's contorted face.

"Is it over?" Breaking his hold, Eleven shoved Felix into the mildew-ridden brick wall behind him.

He steadied himself. "Hey. Easy."

"Easy?" Eleven paced, her gloved fingers fidgeting at her sides. Derelict passersby gave her pause.

Felix pushed off the wall but kept his distance. He licked his lips. "Time, for one, is not on our side." The beginnings of rain stopped his argument. Splaying his arms wide, Felix looked to Eleven. His amusement faltered. "The other travel option was to go by train. Crux mentioned something about motion sickness a while back and—"

"Stop talking as if you know me."

The brave new world assaulted Eleven's ears. Her time in Ceruleman control had left her audibly vulnerable.

"Like it or not, I do," Felix replied. "Creepy? Maybe, but thems the breaks." He surveyed the little he could make out through the darkness. Wiping grime on the hips of his jeans, he added, "Besides, always wanted to try that."

Pacing, Eleven asked, "How does it work?"

"Crux tried to take over a human once with the original. It cremated him. Not a great day."

*The original? Teleportation isn't human technology.*

"V based it on Crux's with a few mods here and there."

"And you're certain we wouldn't have suffered the same fate as this human before?"

Felix shrugged. "We're not exactly human, are we? Come on. I'm buying."

• • • • • • • • • • •

"FINALLY," FELIX SAID.

After ten minutes of walking, the two arrived at their destination: Onward Betty's. The walls were filled with nostalgic throwbacks, namely signs and posters that attempted to master the double entendre. Most surfaces conjured images of tetanus.

Felix made his way to the back of the establishment. Eleven hesitated at the front double doors. Noticing her reluctance, Felix took her by the hand and guided her.

"Act out of place and you'll be out of place," he said.

The farther they went, the dimmer the lighting. Couples and crooks took full advantage of the darkness. But what gave Eleven pause wasn't Onward Betty's seedy clientele. She scoured corners for telltale signs of security.

*Minimal surveillance. Downright criminal.*

Zeroing in on the one free table, the pair approached a booth riddled with peanut shells and half-filled mugs. Eleven sneered at the crumpled napkins and scraps.

"Not up to your standards?"

Before Eleven could reply, a disheveled individual scurried up to their booth. Onward Betty's bartender and waitress, clearly having lost her more endearing qualities long ago, drummed a pen against a worn notepad. "What'll it be, ladies?"

"Ben here?" Felix asked.

"Ben's dead."

"Well, shit."

"Yeah, real sad." The waitress sighed. "Should I come back?"

"No, I think we're ready. Kitchen's open, right?"

"Unfortunately."

Felix chuckled. "Just give us the specials."

"Two burgers, two fries. Real thrill seekers. What are you drinking?"

"Vodka. Best keep the bottle handy."

The waitress scribbled in shorthand. Eleven read the aged advertisement to the right of her.

# SHAKE THINGS UP!

"And a chocolate shake," Eleven added. Felix and the waitress turned to her. Putting her hands together, Eleven slouched against the sagging booth cushion.

"A shake?" Felix asked. Eleven nodded but didn't meet his eyes. "Make that a chocolate malt. More savory, less synthetic." With a quick nod, the waitress walked off as she finished writing down the order. Eleven's mouth flattened.

Felix fumbled with the nearest peanut shell. "Why a shake?"

"Why vodka?" Eleven countered.

"We're at a bar. That's what you drink, isn't it?"

*How does he know all of this?*

The disgruntled worker returned with a bottle, two shot glasses, and a pitcher of water. She put the glasses on the worn table.

"Food'll be right up." She knocked on the table. As she walked toward the bar, she said, "Name's Henrietta if you need anything else."

"Knew someone that used to work here. Got paid in food mostly." Felix poured himself some water. His forehead crinkled as he sipped. "Figured burger and fries was the safest bet. Third-kind food ain't much better."

Felix opened the bottle, pouring its contents with care. The guardian smiled as Eleven caught a shot glass slid in her direction. Vodka spilled over the brim.

"To the other side."

After waiting a beat too long, Felix slung back the shot. Eleven turned her drink clockwise and counterclockwise between her index finger and thumb.

"So?"

"So." Eleven pinched at the point of her hood.

"Can you get drunk?"

"Sorry?"

Smiling, Felix repeated the question. "Can you get drunk?"

"Seems like something an adept person such as yourself should already know."

"Again with the jokes." Felix poured himself another shot. Eleven drank the vodka. "I can't."

"Really?" Felix pushed. The former guardian emptied his glass once more. "What kind of sense does that make? I mean, I can get drunk."

"Because we're not the same."

Immediate regret shadowed her outburst. No matter the alteration, Eleven didn't afford herself the luxury of externally speaking her mind often.

"So they say, Eleven."

Henrietta reappeared with two baskets of food-like products and a tall chocolate malt. By all accounts, the cliché coloring and odors suggested the burgers and fries were edible. Condensation pooled along the sides of Eleven's malt.

Placing a thick stack of napkins on the table, Henrietta said, "Enjoy."

Felix took his greasy burger in both hands. The bun cracked around his grip. With difficulty, Felix gulped it down. "Remind me not to order anything else."

"Doubt anyone comes here for the cuisine."

"True enough," Felix said as he braved a steak fry. He slid the malt toward Eleven. "Can't all be shit." Giving in, Eleven took the offered beverage and sipped.

*Not bad.*

"Ain't got nothing like this on the base, do they?" Eleven looked around. Felix waved off her concern. "Relax. We're in good company here."

The statement threw her. Taking another sip, Eleven said, "You'd be surprised where sympathizers lurk."

*And greed sways.*

"Not here, that's for damn sure." Felix chewed on another fry. "An Onward Betty customer isn't fond of working for third-kinders, myself included."

"Hard to believe, given the company you keep."

"Crux is different."

"How?" Eleven pressed.

"Stick around. Find out for yourself." Felix poured more vodka. He filled Eleven's glass before she could answer. "What do you miss?"

*Right now? Quiet.*

"What did *you* miss?" Felix savored his tall glass of tepid water. Eleven didn't relent. "What kept you on this... *path*?"

Felix chewed on his straw. "Usual stuff."

"Family?"

"Not in the traditional sense. After our parents passed away, we were put in the system. Me and my sister Lani. Managed to stick together for two years." He took another shot. "Lost track of her when I turned eighteen."

Felix's fingers thrummed a hypnotic beat. Eleven took in the features of his face, tilting her head for a better view.

*Can't be a day over 30. That sliver of blue around the corneas indicates he's been dosing for some time now. Years. Maybe a decade.*

"Are you trying to find your sister?" Eleven asked with genuine curiosity.

The interrogation role reversal threw Felix. He shifted in his seat. "Ties like that don't often mean anything. People like Vera, even Crux some days, they're family."

"I don't understand."

"Like you said," Felix replied, his casual demeanor fading. "We're not the same."

*"After our parents passed away, we were put in the system."*

*Children without a home to call their own.*

Though adoption wasn't unheard of, costs seldom allowed siblings to remain together. Many opted for infertility treatments courtesy of Ceruleman medical facilities or no children at all.

*He may not have volunteered... but did Lani?*

"Showed up more than any of the others in my research. One might even say a lot. So what's he like?"

Eleven blinked. "Who?"

"Take a wild guess."

Rather than answer, she hid behind her chocolate malt. Felix began to pour yet another shot. Eleven yanked the vodka bottle away from him.

"Hey!"

"Is alcohol poisoning the purpose of tonight's outing?"

"Eleven."

"Please, do speak louder, *Felix*. I'm sure there are droves of people with that name running about."

Sweat pooled below Felix's hairline. Dark circles underneath his eyes had become more prominent in a matter of minutes. His hands lightly twitched.

*He's drying out.*

"When was your last dose?"

Felix narrowed his gaze. "The hell did that come from?"

"I'm observant."

"That's none of your business."

"Keeping up with your dosage is of vital importance," Eleven pointed out.

"I got the rundown some time ago, friend. I'm well aware of the risks, okay?" Felix reached for the vodka. Eleven moved it to the opposite end of the table. "Hand over the bottle, Your Ladyship."

*He can have a psychotic break when I'm not dependent on his well-being. How should I approach this?*

"Stick to water for the remainder, and I'll answer anything you want."

Felix asked, "This a negotiation?"

"Eight questions, no limits. Once in a lifetime opportunity, one might say." Eleven raised the dwindling vodka supply. "So what will it be?"

The corners of Felix's mouth twitched. He crossed his arms as he leaned back. "Deal."

"First, a precaution." Eleven popped open the lid and proceeded to finish off the bottle. Felix watched in amazement. The locator slid the now empty container to him. "Let's get this over with."

"Okay," Felix said through laughter. "We'll start off simple. Where are you from?"

"North."

"Where up north?"

"Region 3."

*I think.*

Felix sipped on his water. "Family still alive?"

*He doesn't know.*

"No family. Blood ties or otherwise."

Felix scratched at his stubble. "How old are you?"

"Is that information not available in one of your plentiful 'Locator Eleven' files?"

"Says you're 26," Felix replied.

"Then I must be 26."

*Give or take a few decades.*

"Hang on," Felix said. He leaned forward. "You said you'd answer anything."

"And I have thus far."

Altering course, Felix asked, "Weirdest thing you've ever found in a chamber?"

"A kazoo," Eleven answered. "Your guess is as good as mine."

"All right." Felix rubbed the back of his neck. "Why are chambers a big deal to third-kinders? I don't see the benefit."

*You do. Every day. You're just blind to it... as you're supposed to be.*

"That's not for me to say."

"Not really answering the question."

The slight amusement in Eleven's face vanished in an instant. She thought better of shutting down, determined to keep to her word. "No one knows how they came into being or why. Not even me."

"Crux says they provide hope."

*"For the people, never for profit."*

Eleven rolled her eyes. "To some, I imagine that's true."

"So, I ask again—"

"They're power, Felix." Eleven toyed with the dew on the malt. Another memory threatened to surface.

*"As long as we have you—"*

*Shut up!*

She dropped her hands into her lap. "It's as simple as that."

"Sounds like locators have the upper hand."

In spite of herself, Eleven regarded Felix. There wasn't a hint of sarcasm to his words. Clearing her throat, she said, "Which is why we're… *utilized*."

"Utilized?"

*Just ask the next question.*

Changing tactics again, Felix asked, "Got a sweetheart?"

*Two left. Nothing off-limits, and* this *is what he asks?*

"No."

"Bullshit."

"In case you haven't been keeping track, you have one left."

Adjusting, Felix asked, "Do you miss him?"

*The more things change.*

"Yes," Eleven admitted.

"Ten means that much to you?"

"That makes nine, sorry."

"Don't shut down on me now, Eleven. Things are getting good."

Eleven raised her chin, leveling her gaze at him. She leaned a temple against the palm of her hand. Though nowhere near intoxicated, the day in the sun, teleportation, alcohol intake, and ever-changing conversation had begun to take their toll.

*Have they even let him remember me?*

"We'll get him."

Sighing, Eleven asked, "Same way you retrieved me?"

"Probably."

"Excellent. I look forward to a reunion in the next decade or so."

Felix chuckled. "What? You got somewhere else to be? Near as I can tell, we just blew your schedule wide open."

"And I suppose you're wanting a thank you?"

"No," Felix replied. He waved a hand in Eleven's direction. "Brilliant idea though."

*Maybe I should've just let him drink himself to death.*

"Did your superior put you up to this? Are you going to give me the full pitch now?"

"Nobody tells me what to do. Crux isn't my boss," Felix said in a rush. He pulled at the hem of his leather jacket. "He doesn't know we're talking. Though, he's probably got some inkling about now. And, for the record, Crux would relish the chance to pep-talk it up. Granted, he'd leave out choice 'fucks' and 'shits.' All I'm saying is the rest'll make it out of there. Maybe even sooner with your help."

"And then what?"

Felix was saved from responding by their waitress. Henrietta laid down a small, flat portable. "Ready when you are." Felix waved his wrist over the aged gadget. With a couple digital clicks and a swipe, Henrietta nodded. "Thank you, Mr. Stephens."

Brushing his palms together, Felix said, "Add twenty percent for yourself."

"Much obliged," Henrietta said over her shoulder.

"Mr. Stephens?" Eleven asked.

Felix lazily threw her a salute. "Patrick Stephens, civil servant. Nice to meet you, ma'am."

Grasping for the last precious bits of malt with a less than cooperative straw, Eleven stopped. A piercing sensation hit her right between the eyes.

"Ice cream headache? Hate it when that happens." Felix picked at her stale fries. He pushed the basket in front of Eleven. "Try something solid. Your cast-iron stomach will serve you well."

*I should be hungry. Starved.*

"You could make a difference with us."

"And what leads you to believe you're *making a difference*? That any of you in this *movement* can stop them?"

"I have faith," Felix answered.

"I'm sure that did wonders for your sister."

The hurt in Felix's eyes spoke volumes. "What I do and why I do it don't matter to you."

"Felix, I—"

"You're not sorry, so don't bother. Like I said, I've done my homework."

Neither spoke for the next few minutes.

"Regurgitating some pathetic company line won't inspire me to join you." Leaning away from the table, Eleven crossed her arms.

Felix chugged down acidic water. Refilling his glass, he said, "How does personally screwing over every one of those smug bastards sound? Cutting them at their damn core."

"Freeing locators does that?"

Pressing his forearms against the table, Felix leaned toward Eleven. "It's a start. Pull a seemingly insignificant thread, no big deal. Keep pulling? No more afghan."

"You knit?"

"No more locators, no more chambers. At least not for them."

*Just complete control of a world that embraces them with open, pudgy arms.*

"We're not all suckers," Felix added. "I'm living proof of that. Otherwise, you'd be getting a shiatsu right about now or going over mission parameters with the region's finest. I've seen what you can do, and I know the kind of person you are. You've got more power than you know what to do with."

"Please make no references to being chosen."

"Fuck being chosen. Who the hell wants to work with some fucker doing shit out of obligation? If you're gonna do something, do it because you can't see yourself doing anything else."

The tired locator tilted her head. Felix's drunken attempt to sway her brought more questions than answers.

*"I'm not here because I have to be."*

*You'd have said yes, wouldn't you?*

Felix deflated. "For what it's worth, Crux put a shit-load of eggs in the locator basket and he's never wrong. Except when he is." He continued to melt into the bench. "What have you got to lose, Eleven?"

# 8

HINTS OF DAWN LIGHTENED THE CITY HORIZON AS
Eleven and Felix hurried back to the deserted alley. Returning to
the shipyard proved difficult. Other than inputting coordinates,
Felix was no help in teleportation instruction. Luckily, Eleven
had paid close attention during their initial outing. She left the
rest to chance. They materialized on the lower level of her
container-turned-quarters.

"Not bad." Felix fell, taking a pile of books down with him.
"I'm good."

*The alcohol must've burned up most of his dosage.*

With jerked fluidity, Felix stood. His brow furrowed as he
took in the state of the room. Creating a path with heavy boots,
he kicked his way to the corner ladder.

"Felix?"

He rested a foot on the lowest step. "Yeah?"

*Just let him go. He isn't your responsibility.*

"Everything okay?" Felix asked.

"I'd dose if I were you."

"But you aren't me," Felix snapped.

*See where being nice gets you?*

Turning back to the ladder, Felix focused on the rung he gripped tightly. "Look, you're not the first person to baby me on my meds."

"I'm not trying to—"

"I've been on it for years. I think I know what I'm doing by now."

"Is that why you're shaking?" Eleven replied.

Contrived amusement fell from Felix's face. "If I want help, I'll ask for it."

Soldiers in the field often sustained injuries. The dose provided and created by Cerulemans limited the need for medical attention. And thus, guardians came into being. Humans with the ability to heal.

A drawback, however, came in the form of addiction. Once introduced to the bloodstream, the human body craved this so-called miracle. Guardians never reacted well when going through withdrawal. Eleven knew that better than most.

Shaking away a response, Felix crawled up the ladder. Eleven kept a firm stance until the sound of him dwindled.

Seconds after her door closed, Eleven climbed to the upper level. Falling onto the small cot, she took the teleporter from her pocket. She examined it against the nightstand's dim light.

• • • • • • • • • • •

ELEVEN RUBBED HER EYES WHILE SIMULTANEOUS-ly growling in frustration. She pushed herself upright as dissonance across the way erupted.

"Oh, I'm sorry," Vera said.

*Where are stoppers when I need them?*

Much to Eleven's dismay, Vera continued to make a racket in the kitchen. "Is this bothering you, Unger?"

*I could live a millennium and still not be a morning person.*

"Damn it, V. Not now."

"You've got a lot of nerve," Vera snapped.

"Just needed to let off some steam."

"Yeah, I bet," Vera replied. Gas burners flicked on. "Making eggs."

"Real or powdered?"

"What do you think?" Thick liquids whisked and stirred. "Next time you take a toy without asking, I'm gonna stab you a little. Capiche?"

A graveled chuckle escaped Felix. Eleven did a double take when she looked to the nightstand. She leaned over the cot's edge before searching her sheets and pillowcase.

*It's gone.*

"Good night?" asked Vera.

"I've had better," Felix replied. He sipped loudly. "Had worse." A thick-coated skillet landed hard on a burner. Even Eleven jumped. "Jesus, V. You're at a 10 and I need you at a 2."

"Got a never-ending pile of crap to get through. This place isn't near where it needs to be. I'll need your help with inventory later."

"Do I get my own clipboard?" Felix asked.

"Jackass."

"Didn't you just do inventory?"

"Salvaging does wonders to stock. Add that to whatever the hell Crux is doing—"

Felix cut her off. "What is he doing?"

"You'd have to ask him."

"We'll manage, V. Always do."

"Stuff ain't getting any easier to find, *Designation HD62*."

"Do not call me that. Stupid name."

Vera lightened her tone. "More like a fucking ISBN."

"Those don't have letters, V. Any more coffee?"

"Add it to the list."

Slurps and scrapes wreaked havoc on Eleven's superior hearing. She leaned against the ridged wall next to her cot, annoyance deepening her frown. Drowning out external noises at certain times was effortless, especially when unintentionally eavesdropping.

*Whoever took the teleporter had to be quiet.*

Vera interrupted Eleven's train of thought. "How's Her Highness?"

"You've been reading her files," Felix replied.

"Skimmed here and there."

"So you know how much she hates that."

"Who wouldn't?" Vera asked through chews. "You might want to take it easy with the whole nice guy act."

"Who says I'm acting?"

Vera scoffed. "Anyone that's known you for more than five seconds."

"She's good. Green, but she'll get there."

"What the hell makes you and *him* so sure of that? Snagging alien goodies doesn't make someone any better than the rest of us *homo sapiens*."

"Not even sure she's human."

"Could say the same thing about you these days, Unger."

What Vera hinted at in her less than subtle comment hadn't gone unnoticed by anyone in the room. Or within earshot.

"Heard from anybody else?" Felix asked.

"Outside normal check-ins? Not for a while."

"Might need to trade this and that. Maybe do a barter type of thing."

Vera hummed to herself. "Anything springing to mind? Operating under the assumption that *Her Highness* will be staying, we'll need more food than other posts if that's what you're getting at."

"Partially. Don't get me wrong—being on the mend does

things to the metabolism. We should also consider the state of our arsenal and—"

"Just fucking get to the point already. Off the charts IQ, Unger. Though it doesn't take a genius to figure it out."

"Vera."

"*Felix.*"

A chair screeched against the kitchen floor. Silverware clanged into the steel sink. Curiosity piqued, Eleven leaned in the direction of the kitchen.

"Eleven?" Crux called through the door. Eleven bolted upright. "Are you presentable?" Without waiting for a reply, he entered and closed the door behind him. Crux examined her dingy room. "Your heartbeat is irregular."

On cue, Eleven took deep breaths as she turned from the crimson man. Pulsations slowed to a steady pace.

"Breakfast?" Crux presented a wrinkled, greasy bag. "I always buy too much. Joining me would be a kindness. We could even stay in here if you prefer."

Eleven's hunger for information as well as food resulted in her sitting cross-legged opposite the offworlder. To her surprise, Crux's presence didn't bother her. But she still avoided his gaze.

"Curious thing, a burrito." Crux assessed the wrapped filling in his broad hand. He picked at bits that threatened to drop while he sat in the middle of the room. "Best when eaten fresh, which is a rarity for me."

*Glad to see I'm not the only one that's rubbish at pleasantries.*

"I trust your expedition devoid of escorts proved fruitful?" Eleven met Crux's lilac irises. He chewed on his burrito. "If I recall correctly, I was not skilled in the art of camouflage when I first arrived."

"From?" Eleven asked.

"I take it you are familiar with the scrolls of Aqandrose?"

"I am."

Leaning back on his hands, Crux said, "Enlighten me."

"It was a historical account of Dusslore. The planet itself was destroyed centuries ago."

"*Was* a historical account?" Crux asked.

"The parchment was lost in a chemical fire."

"According to whom?"

"It's a matter of record."

Crux dropped his gaze. Pain matured his face, causing deep lines to burrow. "Do you know the specifics as to how Dusslore was decimated?"

*The scrolls indicated foul play, but the details were few. Something about… Cerulemans.*

"How did they do it?" Eleven asked.

"Cerulemans have their methods."

"Is that why you're here? Vengeance?"

He shook his head. "Mine is a mission of peace."

"Peace?"

Crux rested his forearms on his legs. "Before Ceruleman intervention, my people were amicable."

*Which no doubt contributed to their downfall.*

"I sought refuge," he added.

"This world offered asylum." Eleven thought back to the Märchen chronicle.

*Nothing to fear. Nothing to fight. Now they are nothing.*

Aqandrose scrolls cited Dusslore's demise plainly. Reality appeared to be much more complicated.

"Given the information within their pages, one can assume your captors destroyed the scrolls."

*All hints and half-stories. It isn't enough.*

"I wish to discuss your stay here. If you had planned to leave, I suspect you would have made use of the teleporter formerly in your possession."

Stopping mid-chew, Eleven asked, "*You* took it?"

"Mr. Unger seized an object he had no claim to. Fortunately for him, I have an urgent matter to attend to." Crux took the teleporter from his coat. Tossing it back and forth, he maintained eye contact with the woman across from him. "How would you have fared without him? We only know what has been observed during your captivity. Have you ever been without a companion?"

*Does no one think I can endure alone?*

"Don't confuse fleeting naiveté with commitment."

"I would be a fool doing so," Crux replied through a chuckle. He pushed himself up then extended a hand to Eleven. "It is not a weakness."

"Companionship?"

"To acknowledge shortcomings."

Shaking her head, Eleven grimaced at her shortage of options. Crux watched her, but not predatorily. Curiosity flickered within his purple eyes. He pulled Eleven up with minimal effort.

She wiped moist palms against the crests of her hips. "I understand I'm in your debt. Make no mistake, I am grateful for what you've done."

"However?"

"*However,* my gratitude has limitations."

Crux waved her words away. "You need not explain yourself. You are more than welcome to make an informed decision."

"Were you given a choice?"

"The people we work with think me a leader. A beacon for change. I am one being, Eleven."

"Blood is being spilled by those following you. If it's peace you truly seek, this isn't the way."

Crux looked to his feet. "Yet there is no alternative. People precious to me reside here. I count you among them."

*Me?*

"That makes this world my home, and I refuse to lose another."

Ten came to mind at Felix's mention of family. Eleven contemplated what she'd do to keep him safe. What she should have done.

*Is he reason enough to stay?*

"I have a request." Gathering muster, Crux's tone eased. "I am uncertain how long I will be gone. Would you watch over Vera until my return?"

Eleven squinted. "She can more than handle herself from what I've seen."

"What one can do is not a direct correlation with what one should."

*He sees her through a father's eyes.*

"You trust me this much?" Eleven asked.

"Entirely."

"You shouldn't."

Crux approached, stopping just short of touching Eleven. "You are my kin. That carries weight."

*What is the fascination with family?*

"Continue to think us monstrous?" he asked. Crux's question mirrored Eleven's earlier blank slate inquiry. His distinct fingertips piqued her interest. The Dusslorean took a deep inhale and closed his eyes. "We share a bond few are capable of possessing."

"Say it, Crux."

"We called ourselves seekers. Surely you didn't believe humans were the first to be gifted the chambers."

Unable to move, Eleven asked, "How many?"

"Only eleven are operational."

"That isn't an answer."

Exhaling, Crux replied, "No. It is not."

*How many others? Are more here? What did the Märchen chronicle say?*

*World after world.*

*Do Cerulemans know of this? What am I saying*—Of course they do.

Crux smiled. "When I return, we will begin your training."

"I am already trained."

"Even in the realm of combat, that is debatable given the details of your arrival here. There is so much more to learn, both in and out of battle." Crux sauntered to the door. He stopped as he reached for the knob and turned to face Eleven. "Do I have your word?"

*I need more. This* kin *of mine might be inclined to share if I prove myself.*

"Yes. I'll watch her."

# 9

FAR-OFF STIRS WOKE ELEVEN. SHE TURNED ONTO her stomach, burying her face into a poor excuse for a pillow. Covering her ears with the cushion's edges failed to drown out Vera's curses and Felix's placid responses.

*Third night in a row. You have got to be joking. Just kill each other and be done with it.*

Vera berating Felix had become commonplace. Location and distance suggested both hoped to go unheard. With Eleven keeping to herself and speaking when deemed necessary, the indignant pair carried on unaware that anything muttered went noticed. Eleven's combing fingers caught on the knotted ends of her curls.

*How does the Dusslorean handle this redundant disarray?*

A return to sleep eluded Eleven for the better part of an hour. She opened her eyes at the sound of boots against steel.

*Too light for Felix. Has to be Vera.*

Eleven froze as the steps drew closer. She waited for the doorknob to turn. A loud thud jolted her.

Moments later, the boots descended.

Eleven opened the door a sliver, suspicious of what awaited her on the other side. Six books bound together in oil-soaked twine stood at the edge of the ladder opening. A blank sheet of paper waved and crinkled as the air system ran through its cycle. Eleven knelt down and snatched at a corner. It had one word.

HOMEWORK.

• • • • • • • • • • •

"WHAT ARE YOU READING?"

Eleven ignored Felix's inquiry. She attempted to find where she'd left off. She squinted at the writing. Today's reading was a manual that had been scribbled over in blue ink.

*The first partner with entitlement. To think they—*

"Fine," Felix continued. He stood over multiple burners. "Don't tell me. I'm just the jerk making you breakfast."

Fighting a chuckle, Eleven followed along a bumpy line of text with her finger. Vera walked in covered in miscellaneous lubricants and greases. She threw an oily rag over the pages of Eleven's morning read.

"That really what you're spending your time on?"

*I said I'd watch her. There was no assurance that I had to enjoy the undertaking.*

"I'll get to your recommendations eventually, Vera." Pinching at the driest patch, Eleven chucked the rag to the floor. She dog-eared her page before shutting the book.

"Rounding out the week here and you've done jack shit to contribute."

"V."

"Felix Maxwell Unger, don't you even try," Vera warned.

He inverted his lips as he turned off burners and went in search of plates. Taking the seat across from Eleven, Vera made a show of crossing her legs as she sat.

Eleven asked, "In what way do ill-constructed texts on locksmithing and the like qualify as a contribution?"

"If you're half as smart as this cockhole seems to think you are, shouldn't take you long to figure it the fuck out."

Felix, a welcome distraction, placed plates in front of the two. He sat between the women and attacked his own breakfast. Eleven pushed her book aside, twirling a fork as she dug in.

"You know," Felix started, "might be useful if we can pop locks. Make use of people's forgotten?"

*A lot of help you are, guardian.*

Snatching a bundle of silverware, Vera took her plate and approached the door. "Thanks for the grub," she said as she exited.

Felix and Eleven ate in silence until hearing a door shut. Felix dropped his fork. He leaned an elbow against the table. Vera always left him with a similar melancholy. Eleven continued to chew, avoiding his worrisome face.

"Doubt any of that was about you," Felix said. He picked at his plate. "Just her with a pinch of me for flavor."

*Let it go. Don't engage.*

"Why does she want me to do this?" Eleven asked.

Felix shrugged. "Why does Vera do anything? She's a fan of playing up the mystery." He sipped on his coffee. As he lowered his mug, a sly grin formed. "Besides, it's not like you aren't interested. The task involves reading and working on your own."

*Sans incessant coddling? Tempting.*

"Maybe this is your calling."

*Oh, how healing and the fourth dimension pale in comparison.*

Eleven made quick work of her food. She dabbed at the corners of her mouth after clearing her plate.

Felix watched as she slurped down a tall glass of instant orange juice. "Just think about it, Eleven."

• • • • • • • • • • •

AFTER BREAKFAST, ELEVEN RETREATED TO THE comfort of her room. She paced near her cot, staring at the short stack of books on her nightstand. They were on picking locks, making use of scraps, living off the grid, and so on. Vera had gifted Eleven a care package on becoming self-sufficient.

Eleven lifted her pillow at two corners and shook. A leather bound volume tumbled onto her sheets. She brushed her fingertips along its spine.

*Who needs to know of locators throughout the universe when I can learn how to purify water with iodine?*

Eleven slumped onto the cot, dragging the back of a thumb against her temple. She sighed. Tossing the book aside, she reached for the smallest book lying at the top of the heap. The beginner's guide to locksmithing featured more diagrams than words. Its aged pages gave some relevant information. Black ballpoint handwriting filled in what weathering had erased. Additional notes and references had been scribbled down in open spaces.

*Tweezers, followers, gauges, shims. They long to turn me into a common criminal.*

Her expression eased as she read on. The simplicity of design in most locks—key and keyless—intrigued Eleven. She rarely encountered latches bound by anything other than passcodes and interfaces. Though she questioned the extent to the use of such knowledge, Eleven absorbed line after line. Within twenty minutes, she'd reached the last page. On the inside of the back cover read:

*Why stop here?*

*That handwriting.*

Eleven searched for the note that had lain on top of the book stack upon its arrival at her door. The homework note had been lazily scribbled in a poor excuse for print, while the notations and back cover inquiry were in thick-lined cursive. Comparing the two samples left no room for doubt—this involved two penmen.

*Did Vera want me to read these or Crux? And what purpose could any of this possibly serve?*

An intense ringing claimed Eleven fully. She panicked, covering her ears, but the invasive sound persisted. She fell to her knees and began to feel faint. Trying to focus on the flaking, rusty floor, she watched red droplets splatter. Eleven withheld a guttural scream.

Moments later, the sound ceased. Eleven wiped her nose with the back of her hand. She found it coated in blood. The whole of her body shivered with a savage hunger. She wrapped both arms around her stomach.

*What is this?*

A loud thrash from the ground level ricocheted through the complex. Felix and Vera were in some kind of struggle. Eleven hustled down the ladder, unsure of what she'd find when she got there. She worried about keeping her promise to Crux. For whatever reason, it mattered.

"Are you brainsick?" Felix's feverish voice traveled up the laddered column.

Vera grunted. "Back the fuck off, Unger!"

Eleven took a deep breath.

*This is going to hurt.*

She retreated from the ladder, collapsing onto the complex's lowest level. Eleven landed on her side and bit back an imploring vocalization. She looked to the open door of Lab 1. A shortage of sound brought her to her feet.

"Hello?" Eleven called as she passed the threshold. She found Felix cutting off Vera's circulation in a chokehold. "Felix, no!"

Felix tightened his hold as Eleven neared. "Don't." Similar to Eleven's blood loss, he also had red dripping down his ears and nose. His fingers trembled.

*It burned through me—through him. I've seen this craze before.*

"You don't want to hurt her." Eleven raised her hands as she approached. Felix's rough grip suggested he could easily snap Vera's neck. "Let her go, Felix."

Fear and uncertainty flooded Vera's bloodshot eyes. In a panicked last effort, she reached to Felix's back pocket and took his knife. With one flick, she secured the blade and drove it deep into his thigh. Vera, taking advantage of Felix's loosening hold, elbowed his nose. She gasped as he threw her to the floor.

*His dose. He'd have at least one on him just out of habit alone. There might be a chance.*

Eleven lunged for Felix before he could recoup. She didn't react when he stuck his bloodied blade into her side. Her fists landed blows to his jaw and cheekbones. With Felix disoriented, the locator hurried to get the upper hand. Keeping him down with her knees on his chest, Eleven checked the inside of his jacket pocket. She found a blue vial.

*You'd better pray this works.*

As she retrieved Felix's dosage, he rolled Eleven to her backside. The sweet disposition she'd come to know was nowhere in sight. Felix's facial tics added to his rabid demeanor. Eleven flicked the cap off the vial and jabbed him in the neck.

Felix squeezed both hands around Eleven's throat. Again, she didn't respond to his attack.

Vera approached, raising a shaky gun to the back of Felix's head. A shudder ran through him.

"Wait," Eleven exclaimed.

When Felix opened his eyes, the cloudiness around his irises dissipated. He released Eleven.

"Are you back?" After nearly a minute of shifting and shaking, Felix nodded while hovering over Eleven.

She struck him hard enough that his skull audibly cracked. Felix tumbled to the side of her as he lost consciousness.

"Explain."

Lowering the gun, Vera's gaze landed on Felix. "I forgot to shut the door." She limped to the nearest chair. "What I'm working on... it ain't easy on guardians, which is kind of the whole point. Locators too, if I had to guess."

*This isn't just to incapacitate someone.*

Eleven's ears pulsed with the memory. She'd never encountered anything like it. "How does it work?"

"What'd you shoot him up with?" Vera asked, ignoring Eleven's question.

"What do you think?"

Vera dabbed a sleeve across her forehead. "He's weaning himself off."

Eleven laughed. "Weaning?"

"Yes." Complete and utter disgust radiated off of Vera.

The locator chuckled again as she stood. Pulling the knife from her side, Eleven tossed it to the ground. She rubbed her torso.

*Another sullied blouse.*

"This isn't some run-of-the-mill street nectar, Vera. There is no *weaning*. No end. Felix had to have known that from the start."

"The hell do you know about it?"

"More than you."

Vera licked her lips. "If anyone can do it, he can."

"The discoloration taking shape underneath your jaw tells a different tale."

*He almost killed her.*

"This uncharacteristic bout of optimism is best utilized elsewhere." Eleven pointed to Felix. "Whatever you did triggered one of the more tame reactions I've had the pleasure of witnessing."

*What a trio we make.*

"Designation BI36 had a similar strategy," Eleven continued. "We were pinned down and she'd forgotten to dose. To make matters worse, she'd been injured." She kept her voice steady. Her eyes stayed glued to an unconscious Felix. "I awoke just in time to see her tear off her eyelids because she wanted to stay awake. When they grew back, she did it again. And again. And again."

"Shut up," Vera said more to herself than Eleven.

"Designation SC42 convinced himself that since I didn't need meds, he didn't either. Within a week, he jabbered on incessantly that his head hurt. He cracked his skull with the pommel of his blade to 'relieve pressure' if you can believe it."

"I preferred you quiet."

"If you care for Felix as you've adamantly claimed, stop trying to change what can't be undone."

Eleven realized only after the words escaped her that she'd come to care for Felix herself. Had it been anyone else, the locator would not have hesitated to go for the kill.

The gun shook in Vera's hand. "This is where you get the fuck out of my sight."

Without hesitation, Eleven strode out of the room. Vera's all-too-familiar judgmental stare clung to the locator more than her blood-soaked shirt.

*In the end, it would've been a mercy.*

· · · · · · · · · · ·

"ELEVEN?"

Having packed all the materials she could into the duffle her secondhand clothes arrived in, Eleven had hid away in a shipping container at the edge of the perimeter. Her latest interaction with Felix and Vera had led her to the conclusion that she did not do well with roommates. Eleven lay on her stomach in the center of the rectangular surface.

"I know you're in there."

Sunset had long since passed. A flashlight pointed to the ceiling. Eleven kicked up her feet and rested her face in her palms. She scanned her latest how-to guide.

"Please let me in."

"Speak your peace and be done with it," Eleven said.

Felix coughed. "Kind of difficult given the stink out here."

Eleven's hasty decision to leave the complex had not been an easy one. She had debated leaving entirely but recalled her promise to Crux.

"I'm not going anywhere until you talk to me."

*Why did I think this would deter him?*

"Brought dinner," Felix added.

Eleven's stomach rumbled at the mention of food. Closing her eyes, she knew shutting him out would prove fruitless.

*Persistent bastard, I'll give him that.*

Felix shoved past Eleven the instant she opened the door. His lantern brightened the room considerably. Lowering the large cooler he'd brought with him, he admired every direction Eleven wasn't.

"Figured you might be hungry," Felix said as he interlocked his gloved fingers. "When I woke up, I was starving."

"Been awake long?"

"Couple hours."

Harsh wind hit hard against the shipping container. Bits of debris chimed as the two occupants faced one another. Eleven inverted and righted her ankles in her stance. Unspoken words charged the silence, making it almost palpable.

"I'm sorry."

Eleven blinked. "Why are you apologizing?"

"Least I can do. V hasn't been very forthcoming, so I took a look at the feeds."

"Whatever Vera's experimenting with—"

"This wasn't her fault." Felix sat on top of the cooler. Pulling off his gloves, he took a vial from his pocket. "You were right. There's no stopping it."

*Video* and *audio surveillance. I'll have to remember that.*

"What is she working on?" Eleven crossed her legs as she sat.

Felix forced a laugh. "Something pretty damn effective."

"Meaning you don't know. Does Crux?"

He shrugged. "Ain't much those two don't tell each other."

Eleven suppressed the snide comment that presented itself. "Apology accepted."

"It's that easy?"

Finding common ground with a guardian left her reeling, as did the ease she'd begun to feel in his presence. "If you reviewed the footage, you may have noticed you weren't the only one affected."

"Still—"

"How long do you intend to brood?" Felix halted his prepared response. The locator pushed her shoulders back. "I'm not certain how long either of us will be here, but if this is to become a regular occurrence, I may very well cut ties now."

"Not used to cheering people up, are you?"

Eleven broadened her gaze. "Don't let it happen again. This is who you are, Felix. Pretending to be anything else will just get you and those that surround you killed."

Readjusting to the ground, Felix opened the cooler. He threw the locator a wrapped sandwich.

"Hope you like things trying to taste like chicken." Not waiting for Eleven to join him, Felix chomped down on his own bit of bread. He washed a chunk of sandwich down with a beer. "Sounds like you've experienced some heavy shit. How did today measure up?"

Eleven busied herself with the plastic trappings of her sandwich. Felix waited for her to elaborate. "Tales of guardian misadventures would hurt your appetite. Trust me."

Taking another swig, Felix pressed on. "A man's got a right to know, don't he? Know what he's in store for?"

"Surely, as with all things it would seem, you've done your research?"

"Certain things are easier to find than others. There's tons of lore on the risks of dosing, but not for instances. Starting to see why that is."

*Isn't as informed as he claims to be. Good.*

"Please."

The quiver in Felix's plea threw Eleven. She never did well in delicate matters. This, along with countless other reasons, stopped her from telling him everything right then and there. His thumbnail picked at the corner of the beer bottle's label.

"Why did you become a guardian?"

"Didn't have a lot of options at the time," Felix admitted. "I had a lead on Lani's whereabouts... but it didn't pan out."

"Was it worth all of this?"

"I'll have to get back to you on that one."

Eleven sighed. "What do you want to know?"

# 10

BY THE END OF THE FOLLOWING WEEK, ELEVEN had made great strides in her studies. Both Felix and herself remained on shaky ground with Vera. In turn, the resident tech expert hardly left the confines of the laboratories.

The bulk of the reading materials had, at the very least, been skimmed through. Crux's personal accounts and chronicles, paired with Vera and Felix's suggestions, had caught the locator up on the world at present.

Eleven had also developed a knack for picking locks, though she hid her amusement. She spent much of prime daylight hours perusing the shipyard to test whatever lock she came across. Using a set that Felix had fashioned for her out of discarded metals, few locks resisted Eleven's persistence. Most shipping containers yielded negative results as far as "useful forgotten."

One, however, eluded her. Residing at the farthest corner of the complex on the highest level, the contents remained a mystery. Its lock was unlike anything she'd come into contact with or studied.

For three days, Eleven visited the container in the hopes she would unlock the curious latch. As dusk approached at the end of the third day, she'd had enough of her losing streak. Taking bolt cutters from Felix's workshop, she attempted to tear open the shackle. Her efforts resulted in the breaking of the bolt cutters themselves.

*It's just a pin-and-tumbler lock, for crying out loud.*

Dropping halves of the bolt cutters to either side of her, Eleven wiped away thick beads of sweat from her face. Something about this container differed from the rest. She would not be deterred from learning the contents.

"Plan on staying up there all night?"

She glanced down at Felix. Holding a gargantuan lantern, the guardian angled his head up. Eleven's nostrils flared as she took one last look at the troublesome lock.

"I don't relish the idea of you breaking your neck on the way down. Healing or not, it's gonna hurt like a bitch." Felix grinned at Eleven's frustration. She weighed her options. "Come on. I know you're hungry. It'll still be there tomorrow."

*Food. He'll always use that angle... and it'll always work.*

• • • • • • • • • • •

FELIX AND ELEVEN SHARING A MEAL HAD BECOME habit. As they let their guards down, conversations turned from light to meaningful. Silences were few and seldom awkward.

Eleven went to sleep shortly after dinner.

A dim drone teased Eleven's ear. She rolled from her back to her side on the lumpy cot. The signal of the curious noise strengthened. Eleven sat up.

*Vera?*

The heavier Eleven's concern, the louder the occurrence. It called to the locator like a beacon. This wasn't akin to the effects of Vera's weaponized sound waves. She caught on to a beat in tune with her heart.

After putting on clothes, Eleven pocketed her pick set and a jagged blade Felix had given her. The locator searched all three laboratories before expanding her search.

*It couldn't be a chamber... could it?*

Eleven climbed to the highest point, quickly exiting the structure. Her lantern barely lit enough to combat the heavy fog. Upon reaching the same troublesome tower of shipping containers at the very end of the complex, she lowered the lantern.

*Three days and now it decides to get interesting?*

The rhythm quickened as Eleven ascended. Using limited moonlight and her sense of touch, the locator slipped more than once. She counted herself lucky that no one witnessed her ineptitude. Seven levels of shipping containers later, she reached her destination.

Taking the tension wrench from her kit, Eleven tested out the taxing lock. She did her best to disregard tricks she had formerly depended on. Like earlier attempts to open the lock, Eleven cursed as she applied pressure to it. Being unable to see forced her to rely on her hearing. Springs played merrily with the pick in play.

Eleven's determination fought doubt as she went through the motions. She listened closely, moving only when the mechanisms demanded it. As Eleven questioned her ability to open the lock that had caused her so much grief, the shaft jerked open.

Wasting no time, Eleven lifted the bulky latch and tried the handle. Unlike other shipping containers, the doors opened inward. A familiar percussion echoed. Darkness unsettled Eleven. The reverberations weren't like the ones she'd grown accustomed to in similar spaces. Shutting hard behind her, the door she'd just unlocked secured itself.

*This isn't right.*

Darkness faded out as illumination crept in. The bright lavender lighting stung Eleven's eyes at first. She squinted in her vigilance to explore the space. Shelves stacked on top of one another occupied the whole of the back wall. The first row carried thick leather bound journals and miscellaneous files. The space free of literature held jars of sand, rock, debris, metal, along with other elements. In front of the shelves sat a metal desk and a tall leather chair with its back to her. Clattering drew Eleven to a compartment at the desk's side.

"Excellent timing."

Eleven gasped. The rarity of someone being able to surprise her disturbed her more than the act itself. Crux turned in his seat to face her.

"Your preparations appear to be on schedule."

Forcing herself to relax, Eleven took a deep breath. "How long have you been here?"

"Just a few hours," Crux answered. "I trust you found a way to keep yourself entertained in my absence."

*No one is that quiet.*

Crux leaned over and opened a drawer. The fast-changing pace carried a less melodic beat, making it difficult to adjust to. An inventory of sensations revealed that it remained in tune with her heart. Crux revealed a clear crystal with multiple interior cracks. A wave of his hand terminated the sound. Pressurization in the room altered in the hum's absence. "Did I frighten you?"

"Was that not your intention?" Eleven replied.

"My apologies." Crux pushed away from the desk. He circled to the front of it. Leaning against the table's edge, he said, "Do make yourself comfortable."

Eleven turned to a wooden chair that she'd missed when entering. She rested a hand on either hip. Amused by her defiance, Crux took the mysterious crystal and displayed it in his palm. "Curious as to what this is?"

"Yes," Eleven admitted.

Crux tossed it to the opposite hand. "Rightfully so."

Quirking her head to the side, Eleven debated delving into the matter. Crux stood as he pocketed the item. "Frustrating, is it not? The unknown."

"Perhaps I don't need to know."

"That logic is for your lesser. Seek the unknown."

"I'm here, aren't I?"

A corner of Crux's mouth twitched. "True enough."

The wall behind Crux caught Eleven's attention. Jar after jar filled shelves to the brim.

Crux faced the containers themselves. He moved to stand side by side with Eleven. Crossing his arms, he said, "I am a collector."

"Of gravel?"

"Fascinations are often odd to an observer."

Somehow, the room in its entirety calmed Eleven. The reason for this was on the wall of mystery. Where the filled glass intrigued her, the books perplexed. The Dusslorean treasured them enough to keep them under lock and key. Eleven thought better of prying.

"How goes the adjustment process?" Crux asked.

"You tell me."

"Not fond of revealing much, are you?"

*How observant, not to mention hypocritical.*

"I'm fine," Eleven said.

"Just *fine*?"

"As well as can be expected, Crux."

"I am still fairly incompetent with sarcasm." He walked to the door, dragging lazy fingertips against the rust of a nearby wall. Stopping at the entrance, Crux said, "Cynicism can be difficult to decipher."

"Merely stating facts."

"And my associates?" Crux turned his head. The late hour further darkened Eleven's mood. "I am just making conversation, Eleven."

"They're toxic," Eleven said.

"Toxic?"

"You couldn't have planned for a less cohesive grouping."

"Who is to say I did not do just that?" An all-knowing smile slid across the Dusslorean's face. He threw his hands into the depths of his coat. "Petty bickering aside, Vera and Mr. Unger are ideal companions. Like you, they have a tendency to alienate those surrounding them. Though for very different reasons."

"He nearly killed her."

"Nearly," Crux reiterated.

"You knew?"

"Surveillance feeds."

Eleven inhaled. "You shouldn't dismiss—"

"What do you think you know of guardians? The treatments, their pitfalls, their origins?"

"They aren't us."

"Try as they might," the Dusslorean said under his breath.

"If stability is problematic, why have them?" Eleven asked. "Why put one in the direct line of fire?"

"You seem concerned."

Eleven dropped her gaze to the floor. "I've had my fill of carnage."

"Quite young for such a statement."

*How old is he?*

"I'm really not."

"Nor am I," Crux said through a chuckle. He soon righted himself. "Why do you think I asked you to watch after Vera? Contrary to what she has claimed on multiple occasions, Mr. Unger blinds her to reason."

"And that makes them ideal companions how?"

Crux ignored Eleven's derisiveness. "Return to your quarters and rest."

"I'm fine."

"Your body says otherwise. It requires sleep in order to function properly."

Eleven looked to the shelves again. For reasons unknown, she didn't want to leave the space. A multitude of objects called to her. Books begged to be read and trinkets yearned for examination.

"To bed with you," Crux pressed.

He placed a hand on Eleven's shoulder. She shrugged him off. Crux walked to the shelves at the opposite end of the room. He took one of the thicker volumes from the top shelf.

"Does the word 'ophidian' mean anything to you?"

"A serpent?"

Handing the ebony-covered text to Eleven, Crux said, "There is not a direct written translation for what he is called in my native tongue. We refer to him as Ophidian in most of our accounts."

"Who?" Eleven asked. Gripping it with care, she tucked her new reading assignment under her arm.

"See for yourself." Crux led the way to the exit. "After daybreak."

Sunlight already hinted at the horizon. Crux watched as Eleven descended into the polluted mist. When she reached the ground, the doors to his mounted lair closed.

• • • • • • • • • • •

LAUGHTER ROUSED ELEVEN FROM A DEEP SLEEP. The bizarre sound had the locator convinced she was still well within the confines of slumber.

*That* cannot *be Vera.*

Crux regaled Vera with tales of his travels. The Dusslorean

already making his return known surprised Eleven. She leaned an ear toward the door, waiting for Felix's voice to enter the fray, to no avail.

Eleven walked in to find Crux, Vera, and, much to her surprise, Felix sitting at the kitchen table. He occupied the seat farthest from Vera and Crux.

"Good afternoon," Crux said to Eleven.

*Afternoon? This is what happens with no windows or alarm clocks.*

Nodding in acknowledgment, Eleven made a plate and took the lone empty seat by Felix. Their knees brushed against one another's underneath the table as she settled in.

Ignoring Eleven, Vera continued her conversation with Crux. "Move it into the main hall."

"We have discussed this at great length, Vera."

"Don't I know it."

"I require minimal external influence," Crux told Vera. "The workshops and laboratories alone are counterintuitive."

Vera sipped her coffee. The Dusslorean beamed much like a father would at his child. Felix pulled his mug close.

"None of the outer units are equipped for—" Vera stopped. Crux said nothing to fill in the blanks. Vera glanced at Eleven. "For whatever it is you got planned."

"Vera, you need not concern yourself."

"Easier said than done." Vera kept her eyes on Eleven.

Her attempt to intimidate the locator didn't go unnoticed. Eleven pushed aside her plate. Without a word, Felix poured her a glass of orange juice.

Crux stood. Extending a hand to Vera, he said, "Show me what you have been working on. Your clandestine correspondence has my interest piqued."

"Sure thing."

Vera allowed Crux to guide her out of the cramped commissary. The two remaining occupants noticeably relaxed with the chattier individuals gone. As Eleven began to speak, the guardian placed two fingers over her lips.

"If his hearing is anything like yours, this is probably a safer bet," Felix signed.

Eleven smirked. It seemed like a lifetime ago since she'd signed anything. She found herself glad that the skill hadn't gone to waste. "Everything all right?"

"Never better," Felix replied with swift movements. The locator watched as he finished his coffee. Unconvinced, Eleven tapped her fingers against the plastic table.

"The concern is appreciated, but don't worry about it," he signed.

"Why would I worry?"

Felix chuckled. "Sounds like you're about to be very busy."

"Is that right?"

• • • • • • • • • • •

FELIX RETIRED TO HIS UNDERGROUND WORKSHOP soon after his brief exchange with Eleven. The guardian's go-to retreat held a hodgepodge of all things miscellaneous. No rhyme or reason to the disarray, at least not to an outsider. Eleven thought better than to press him for information. Something had happened in the few hours she'd slept, and she knew he would tell her the details at some point.

Eleven lay on the lower level floor of her quarters. She had made it a habit over the course of her stay. Being surrounded by books, even ones she'd read, pleased her.

Today's text: **The Ophidian**.

Unlike previous homework from Crux and the others, scribbles did not overlay preceded print. This was a true journal. Its pages, the material itself offworld, proved problematic in discerning. Familiar with Crux's handwriting, Eleven didn't recognize the contributor of this text. Before now, Eleven had depended on her fluency in numerous foreign languages. These longhand sentences, far from perfect, had been written by someone less than articulate with her native tongue.

OPHIDIAN FOREVER FOUND HIS OWN.
HE CLAIMED THIS IN BOAST.
HIS OWN. THAT IS HOW
HE REFERRED US.

I HAD KNOWN HIM FROM MY STARTING.
THAT WAS THE FEELING HIS PRESENCE
TOLD ME. MUCH LIKE MY BELOVED IN
MANY WAYS. BUT I DID NOT KNOW HIM.

DISSIMILAR IN FORM AND BLOOD
YET WE WERE THE SAME.

WE WERE ONLY TWO BEFORE. MORE
THAN PLEASING. BUT TO DISCOUNT HIM
WAS CRUEL. SELFISH. MY BELOVED
DISLIKED HOW SCARCE WE WERE.

MY BELOVED ACQUIESCED FIRST.
WELCOMED HIM. CALLED HIM KIN IN
WHAT FELT LIKE ONLY MOMENTS.
WE BECAME THREE. THREE TO
HELP. THREE TO PROTECT.

Eleven ran her fingers along each of the words. Though she'd become something of a speed-reader over the years, she took an inordinate amount of time on the written words.

BEFORE HIM, INSTINCT DROVE US.
OBJECTS OF THE FOURTH BECKONED
AND WE RECOVERED THEM. SOUGHT
PIECES WANTING TO BE FOUND.
PROCURED THESE CURIOUS THINGS

THAT BENEFIT AN EQUAL.
HENCE THE NAME "SEEKER."
OUR PEOPLE NAMED US
THIS UNDETERRED BY OUR
DISINTEREST FOR BRANDING.

I PREFER THAT TO LOCATOR.
PURSUIT. THAT IS WHAT IT BECAME.
A HUNT.

LIKE THE LOCATORS HE ONCE
KNEW. HIS FORMER KIN.
LOCATORS.
THAT IS WHAT HE CALLED
US. NEVER SEEKER.
WHAT THEY CALL US.

Looking away from the page, Eleven squinted.
*Where does Ophidian fit in?*

HE SHED LIGHT ON OUR BEGINNING.
ON A GREAT MANY THINGS.
KIN DOESN'T QUESTION.

YET I DID.
THE CONNECTION CLASHED WITH
DOUBT. TO ME, NOT MY BELOVED.
TRUST COMES TOO EASILY TO HIM.
IN A WAY, I AM GRATEFUL.
IN OTHERS, I PITY HIM.

OUR EQUALS VIEWED HIM AS I.
HIS VOICE CARRIED PROMISE, BUT
REVERBERATED SOMETHING NEITHER
MYSELF NOR MY BELOVED FATHOMED.

*Not until time betrayed us.*
*Time and more.*
*Earliest of us and yet—*

A knock from above pulled Eleven from the book. She snapped it shut as if its contents would escape otherwise. The opening of her bedroom door resonated off the walls.

Crux peered down the ladder. "Am I disturbing you?"

"No," Eleven answered. She wedged the book between two others.

"Meet me in my office."

"Office?"

"Your most beloved crate, if memory serves."

Eleven scowled. "Why there?"

Crux didn't answer.

*Locators.*
*That is what he called us. Never seeker.*
*What they call us.*

*"Locators, as they call them, are a treasured asset to Ceruleman kind."*

*Earliest of us…*

*Was the first locator Ceruleman?*

# 11

FOR THE FIRST TIME IN FAR TOO LONG, ELEVEN'S nerves got the best of her. She hadn't expected training to immediately follow Crux's return. Vera's reading assignments and Felix's occasional lesson in survival were, for the most part, welcome surprises. This new unknown had Eleven second guessing how much she wanted answers.

The Dusslorean appeared to keep Vera and Felix oblivious to the life of a locator. Knowing that she and Crux shared an uncommon trait appeased her.

The sun's highest point had already begun to fade as Eleven ventured toward Crux's office. As she reached the desired container, Eleven found a mason jar in front of the tower.

"Welcome."

Eleven squinted up to see Crux standing at the opening of his office. The Dusslorean pounced from his makeshift workspace, landing in close proximity to the jar.

"Shall we begin?"

Shifting her weight, Eleven placed her hands on her hips.

Taking the lidless container at his feet, Crux angled the opening toward her.

"Physical encounters will not be our focus today." Crux turned his head to the side. "Comfortable?"

"Much as one can be."

"What have you read?"

"Of the collection in my room?" Eleven asked. Crux replied with the simplest of nods. "Almost all?"

The Dusslorean swaggered forward. "Are you asking or telling me?" Walking past Eleven, he stopped when their backs faced one another.

Eleven clarified. "Out of the approximately 745 books that were there upon my arrival, all but 30 remain untouched. All 23 of Vera's *suggestions* have been scanned through."

"Mr. Unger did make a note of your appetite for the written word." Crux withdrew from Eleven. He circled back to his original position. "Any thoughts?"

*On the circumlocutory history of chambers and lost worlds?*

"Riveting," Eleven said.

Crux chuckled. "Now that was sarcasm."

Reaching into his pocket, he revealed a lock, the same one that Eleven had been cursing for the last few days. Crux chucked it to her. Displaying it with an open palm, she examined the bizarre bolt.

"I am pleased that your fascination with locks is not exclusive to chambers. It is not always the case with us."

Eleven gripped the lock. "A test?"

"Yes."

"The intention being?"

Crux's thick fingernails tapped the jar's glass in a tuneful manner. "To gauge aptitude." He swayed from side to side, the sternness of his voice waning. "You have been done a great injustice."

*There's a loaded statement.*

Muscles in Eleven's neck tensed. She had pushed back the emotions associated with the countless transgressions that had befallen her.

Crux readjusted his position. "We are to resemble that of our world's dominant species. Yet our sensibilities are unlike that of our fellow man. Why?"

"If the whole point of this endeavor is for me to learn, there isn't a benefit to asking me questions I don't have the answers to."

Eleven opened her eyes to find an unamused Dusslorean standing directly in front of her. "Excess hinders," Crux said.

"Meaning?"

"Guardians."

"They overindulge?"

Crux looked skyward. "They *are* the overindulgence. Surrounding yourself with them has spoiled you."

*Yes. Because that was my decision.*

The temper Eleven attempted to reign in surprised her. Since the night of her liberation, the locator had become more emotional. A fact she had hoped to conceal from everyone.

"They sought them for you, did they not? Our coveted chambers?"

"More or less."

Unaffected by his pupil's conduct, Crux closed the gap between them. "In being led astray, you have missed one of the best—"

"I've missed a great deal," Eleven interrupted. "That has been firmly established."

"I have offended you?"

Eleven turned from him. "No."

"Good." Crux nudged the jar against Eleven's abdomen. She took it from him. When her eyes returned to his, Crux backed away several paces. "Regardless of admission, you still see yourself as a sufferer of the human experience."

"I'm not human," Eleven said.

"Technically, you are. Just as I am *technically* Dusslorean. Complications give way to hazards and routine. Doubt delays progression."

*Speaking of delays.*

Crux zeroed in on the jar in Eleven's grasp. "Do not confuse the impossible for what one is simply unable to achieve without effort. Tell me you understand."

"I understand."

"This will take time and practice before any true result." Crux lowered himself to sitting. As he crossed his stocky legs, he said, "You are capable of such a feat."

"Crux."

"Sit."

The Dusslorean motioned to the ground. Eleven's thirst for answers, Crux's and her own, deterred any reservation she had. She sat.

"Choose from the basin."

Examining the clear container she held, Eleven tipped it toward her. She settled for the first item to fall out. An aged, hardened dollop of plaster irritated her filthy palm.

"Where is it from?" Crux asked.

Eleven's forehead creased. Glancing from Crux to the plaster, she lifted the item. No matter the angle, its significance failed to present itself.

"Do you wish to know, Eleven?"

"Yes."

"Shame."

Giving Crux her full attention, Eleven's hand dropped. "You're not going to tell me anything, are you?"

"How would you learn if I did?"

Eleven tossed the item of mysterious origin to the ground without care. Crux's gaze fell to it. He adjusted his posture. "A forward-looking mindset is for your benefit as much as mine.

Stay cross-legged and face me."

"For what purpose?"

"Instruction before clarification."

*This* is *what you wanted.*

Eleven sighed. Her modified position mirrored Crux's. The locators glared at one another.

Crux lifted his chin. "Be comfortable in your pose, but remain still. Keep upright."

*Are chakras next?*

"Eyes closed." Crux's composure resembled that of a monk. Eleven's eyes shut as his did. "Be conscious of your breathing. Exhale long and thin through your nasal passages. Inhale slowly."

*If anything could kill me, it's this wretched stench.*

"Do not let environment take control."

The air refused to relent in pungency. With the dryness of her throat progressing, tears streamed down Eleven's face. Still, she did as Crux instructed. Eleven suppressed a gag as her nose took on another polluted assault.

*If he can handle it, so can you.*

"Pause," Crux said. "And again."

The majority of their lesson consisted of breathing. Despite Crux's numerous requests for complete silence, Eleven muttered rebuttals. It continued as such until dusk approached. Crux offered a flask of water at the end of their first day.

· · · · · · · · · · ·

A BOUQUET OF APPETIZING SCENTS HIT THE LOCA-tors as they reentered the main complex. Felix had a knack for working with limited ingredients. Tonight would not be the exception. Eleven leaned against the kitchen's threshold as Crux continued toward Lab 1.

Adding a pinch of salt to his latest concoction, Felix sa-

vored his work. The guardian's face scrunched. "What the—"
He stopped as he turned. Snickering, he said, "I'd say I've
smelled worse, but... *damn*."

Eleven rolled her eyes. "Thank you."

Felix carried on with dinner preparations. Eleven kicked a
leg of the nearest chair out. Dust misted off her as she sat.

"Had to check the video feed to make sure nothing went
wrong out there." Felix smirked at the puzzled locator. "Can't
remember the last time you skipped a meal. If you've seen my
notes, you'd know that's saying something."

Pursing her lips, Eleven said, "It wasn't by choice."

"Yeah, I figured." Felix motioned to the refurbished fridge
in the far corner. "If you get a midnight hankering, I saved you
some lunch."

His old-fashioned cordiality always amazed Eleven. In defiance of plentiful grievances, Felix often armed himself with
nothing but a grin.

"Ow! Son of a—" Felix jerked back his hand.

Eleven peered over Felix's shoulder, never leaving her seat.
A burn on his hand sizzled. For a first-degree injury, it healed
slower than it should have. Switching off the stovetop, Felix
then rubbed at the mending area with a calloused thumb.

"Let me see," Eleven said.

"Don't bother."

Eleven charged at Felix. Taking a still cooling copper spatula from the stove's spoon rest, she placed it on the top side of
his forearm.

"What the hell are you doing?"

Before Felix could retreat, Eleven placed her hand over
the spatula. Their singeing flesh created a distinctive smell.
Overcoming his shock, Felix used his free hand to push Eleven
away. The spatula clanged as it landed at their feet.

"Have you completely cracked?"

Eleven raised her nearly healed hand. "Show me."

She snatched Felix's arm, pulling back the sleeve that'd unrolled in the struggle. His burn had several minutes left before a complete restoration. She shoved her friend's limb away.

"It's not what you think."

Eleven motioned to his arm. "Evidence to contrary."

"I promised I wouldn't try anything like that again."

"How many?"

Felix licked his lips. "Vera's got a couple leads on suppliers. But nothing concrete."

"How many doses do you have left, Felix?"

"One," he admitted. "This is why I didn't want to tell you."

One *treatment?*

"Do you think Vera has what it takes?"

"To what?"

"To *end you*, Felix." The locator turned to him. All manner of readable expression fell from his face. "If you don't maintain your condition, that's what you're forcing her to do."

When Felix didn't reply, Eleven moved to the refrigerator. The locator blankly stared at the contents within. She snagged a container from the middle shelf and made a break for the exit.

"Could you do it?" Felix asked. Eleven stopped just as she passed the dining table. The guardian pushed off from the counter.

Keeping her feet in place, Eleven leaned toward the table. She snagged a fork, butter knife, and a cloth napkin. "I told you my stories, Felix. You'd hardly be my first."

• • • • • • • • • • •

*HE'S SPEAKING TO US.*

*E* ARLIEST OF US AND YET LIMITED.

*THANKFUL FOR MANY THINGS,
OPHIDIAN'S DISADVANTAGE
IS HIGH IN RANK.*

*WE, TOO, FEEL INFERIOR
TO YOU, HUMAN SEEKER.*

*YOU LOCATOR.*

*YOU ELEVEN.*

*He's speaking to me.*

Eleven investigated the pages themselves. Clues as to the age of this latest chronicle were few. Though paper had been uncommon for decades, the sheets looked somewhat new. The cost alone forced most to favor digital over analog in regard to most purchases.

*THE FOURTH CAN ONLY BE
REACHED THROUGH PREVAIL.
BY ONE OF RESIDENCE.
I NEED NOT ARRIVE
HERE TO KNOW THIS.*

*OPHIDIAN SPOKE OF HIS SHORTCOMINGS
IN FREQUENCY. THIS FOOLED MY
BELOVED TO THINK HIM TAME.*

*WE CAN NOW ATTEST OTHERWISE.*

*HE WAS NOT.*

*WE ARE NOT.*

*YOU WILL NEVER BE TAME.*

Eleven moved away from the pages of her burdensome read. Scooping up the last of her cold meal, thoughts stayed with the text lying in front of her.

*Ophidian used these seekers because he could no longer*

*access the chambers.*

*"Only eleven are operational."*

Operational. *That's how Crux put it. He can't open them himself. Not anymore. Is that why he's freeing us?*

Books surrounding Eleven, most of which she had already perused, centered on missions of Crux and the other seeker. Both Dussloreans had gone into great detail on chambers, their contents, and how items from them were utilized. This read another way. More personal than a matter of facts.

To hear Ophidian speak of his people, the beings from a distant world, was heavy on the heart. He spoke of unrest, revolution, and betrayal.

Scarcely did he talk of kin. Those like him.

Like us.

He remembered them fondly at times. In talks with my beloved, never myself. Soft words hinted at sorrow, but the facts were few.

We only knew he was now alone. Had my beloved and I been granted the equivalent amenity, the potential prospect is sickening. As is the horror of our constant reality.

One you now find yourself in.

It pains me to scribe so harsh a matter. Yet ache is a given for us.

*If* not for allies having rightly earned my trust, *I* fear my soul would have soured long before our arrival here.

*Do* you believe we are capable of carrying one? *Does* the seeker reading my scattered thoughts hold a soul?

*K*now this: *O*phidian lacked many things.

*A* soul most of all.

*A soul... what a human concept.*

# 12

IN THE DAYS THAT FOLLOWED, ELEVEN ENDURED the pollution outdoors in full. By the third day of so-called training, her protests diminished—at least in words spoken aloud.

*"Grey matter increases..."*

*Locators are in need of evolution? Is healing from any wound and accessing chambers not enough for you, Dusslorean?*

*"Emotional regulatory..."*

*Annoyance is an emotion, correct?*

*"Boosts in cortical thickness, namely in relation to attention span..."*

*Where does he find these ridiculous articles?*

*"Deep contemplation improves introspection and self-control..."*

*Case in point.*

Crux's breathing exercises were the precursor to meditation. He referenced countless studies and offered his own theories to various sequences. His deductive reasoning was anything but to Eleven. She surmised this to be one of his many quirks.

*Two and a half weeks... has it really only been seventeen days?*

Within seconds of Eleven's arrival, Crux sat across from her as he had done time after time. She awaited instruction. The locator fidgeted as minutes passed. He pulled an item from his coat pocket and threw it to her. Catching the thrown object, Eleven examined the piece. She recognized it immediately.

*Not this again.*

"Where is this from?" Crux inquired.

It was the same question he'd asked during their very first lesson. Again, the unchanged bit of plaster rested in her palm, its origins still unknown. Eleven gripped the fossilized adhesive, careful not to damage it. When she still had no answer, the locator closed her eyes.

*Perhaps I should cite facts and figures on the benefits of breathing to it. That seems to be the way of things.*

"Care for a hint?" her instructor asked. Kneeling before her, Crux took her hand into both of his. "This and everything else in that particular basin are linked to the eleventh human locator."

"How?"

"Think back. Recall a mission that took you to a warehouse along one of the region's borders." Eleven tried to withdraw her hand, but Crux wouldn't relinquish it. He raised their hands slightly. "Answer the question."

"I would if you gave me a moment."

"The chamber," Crux said, disrupting her thoughts. He squeezed her hand. "What was it?"

Eleven shook her head. "That was ages ago."

"You complain to me about the passage of time? Is this another attempt at jesting? Think, Eleven. You are capable of this." The tips of his fingers brightened as his hold on Eleven constricted.

Wincing, she said, "Hard to think with your sweaty palms on me."

"Shall we approach this in a different manner? My paramour suggested another methodology I have yet to implement. Further research—"

"Enough with your research," Eleven snapped.

"Then stop wasting time and tell me what was inside the chamber."

*It was… a warehouse! But where? No, not a warehouse… a factory. Closed down and—you're joking.*

"A kazoo," she answered. "Well, a version of a kazoo."

The Dusslorean kept on target. "Where is it from?"

"Terraformed planet. The name escapes me."

Crux freed Eleven's hand. He snatched the damp plaster as her fingers unfurled. Leaning in, he asked again, "Where is it from, Eleven?"

*Starts with a "W"… or an "M."*

"Majort," Eleven whispered. Both eyebrows lowered. Looking to Crux, she said, "It's from Majort."

"Reverberations," Crux started. "Anything in proximity to a chamber has them."

"No matter the material?"

Stretching his pupil's hand, Crux returned the plaster to Eleven's palm. He stood and backed away several paces. "Familiar with the frequency a chamber emits?"

*Rubbish-filled preserve jars, breathing, now frequencies?*

"When in its presence, have you ever known the contents before unsealing a chamber?" Crux recognized her confusion. He searched for the right words. "One harboring weaponry carries a different quality than that of another holding an elixir or text."

144

"And you know this how?"

"Years of absentmindedness, a *very* forgiving partner, and—" The Dusslorean stopped himself. His grin faltered. "Many factors came into play."

*He refers to the other in the past tense. The one who calls him "beloved." The seeker who speaks of souls.*

"Factors your Ceruleman hosts made certain to keep hidden."

*With great effort.*

"I am not a quick study. The same cannot be said for you," Crux continued.

Thrown by the compliment, Eleven looked to the item in her hand. Crux searched a hidden corner to the side of him, soon returning with the same jar from before. Eleven noticed etchings carved along the bottom of it's rim. Narrowing her gaze, she spotted two crudely carved numbers.

$$//$$

*Everything in there is from chambers I've opened. Do the others have jars waiting for them?*

The Dusslorean took a rusted, warped piece of metal. Crux switched plaster in favor of this new challenge. Its corroded ridges stained Eleven's palm.

"Without overthinking it, tell me what you feel."

*Rust.*

"Eleven."

*Exhale… inhale… pause… again.*

Minutes went by like seconds.

"Well?" Crux asked.

"Nothing."

"Not to worry." Without breaking contact, Crux took a crystal from his coat.

"And where should I recognize this from?"

"Putting aside the brief encounter upon my return some days ago, this is not known to you." Crux pulled a miniature, flat panel from another pocket. Its sheen was similar to obsidian.

The Dusslorean placed the onyx sheet onto his palm. Eleven watched as he waved the crystal over it. With a vengeance, the hum she'd heard on Crux's first night back returned. The pressure around them altered.

*He isn't reacting. Is it just me?*

Crux moved his hand over the metal in Eleven's. Again, her senses went into overdrive.

"Think of it as a chamber, Eleven. Seek. Find it as you always have."

*A chamber.*

She refused to give into lingering apprehension. Eleven depended on her lessons in concentration and breathing.

"I feel… something."

"Good. Something is good." Crux pocketed the crystal and onyx obscurity, but the sound remained. He swiped the metal from Eleven. "Astonishing, is it not? However minuscule, it still carries an echo."

Eleven fought to hold onto the fading frequency. Straining her ears, she rubbed her thumbs and fingertips together. Sensations akin to finding the sweet spot of a chamber begging to be unlocked sped up her pulse.

"Region 3, District 7." Eleven glanced up to Crux in realization. Nostalgia curled her lips. She continued. "A crop field with equipment, tractors mostly. I was an active locator then. The chamber had seeds from Raupe."

*This is amazing.*

Crux wiped at Eleven's cheek with the back of his hand. Then she noticed the tears streaking her face. Steady streams impaired her vision. Out of habit, Eleven tried to hide. Determined arms hurled her toward him. Escape from his clutches would have been near impossible.

"As I said—quick study."

• • • • • • • • • • •

THE LESSON ENDED NOT LONG AFTER. IN THE AF-termath of Eleven's uncommon display, she felt foolish. She viewed outpourings as flaws. A weakness that needed to be improved upon.

Refusing to allow Felix or Vera to see her in such a state, Eleven sat in the chair opposite Crux amidst his towered office. She granted herself nothing more than short glances at the Dusslorean as he kept busy documenting. He had just begun a new journal, the first few pages already full.

*Is he writing about me for whatever world follows this one?*

A small tray of beverages sat between them. Eleven sipped on a canned soda while Crux appreciated a foul-smelling liquid served in a cracked teacup.

*If there is another world to follow.*

"Still enjoying the Ophidian text?" Crux asked.

Eleven cleared her throat. "Not sure your partner's words were meant to elicit joy."

"They were not."

"It's... enlightening."

Crux leaned back. "In what way?"

"You and your partner have been very detailed."

"Helot."

Eleven arched an eyebrow. "Sorry?"

"Vera called him Helot." Crux sipped on his concoction. He wiped at the brim before setting it down. "The other of my kind."

*Locators without purpose.*

Eleven's reading gave her insight to the Dusslorean seekers.

They had arrived centuries earlier. Their first few decades kept them in shadows. They busied themselves by gathering any and all information regarding humans, the planet's dominant species.

Then Cerulemans arrived.

Their presence was an affront to what they'd foregone—all that had brought them to this world of humans. Unlike their arrival on Dusslore, the Ceruleman race painted themselves as people of peace. Humanity embraced their presence with minimal opposition. In a matter of years, they had entangled themselves in practically all facets of everyday life. Even worse, Cerulemans monopolized the human seekers.

A quasi-universal acceptance of extraterrestrial life led the Dussloreans to make themselves known to some. Those outside the top tier of society shared a distaste for Ceruleman intervention. The pair soon became go-tos in regards to hiding and secrets.

*"Vera called him Helot."*

Twenty years ago, a family of three came to the seekers with the hopes of relocating unnoticed. Ulva Ross and Simon Dao were former soldiers unaffiliated with Ceruleman ranks. The couple's knowledge pertaining to defense strategies made civilian life near impossible. Though neither Simon nor Ulva could give a tangible reason why, they feared for their child's life as well as their own.

As the couple finalized arrangements out of the region, they placed their daughter Vera in the care of trusted friends. Though Crux and Helot considered themselves undeserving of such confidence, the Dussloreans cared for her all the same. Neither Simon nor Ulva ever arrived to pick up their child.

Recalling the pages mentioning Vera, Eleven thought back to one sentence:

*P watched V as we sought.*

She questioned the relevance of "P" but never asked. She never brought up anything she read in the chronicles unless Crux did first.

"Eleven?" Leaning forward, Crux asked, "Still unstable?"

"Helot had a lot to say about Ophidian." Inverting her lips, Eleven pondered how to phrase it. "Though I'm not sure how objective he was."

"Hard to be objective where *he* is concerned."

Another passage came to mind:

*My beloved wishes me to be thorough in my storytelling. No event untold. His desires once imaginative reduced for survival. I wish for nothing. Nothing moral.*

"Did you want to be?" she asked. "Objective, that is."

"Want is—"

"Irrelevant," Eleven finished. "Yes, you've mentioned that once or twice."

Crux regarded her. "Did you know yours well?"

"Mine?"

"Those like us. Like you."

Eleven reigned in her annoyance at the change in subject. Her soda's condensation offered a distraction as she thought about the others. The human locators.

"I've only met the men."

"Not a single odd number?" Crux asked. "How strange."

Eleven rested her soda can on a desk corner. Rubbing at her temple, she added, "Two during a transfer and, again, when he passed through 5 on assignment. He's never been fond of me for some reason. Worked a chamber cluster with Six once. He is very quiet. Four and Eight here and there, but nothing stands out."

*Don't you dare mention* him.

The lines on Crux's face deepened. "In all that time, you never encountered another female?"

"Never." Eleven sank down in her chair. "They're just stories to me."

"Anything worthy of note?"

"I'm sure there's a file for each of them at your disposal."

"There is not," Crux replied. "Not all are as easy to study."

*Thanks for the reminder.*

Eleven grinned when recalling an incident involving Seven. Coupling the seventh locator's aptitude for chemistry with her hatred for Banaedrut soldiers resulted in a massive explosion. Many Ceruleman lives were lost.

The Blue Blood in charge of Region 1 kept Three close. Rumors of his infatuation with the third locator unsettled most, though no one had any concrete evidence. Any guardian originating from Region 2 spoke fondly of Five, but the reasons continued to be a mystery.

The ninth locator and Eleven had the closest resemblance to a real connection. No matter the reset, alteration, or distance, Nine was never far from Ten. Both deeply cherished one another. Their bond survived all that threatened it.

*Maybe when this is over, they might actually have a chance.*

Eleven dismissed the hopeful thought. Optimism benefitted no one. She ignored the inquisitive Dusslorean behind the desk.

"What do you know of them? Any of them?" Eleven inquired.

Crux rested his forearms against either side of his drink. He intertwined his fingers. "Only what those like Mr. Unger have assembled for the most part." Eleven's gaze went to shelves behind Crux. "Your original is quite remarkable."

*Original?*

"The first of your kind," he clarified.

"One."

Crux nodded. "We never spoke, mind you. Helot and I discovered her whereabouts too late."

*More secrets.*

"Our differences never cease to leave me flabbergasted. The similarities have a comparable effect."

"Where is she?" Eleven asked.

"Her location is currently unknown."

*More mystery.*

Crux blanched, his hands stiffening into a tight clasp. "We are meant to protect these worlds. Granted, some of us have been more successful than others."

The chronicles alluded to characteristics of a Dusslorean. They regarded themselves as people of peace. Ceruleman kind setting foot on Dusslorean soil altered their perspective.

"You wish to know more of him."

"Of course," Eleven answered. "Helot's writing has intrigued me. It might be beneficial to—"

"Not Helot. You wish to know more of Ophidian."

It wasn't an inquiry, but a declaration. Ophidian intrigued Eleven more than any character, fictional or otherwise, ever had before.

Crux shot Eleven a look, unamused by her passive attempt to avoid responding. She leveled her glare. "What did you call him?"

"Before seeing his true nature?"

"Yes."

"Ordinarily, creators brand their achievements," Crux said to Eleven. He closed his journal, trapping the writing instrument between pages. "Our equals coined him Verraadr. The epithet changed with the undercurrent."

*The language is Oudesloy... means "wanderer" if I'm not mistaken.*

"Verraadr."

The Dusslorean smirked. "Not all names can be as blatant as *Crux*. Vera chose what so many call me now. It was her first bout in gumption."

Crux blamed himself for the loss of Dusslore. He wore the guilt in his eyes. Helot said as much in his writings.

DESTRUCTION.
PROMPT FOR MANY.
PERPETUAL FOR FEW.

FEW LIKE US.

DEATH IS CARRIED IN THE
EYES OF MY BELOVED. EYES
HEAVIER WITH LOSS.

ONE WOULD THINK IT WAS
DIFFICULT. THE CHOICE TO RID
OUR WORLD OF THE FOURTH.

IT WAS NOT.

NOT FOR MY BELOVED.

A SIMPLE ACT.

BETTER NOT TO TRUST THE
ALLURE OF SIMPLICITY.

OPHIDIAN KNEW, AS DID I, THAT
NOTHING WAS WITHOUT PRICE.

MY BELOVED DID NOT KNOW.

THEN CAME THE RECKONING.

"You regret it," Eleven said.

Ambiguity ingrained Crux's face with unflattering lines. Eleven's gaze fell to the edge of his desk.

"Easy decisions are a fallacy." He sipped on his drink with caution. It had long since cooled, yet Crux drank it as if worried he would scorch his tongue.

"Where is Ophidian now?"

*Or Helot for that matter.*

"Gone."

According to Helot's accounts, the Ceruleman locator didn't follow them or his people to this new world. Details of his fall or demise were not mentioned anywhere.

"Few have been made privy to this knowledge."

Eleven gave a curt nod to the reticent Dusslorean. Though she'd learned plenty, the longing for more dried the back of her throat. Ophidian was just the beginning.

"Never been one for gossip," Eleven said.

*He'll tell me. He has to. The rest will come in time.*

# 13

ELEVEN SNUCK INTO THE MAIN COMPLEX AS THE sun set. A curious scent filled her quarters, impossible to ignore. The broken armoire that housed the bulk of her clothing had been disturbed.

*What fresh hell is this?*

Unlike previous days, Eleven entered the crude canteen opposite her room with the intention of engaging the kitchen's inhabitants.

"Who's been in my quarters?"

"Good evening to you too," Vera said.

Felix shook his head as if in pain. Both women faced him with concern.

"You cracking again, Unger?"

He cringed. "You hear that?"

Vera shrugged. "Don't look at me."

A recognizable resonance hit Eleven's lobes, much like they'd presumably hit Felix's. The contents of her pocket had shifted, causing a new jar item to connect with the black square

Crux had lent her.

"Unger?"

Felix waved away Vera's concern. "It's gone."

"Gone?"

"Guess a rogue frequency or something. Maybe a craft or—"

"We good or what?" Vera asked.

"Everything's gravy, V."

Zeroing in on the locator's agitation, Vera left the table. She quickly patted down Eleven. Vera swiped the onyx curio from Eleven's jacket without so much as a word. "Now what do we have here?"

"Hey," Eleven shouted. "That doesn't belong to you."

"Unclench your delicates. Just curious is all." Vera brought the item close to the light hanging over the table. Eleven fisted her hands but thought better of snatching it back.

"Offworld tech," Vera speculated. She tossed the square to Eleven. "What's it do?"

Eleven scrambled to catch it in time. "Careful."

"Seriously, V?" Felix asked.

Vera didn't hide her amusement. "Well?"

"Need to know basis."

The three of them had their own set of issues and none were keen on talking through them. Eleven went to her usual chair in the furthest corner as Vera returned to sitting.

"An item's been taken from my room."

"Sleeping and reading in a spot don't make it yours, wunderkind." Vera and Eleven locked eyes.

"So it's safe to assume you took it?"

The tech expert crossed her arms. "I'm putting the jacket to better use."

"What does that entail?" Eleven asked.

Felix frowned. "Talking about Lani's jacket?"

"Don't worry about it, Unger." Vera sighed.

"V."

Vera glared at Eleven. "I get that juicing has made him thoroughly deficient in a plethora of ways, but what's your excuse?"

Felix's lips tightened. "Little late for that kind of talk, ain't it?"

"Never too late to call a junkie on his bullshit. This isn't a home. Nothing here is yours. The sooner the pair of you dumb fucks grasp this apparently foreign concept, the better for all of us."

*What does Vera want with a jacket?*

"You know what it took to go through Lani's stuff. More than anyone, you should know, V."

*Lani. Why he's in this mess to begin with.*

"I gave that to Eleven for a reason," Felix added.

"And I'll give the precious locator her coveted gift back when I'm finished with it." Vera snagged the portable in front of her and got up from the table again. "Got a complaint, take it up with the big guy."

Then she left.

*I am failing to recall one instance when someone didn't storm out of this room.*

The resident cook shook his head. "Wonderful day to be alive."

*His pupils are dilated.*

"Is it?"

*Hypersensitive to sound... he was able to pick up that frequency before I did.*

Felix turned off the burner. "Dosed this morning. Still leveling off."

*Not sure "leveling off" is the term I'd use here.*

After bringing a stack of plates to the table in one hand and silverware in another, he put the final touches on dinner. Eleven fixed herself a plate from her seat.

"This batch is different."

"How?" Eleven asked mid-chew.

"Don't worry about it," Felix said. When he realized he'd snapped, he backtracked. "Sorry."

Eleven put her fork down. "It isn't right. The way she deflects. Constantly bringing up the dosing—it is not appropriate."

"Doesn't make what she says any less true." Felix shrugged.

"Still, it doesn't—"

"It matters, Eleven."

Eleven waited for Felix to elaborate. When nothing came, she asked, "Why?"

"Think liquor is needed for that story."

"You can't hold your drink," Eleven replied.

The guardian's face lightened as he let out a chuckle. Eleven fought back her own smile. "V's got enough on her plate as it is."

*Yes, this artillery Crux has her creating must be all-consuming.*

"She wants to help Crux," Eleven said.

"Vera's here for all of us. Even you."

*Now that I don't believe. Lani isn't enough motivation to stay on this course.*

"Why are you still here, Felix?"

"Why are you?"

"You know why," Eleven answered.

"Wish she'd talk to me."

*Is Vera enough for him?*

"About?"

Shaking his head, Felix said, "We really aren't the same, are we?" Felix slumped down in his chair. "Don't answer that."

The guardian prepared a large plate for himself and began to devour.

*Pathetic.*

An all-too-familiar rumble teetered overhanging lights. The steel structure shifted as a tremor became obvious to all. Felix pulled Eleven to the kitchen doorframe without a moment's hesitation.

"We're gonna be okay," Felix said.

"Why wouldn't we be?"

The shaky ground shifted dishes and small appliances. Eleven had been through worse. She said nothing as the quake continued for several minutes.

As the convulsions ceased, Felix stepped toward the series of ladders just outside the kitchen. "I gotta check on V."

"I'll see to Crux."

• • • • • • • • • • •

THE DUSSLOREAN DIDN'T RESPOND TO ANY OF Eleven's calls from below. She could barely see the scope of the quake's damage to Crux's stronghold with her lantern.

"Crux?" she shouted again.

The air congested Eleven's voice. Surveying the perimeter, she noted few towers had shifted or fallen. Still no word from Crux.

*He could be trapped.*

Though doubt regarding structural integrity plagued her, Eleven inched forward. She felt the ripple of an echo. Eleven hesitated as steel walls ached.

*What is that?*

She glanced up to Crux's office, then back to the steel opening of the base level. As her breathing and heart rate increased, so did the sound. It became a signal, a beacon.

Shaking her head, Eleven hurried to the door. The lantern light entered first. Glimmering reflections gave no indication as to the container's contents. She gasped as she continued.

Eleven placed the lamp onto the floor. She leaned toward

a barricade made of jars, all filled with items similar to those in Crux's office. Upon closer inspection, Eleven guessed the crate's contents in their entirety with the evidence presented.

Walking backward, a jar from the top shelf fell. A fast-acting crimson grip prevented it from shattering. Eleven jumped at Crux's presence. "Do not be frightened."

"I'm not." Eleven shuffled away from the jars.

"I trust no one was injured?"

"We're fine," Eleven said as she walked outside. The Dusslorean accompanied her.

"Pleased to hear it."

Eleven fixated on the jar in Crux's hands. "Something you want to tell me?"

"Not particularly."

Crux placed the fallen basin at his feet. Snagging the lantern, he latched the door shut. Eleven noted the absence of a lock.

"Crux?"

The Dusslorean turned to face her. "Earthquakes are uncommon in this district, are they not?"

She nodded. "But not unheard of."

"Curious."

"How so?" Eleven asked.

"Hard to say at present." Crux looked up.

"Where were you?"

"Teeming with inquiries tonight... even more curious." A Dusslorean's vision rivaled that of any Vera creation. Crux surveyed the damage. "Assembling provisions."

"Isn't that something reserved for your lesser?" The left corner of Eleven's mouth perked.

"I have no lesser," Crux replied.

*Right. Never attempt humor again.*

Crux presented the lantern to her. "I recall mention of combative skill in previous discussions. That, as well as intelligence gathered by Mr. Unger, suggests you can handle your-self in an altercation."

"Were that true, I might not be here right now."

"Are you capable of proper defense or not?" Crux pressed.

"I suppose." Eleven took the light from her mentor. Holding the portable lamp to the side of her right leg, the angle painted both locators' faces with unfavorable shadows. The grinding of Crux's teeth wouldn't have been audible to anyone other than Eleven.

"Are presumptions necessary?"

"No."

Crux turned, thinking hard on his next words. "Would you be willing to offer a demonstration?"

"Do I have a choice?" Eleven asked.

"The question is rather simple. A 'yes' or 'no' will suffice, Eleven."

*I know that look well.*

"Yes."

"Excellent," Crux said. "Upon your return, inform Vera that I wish to speak with her. Also, new data imaging of seismic disturbances is required. Inform Mr. Unger. That will be all."

• • • • • • • • • • •

*"I HAVE NO LESSER."*

Eleven examined her ageless skin with a hand mirror. Exhausted, she lay on her cot. But sleep eluded Eleven. The locator replayed the day, Crux at the forefront of her mind.

Turning on her side, Eleven set down the mirror. Her focus went to books on her nightstand. She'd continued to learn all she could about chambers, Dusslore, and Helot. Staring at the unread volumes, works Eleven had looked forward to mere hours ago, she felt no yearning to explore. The creak of a low level door perked Eleven's ears.

Two sets of footsteps clambered up the complex's main ladder. Eleven welcomed the ensuing metallic percussion outside her room. Rushing to the door, she pressed an ear against it.

"You're not supposed to go out alone," Felix said.

Vera groaned. "Because I'm the single, solitary mortal. Yeah, I have been made painfully aware of that fact." Both stopped when reaching the room directly below the kitchen. Eleven winced at clangs and clatters.

"At least let me come with you."

"Not happening," Vera replied.

"Where the hell is he sending you now?"

"I'm not telling you shit, and you're not going. Oh, and so we're clear, the grudge bullshit is tired. Drop it."

"If something happened to you—" A sack of objects landed hard on the ground. Miscellaneous gadgets fell from the bag's hold. The tech expert cussed into a labored breath. "Here, let me."

"I got it, okay, Felix? I'm no being from planet Düsseldorf or some super soldier or whatever the fuck that cunt is supposed to be, but I can manage this all by my lonesome."

Neither said anything for several minutes. The ease in stride suggested Vera continued with her tasks as Felix watched.

"Stubborn ass," Felix said.

The methodical stride faltered. "What was that?"

"Did I stutter?"

"You do seem the type," Vera replied. "At least these days."

"What do you want from me? Am I supposed to just sit back and let you get killed?"

Vera growled. "Nobody's dying." Swift footwork halted her breaths. Whispering, she added, "Can't you just trust me on this? For once?"

"I do trust you, V."

"The man knows what he's doing. I'm just taking this shit as a precaution."

"For what?"

"Damn it, Felix. You know I can't tell you!"

"Okay." Felix's voice became muffled. "Okay, I'll stop. When will you be back?"

"Could be tonight, tomorrow, next week. I—I'm not sure."

Both parties often left much unsaid. Today's conversation proved no exception. Eleven leaned against the door. Sliding down to sitting, she hugged her knees.

*What a horrible thing love is.*

# 14

UNCERTAINTY SLOWED ELEVEN'S FOOTING IN HER approach toward Crux. When she neared the clearing, a familiar hum reemerged.

*It's strong... stronger than last night.*

Shipyard steel cast back unforgiving smells. It also significantly turned up the temperature around the complex. Turning the corner, Eleven found Crux centered in a vast circle. Her boots stopped at the makeshift ring's outer layer. Crux's barrier consisted of four rows of jars.

"Falling behind."

"I didn't sleep very well," Eleven replied.

"Excuses are for the function of sympathy. Something neither one of us has time for, Eleven." Crux signaled her forward. "Fixta."

"What?"

"The component I left in your possession. You brought it with you?"

"Of course."

"Show me."

Confusion rumpled Eleven's brow. Crux's hand didn't falter as he waited for the requested item. Pulling it from her back pocket, Eleven gripped it with care. "Still intact if that's your concern."

"It is not," Crux replied. Stretching his arm forward, he said, "Bring it here."

Eleven unlocked both knees but didn't change her stance. She questioned what the day's lesson had in store, something she hadn't done in weeks. "I haven't mastered whatever it is you're set on teaching."

"Now, Eleven."

Her grasp on the fixta tightened. Against the slew of reservations boiling to the surface, Eleven entered the circle.

*Are these all from one shipping container?*

Stopping in front of Crux, Eleven dropped the curious black sheet into his hand. She watched as the Dusslorean crushed the element in his bulky fist. An open palm released dust similar to ash.

"Crux—"

"It is done. There is no other like it." Crux brushed the fixta's offcuts from his hand. "Much like guardian intervention, the fixta would have become just another a crutch."

"What about the others? How will they—"

"They will have you to guide them."

*Me?*

"Do we understand one another?" Crux asked.

This cryptic change in approach worried Eleven. Any attempt to rationalize his reasons was for naught.

"Yes."

"Take a piece," Crux instructed. He gestured to the basins surrounding them. "I want you to tell me where it's from and what the chamber held."

*Because it's that simple.*

Now more than ever, Eleven thought better of vocally questioning Crux's motives. The hum had strengthened during her short time among the glass containers. Looking to the right, she rushed to a jar. Eleven took a spiral shell resting at the top.

"Well?" Crux asked.

Eleven clasped the shell. "I need time."

Blinding pain warmed the top of Eleven's spine. The shell cracked underneath, piercing her palm at multiple points.

*He hit me… he* actually *hit me.*

Her breathing became erratic. Glass rattled. The low drumming didn't appear to alarm Crux.

*More tremors?*

"In the heat of battle," Crux said, towering above Eleven, "a moment is all it takes for your enemy to gain ground."

Shards of shell stayed in Eleven's hand. Her latest contusion slowly healed. Her eyelids grew heavy as she stood.

*I'm going to regret skipping breakfast… again.*

"Do not delay." Eleven's eyes widened in time to block Crux's forearm. She dodged a swing from his opposite arm only to get a swift knee to the abdomen. A grunt escaped her lips. "Is this the skill you spoke of?"

Eleven lurched over. Saliva dripped from her mouth. One hand continued to grip the shell, the other hugged her stomach. The hum's rhythm convulsed jars and their contents.

*This doesn't sound right. Not for an earthquake.*

Stopping another of Crux's assaults, a balled fist aiming for her thigh, Eleven chucked the fragments at his eyes. The Dusslorean's movements had a fluidity unlike that of any opponent she'd faced before. He charged toward her again.

"Incyo!"

Crux screeched to a halt. "Repeat."

"Incyo," Eleven said through clenched teeth. "Scripture."

"You are certain?"

*The shell is common in District 6 of Region 2. More texts*

*have been found there than anywhere else. Incyo was known for its scribes. When did I study Incyo?*

"I will not ask again," Crux warned.

"Yes."

"Do you recall this scripture?"

"No." Eleven grimaced.

"And why is that?"

*Because—because… because I didn't claim it.*

"One of the others must've found it."

The Dusslorean's breath stayed even. "Then tell me how you would know of it."

"I—I don't know."

"Who did this belong to if not you, Eleven?"

"Five, maybe."

"Maybe?"

*No, not maybe.*

"Five found this chamber," Eleven affirmed. She blinked at Crux. "How do I know that?"

He showed no signs of perspiration. Crux motioned for his pupil to choose another item. "Took far too long."

*It isn't just chambers I've come into contact with. It's all of them?*

"Your approach is demoralizing," he added.

*To hell with this pathetic display of virility.*

"Likewise," Eleven countered. "I know I'm right. So do you."

"Shall we continue, or would ruminating be more to your liking? I had hoped my intentions would be definitive. Assuming your claim to having read the chronicles is accurate."

This new method of Crux's went on for hours. Eleven chose from jars, none of which correlated to her. Crux kept a watchful eye. He made certain Eleven didn't see the etched numbers on the glass bottoms. When Eleven delayed, violence ensued. The shaking kept in time with her irregular pulse.

The circle's shadow grew long. By late afternoon, Eleven struggled for balance. She leaned over, propping herself up with sweaty hands on her knees. Crux shifted and swayed on the balls of his feet. "Another."

"No."

"Come again?"

*I'm done suffering at the hands of men that smile as they sting.*

"I've proven that I can do this. Repetition holds no interest. You're enjoying this lesson change. I refuse to participate any longer."

"There is a reason for this, Eleven. You must—"

"Why?" Eleven asked. "Stop this nonsense and, for once, just tell me what you want from me."

"I understand your hesitance."

Eleven scoffed. "You know nothing of me or my reasons."

*What is* any of this *in the grand scheme of things? I can figure out where something is from. I'm a glorified index.*

Crux tilted his head. "Eleven."

"I've given you my terms. As of today, my patience has run out. I'm not doing a thing you demand of me until you show result or headway."

"I will ask one more time," Crux warned.

Eleven did not waver. "No." The ring of chamber debris shuddered. Tiny fractures emerged.

"Very well."

Shifting his weight, Crux charged at Eleven. The speed of his onslaught limited her reaction time. A heavy blow knocked Eleven's jaw out of alignment. Eleven attempted to sweep Crux's legs from under him. His nimble footing allowed him to escape unfettered. As Eleven pushed up to standing, Crux kicked her locked leg. She fell hard on her side.

His calculated offenses gave her no time to counter. Crux took full advantage of every opening Eleven gave him.

*He's too fast.*

Through studies and her own scrutiny, Eleven surmised that Dusslore's gravity was denser. As a result, Crux carried himself with ease. This explained how he managed to surprise Eleven.

Dusslorean fighting style differed from how Cerulemans trained. Most techniques taught to guardians and locators involved only facing human opponents.

Crux swiftly got Eleven flat on her back. He prevented her from getting up by wrapping his coarse fingers around her neck. Eleven tried to push him off, but Crux had her at a major disadvantage. Her vision blurred while surrounding noises became distant. He willed her back to full consciousness with a frantic yank of the neck.

The ring surrounding them distorted. Jars moved, items soared out. A low roar aggravated the earth around them. Crux paid it no attention. Eleven scrambled to think on how to gain the upper hand.

A jagged piece of mirror from a cracked jar lay out of reach. Eleven broke Crux's hold on her neck by sweeping both arms at his locked elbows. She followed with a knee to his ribs before shoving him away.

Eleven gripped the mirror, readying herself for the Dusslorean's next attack. Her heartbeat grew thunderous. The tenderness of Eleven's neck caused her mind to drift.

*"Poor lost girl nearly of heaven—"*

"No," she said.

Crux rushed toward his pupil once more. His violence intermingled with the onslaught of recollections violating Eleven's conscious mind.

"Stop it! Go away!" Neither the memory of Isaac Kepler nor Crux obeyed her commands. "I said stop it!"

Debris and glass flying in a ticker-tape fashion halted Crux's incursion. He hurried to cover himself, while Eleven failed to register the cuts and gashes that accompanied the exploding jars.

"Eleven!" The Dusslorean knocked Eleven to the floor, concealing her head with his hands. A weighty silence trailed the motley barrage.

*"Open your eyes, Locator Eleven."*

"Are you all right?" Crux asked as he sat up. Eleven unfurled from a fetal position. The Dusslorean cupped a side of her face. "Eleven?"

*"What is your name?"*

Clenching her eyes shut, Eleven grazed a hand to her upper thigh where a thick piece of glass remained lodged. She pulled at that and other fragments found throughout her body. Crux awaited confirmation. All manner of sternness had disappeared in the wake of destruction. The miscellaneous shards that'd flown toward them were strewn about.

*The jars.*

Eleven recoiled from her worried mentor. She put her back to Crux as she rose to standing. "This is my doing?"

"You desired results."

"H—ho—how?" Eleven took in the wreckage around them. Her breaths were ragged.

"Our abilities differ. I wanted to see if they did in this regard. The chambers are bound to us just as we are to them. In heightened states, we have been known to—"

"*This* is what you wanted," Eleven said.

"Yes."

*Wretched man.*

"We are tied. Bound, Eleven."

"And the way to show me was to try to break me?" Her voice grew hoarse.

*Just like* he *did.*

Crux approached. "Conceivably not the best course of action to take."

Eleven lunged at him. She forced Crux onto his back. Planting herself on his torso, she hit him again and again with no sign of letting up. The Dusslorean didn't retaliate or protest in the slightest.

*"What is your purpose?"*

Agony fueled her momentum, tears filling to the brim. Eleven had bottled up so much for so long. Her short time amongst Felix, Vera, and the Dusslorean locator had weakened her grim exterior.

Eleven deliberated how much she could trust Crux, or anyone else for that matter, as she continued to beat the susceptible man. After exhausting the little energy she had left, Eleven stopped. Unable to focus, she hovered over Crux.

"Are you better now?" The Dusslorean healed as he watched Eleven mentally careen.

Hyperventilating, Eleven forced herself to breathe through her nostrils. "No."

"I am sorry."

Toppling off him, Eleven crumbled to his side. The two lay there, staring at the putrid tinted sky.

*You asked for this—demanded it.*

"Each of us has a distinct expertise, Eleven. My hope was to bring out yours. Heightened sentiment tends to reveal more than we allow."

"And?" Eleven bunched glops of crud in her hands.

Crux dabbed at the drying blood under his nose. "I have a few theories."

"I'm sure you do," Eleven snapped. She got to her feet. The hodgepodge of debris surrounding them would not be easily tidied.

"Tarrying in the face of rutted terrain no longer suits you, Eleven." Crux sat up. He whisked his tattered coat. "Nor does naïveté."

This tough love spectacle had all been for this simple show. Eleven's stomach turned at the realization. Caustic statements she could take. However Crux warranted the assault, Eleven viewed it as a betrayal.

*Instead you make my blood flow outward. Break and bruise me because my body can stand the abuse.*

"We're done here."

"While I hate to contradict—" Eleven twisted to kick Crux in his side. He clutched loose earth beneath him. Sitting up again, Crux said, "You are more brazen than I originally credit."

"We're supposed to be better than them, aren't we?"

Felix ran toward them, choking on toxins as he advanced. "What the hell was all that? You guys okay?"

"Of course, Mr. Unger."

Felix took in Eleven's appearance. "Not to question you or anything, but this doesn't look so good."

"It is what you do best, correct?" Crux barked at Felix. "*Question* me?"

"The hell does that mean?"

Crux dropped his head. "You have my apologies, Mr. Unger. I am—today has been trying."

Felix rushed to Eleven's side. "What did he do?"

The locators stared at one another. After an eternity, Eleven said, "Don't worry about it."

*Who knew Isaac Kepler came in red?*

# 15

DESPITE HEALING FROM CRUX'S ONSLAUGHT SOME
time ago, Eleven stroked her neck with tentative fingers. She
slouched in her bloodied and filth-ridden clothes, not caring
about the stains they would leave on her linens. The dour locator stared absentmindedly at the door opposite the cot she
rested on. Both temples throbbed, deafening the slight room
noise surrounding her.

"You gotta eat," Felix said as he entered.

"Later."

"Now."

Staring at her knuckles, Eleven whispered, "I'm not hungry."

Felix let out a long breath. "Yeah. Right." He stomped out
but returned seconds later with a plate. "Grilled cheese with
real tomatoes and everything. Impossible to pass up."

*And yet.*

"No, thank you."

Approaching Eleven, Felix placed the sandwich atop the

sturdiest tower of books on her nightstand. "Best when eaten hot."

"Noted." Felix showed no signs of leaving. Keeping her head down, Eleven asked, "Was there anything else?"

"Don't know. Is there?"

Eleven's eyelids drooped. "I would prefer to be alone."

"Just right now or always?" With that, Felix walked backward until hitting the threshold of Eleven's room. He sidestepped the doorframe while simultaneously crossing his arms. Felix leaned against the wall.

"It isn't an unreasonable request, Felix."

"Appears I'm not going anywhere."

Eleven glowered at the sandwich. "If I eat, will you go?"

"It'd be put up for consideration."

The locator's right hand returned to her neck. She caressed it as she weighed her options. Eleven didn't have the energy for their usual banter, nor the wherewithal to physically remove him. Felix's gaze bore into her.

"Fine." Eleven snatched the sandwich from the plate and took a bite.

"Take it easy. Maybe chew."

Moving a mouthful to her cheek, Eleven asked, "Why are you doing this?"

"Me?" Felix stepped in front of the doorway. "You know how I am. Friendly to a fault." By the end of his sentence, the grilled cheese had vanished. Eleven picked at the crumbs.

Felix smiled. "I can make you something else."

"That won't be necessary."

"I know it's not *necessary*. Figured you could use the grub. Especially after—" Felix stopped. His smile faltered. "Whatever the hell it is he put you through today."

Eleven wiped the remnants of food onto her jeans. "I don't want to talk about that."

"Works out for the both of us then because I don't wanna

hear about it. I've decided to enjoy the rest of my day. Crux's exploits tend to make that difficult."

"If you're quite finished, I would appreciate some time to myself."

"Take off your jacket," Felix said.

"What?"

"The jeans aren't salvageable. Top layers might be though."

Looking down at herself, Eleven took in her appearance. The jeans had been shredded. Her legs were visible from any angle. Blood had soaked through the majority of the fabric. Her leather jacket suffered minor scratches. The same could not be said for the dark cotton blouse beneath it. A large gash on the torso exposed Eleven's abdomen.

"Don't bother. It makes no difference to me whether or not you can salvage it."

"Get up," Felix ordered as he approached Eleven. Stopping within arm's reach, he motioned with his right index and middle finger.

"No."

"Just humor me."

Congealed blood bonded skin to clothing. Eleven reluctantly peeled off the jacket from her seated position. She flinched when gorier sections protested.

A thick green mineral-like chunk dislodged from underneath the collar. Neither reached for it as it skidded under Eleven's cot.

After handing over the worn leather, Eleven brushed her bare arms. Felix watched her. "Thanks."

"You're welcome."

Felix scanned the jacket. "Crux doesn't carry much. What did this?" he asked while grazing a rip on the left shoulder.

"Jars."

"Glass?" Felix's brow lowered.

*Mostly.*

Shaking his head, Felix said, "I'd ask further, but something tells me I'm not need-to-know."

"According to?"

"Crux, for starters."

"Since when do you give a damn about what he has to say?" The locator halted at her intense delivery of the question. Her face fell. "I'm tired, Felix."

"Don't worry about it," he said, throwing the jacket to the side. "Never seen you like this."

"You haven't known me very long." The locator stared at the tattered leather.

Felix sat next to Eleven. "In some ways, that's true." He reached for her but stopped short of touching as she tensed.

"That woman—that shell you watched for all those years, that isn't me."

"I'm getting that."

"I've eaten your food, Felix. And I—I'm grateful for your concern."

Felix raised a hand to halt Eleven's excuses. "Too much time alone isn't good for anyone, even a locator."

"Today was... different."

"How?"

Eleven locked her gaze with Felix's. "He bothers you."

"A lot of people bother me."

"But you trust him, right?"

"Most of the time," Felix admitted. "Don't you?"

"I did."

"*Did?*"

Blinking, Eleven said, "I *do*."

"Doing a hell of a job trying to convince me," Felix replied. "Whatever it is, I'll hear you out."

*This isn't his business.*

"The lesson, it—it drudged up something I'd give anything to forget."

*So why can't I stop myself?*

"The recollector brought all your memories back, didn't it?"

"Humans aren't built to remember everything, Felix. It'd drive you mad."

"You built that way?"

"I believe so." Eleven moved her eyes to the doorway. "Part of living like this is learning to repress certain chapters of my life. Things that hold no benefit."

Felix leaned forward. "Intense type of shit?"

"Yes." Again, Eleven stroked her neck.

"We all try for that."

"Doesn't make it okay."

"No." Felix nodded in agreement. "It doesn't."

Eleven's fingers paused when she saw Felix watching the hand massaging her neck. He reclined back, steadying himself on his palms. "At our group home, me and Lani kept to ourselves. Neither of us warmed to the whole situation. Being quiet didn't really sit well with some people. We just didn't give a shit. This one punk, Marvin I think his name was, had it out for me. To this day, I got no clue why, but it was what it was. You can identify with that, right?"

"Perhaps."

"At the time," he continued, "best way to get to me was through Lani. Anybody with a lick of sense could see that much."

*I imagine some still can.*

"Marvin hurt her?"

"He tried," Felix answered. His eyes became dazed, caught in the memory he spoke of. "A second after he laid hands on her, I laid mine on him. Marvin's touch was downright gentle in comparison."

"You killed him?"

"Almost." Felix scratched under his chin. "The month in

confinement flew by. When I came back, Marvin was the first thing that came into focus. Not Lani or the counselors, but *him*. From then on, every time he found himself near me, even just in passing, he'd cover his neck... like that'd stop me from choking him again."

"I'm missing the story's significance."

"Don't act like this is our first powwow. It's called making conversation, Eleven." His grin fell. "Plus, you've been doing pretty much the same as Marvin since you got inside today. Doesn't take much to work out what may have gone down."

"It doesn't compare."

Felix leaned in. "If Crux hurt you, I need to know."

"Do I look hurt?"

"Yes," Felix replied. Eleven blinked. "You've got it in your head that because you can heal, shit doesn't affect you... but the body has a way of spinning yarn when the mind doesn't want to own up to something, Eleven."

"Crux found a trigger. Nothing more."

"Bullshit. The scene I walked up on wasn't *nothing*."

Eleven pressed her lips together.

*I'm not Lani.*

Tilting her head, Eleven asked, "You've always been like this, haven't you?"

"Like what?"

"Always... nice."

"Haven't been paying attention, have you? Forget Marvin— you forgetting about my stabbing you not too far back?"

Eleven noticed Felix sweating more than usual. "Your coloring is off."

"Way to change the subject." Felix wiped his forehead.

"Have you dosed? Or has caring for everything but your own personal well-being distracted you?"

Through tight lips, Felix said, "These aren't regulation. Others have been feeling the difference too. But what're you gonna do, right?"

"Others?"

"There are more guardians playing rebel than you might think," Felix said. "Good and proper batches are manufactured in-house, but we're managing."

"But the formula is the same? This *unregulated* type?"

Felix shrugged. "More or less, I guess."

*He's playing with fire.*

"We have people on the inside. Surely one of those can gain access to—"

"You gotta stop fretting about things out of your control, Eleven."

"I'm not worried about you."

Felix chuckled. "Didn't say you were. Besides, I'm tough. Not as tough as you, but what mere mortal is?"

"Now I'm a god?" Eleven sneered.

"Already got the complex."

"Felix."

"Weren't we talking about you?" Felix tried to steer the conversation away from himself. Like he always did when anyone brought up his medications.

*You're scared for him.*

Relating to the need for avoidance, Eleven took the initiative. "Has it always been difficult? My inadequate knowledge has left me to wonder if the so-called "normal" life is impossible."

"No... not always," Felix admitted. He leaned forward. "Just don't know how good you got it until you're pulled from the thick of it."

Eleven recalled the snippets of Felix's past that she knew. Unlike Vera, Crux had presented no information about Mr. Unger or his beginnings. She surmised Crux viewed Felix as unworthy of note. The more she got to know Felix, the more she disagreed with the Dusslorean's assessment.

Long before a cause or substances, Felix had led a life

uncommon to most, the likes of which Eleven had read about but never seen. He was the oldest of two with loving parents. The Ungers lived in a district with minimum third-kind regulations. Frederick Unger had a flair for invention, though his specialty rested in auto mechanics. Yolanda Unger taught public school and tutored the underprivileged. Both passed away in Felix's late teens. Details of their demise had never been made clear. No one knew the current status of the cherished Lani, who had wished to one day become a dancer but seldom vocalized the dream to anyone other than her big brother.

*"Ties like that don't often mean anything. People like Vera, even Crux some days, they're family."*

"Catch some Zs, yeah?"

Eleven shook her head. "Sleep doesn't come easily."

"I get that," Felix replied as he stood. "But there's no telling what he's got in store for you come sun up. If you plan on keeping up, you're gonna need your strength."

· · · · · · · · · · ·

*"EYES ON THE PRIZE, GLOOM."*

*Kicking a mound of dirt, the frustrated woman glared at her friend walking several meters ahead of her. "Don't call me that."*

*"Smile once, just once today, and I won't." He turned to face her but continued his trajectory. "Keep up!"*

*"Ordering me around does little to improve my mood."*

*Stumbling while walking backward, he said, "It's a gorgeous day, the weather is perfect for our expedition, and we're strolling around shackle-free. What's not to be happy about?"*

**This sunny disposition of his is effortless. I almost envy it... almost.**

179

"I'm out here against all common sense," she snapped. "Care to reveal your reasoning?"

"And spoil the—" An unseen divot caused the man to trip. Righting himself, he chuckled. "Surprise?"

They were the only people within fifty kilometers. Outside wildlife, life was limited to patches of cacti. Blue skies and red earth contrasted their dark colored clothing and fair skin.

**If I leave right now, I can finish my book before my next shift.**

"Don't tell me you don't like surprises."

"As a matter of fact, I don't believe I care for them, no."

"I'll add that to an ever-growing list of things for future generations." He approached her. "It'll go right under kids christening you 'Gloom,' the texture of sweet potatoes, and historical fiction."

She grinned. "Let's not forget townswomen having the audacity to refer to you as 'Handsome.'"

"There's that smile I treasure so." Throwing an arm over her, he pushed her forward. She put up no resistance. "Best pace yourself, friend of mine. You're nearing the territory of wit. Wouldn't want you to sprain anything."

**How did I get saddled with such a person?**

"What do you think about 'Ichabod'?"

Gazing skyward, she asked, "Which one is Ichabod?"

"Me. Well, maybe me. I don't know." He shrugged. "Thought I might try it out. What do you think?"

"I think this obsession with names is no longer endearing."

Her friend groaned. "So that's a 'no,' I take it?"

"A firm one."

He gave her a squeeze. "You can't keep shooting them down."

"It doesn't suit you." She looked ahead. "None of them do."

His pacing slowed. "My suggestions or names in general?"

"They aren't for us. Such things are for humanity. Make no

*mistake. We only look like them."*

*"Then what does suit me, huh? Should you refer to me by rank? Maybe some amalgamation of letters and numbers with no personality whatsoever? No heart?"*

*Waving off his displeasure, she said, "You're beginning to irritate me."*

*"Yeah? Likewise."*

*She hesitated. "No need to be brazen."*

*"There's more to life than the town library." He pushed forward with hurried movements. He pointed off in the distance. "Those pages you hold so dear got nothing on this view, gloomy girl."*

**He's trying my patience.**

*He kept on. "Get moving."*

**Attempting to prove some overinflated point yet again.**

*"We're too exposed out here."*

**Have it your way, then.**

*Minutes passed before he realized she was no longer following. She had turned around, stomping through the flat terrain with abandon. Her brow pooled with sweat as she rushed her footing.*

*"Hey!" He jogged toward her.*

*"Go on without me, Ichabod."*

*"I am definitely not an 'Ichabod.' You're right, once again." As he neared her, he attempted to take her by the elbow. She veered away from him. "Come on, gloomy girl. We were almost there."*

*"I don't care."*

*"Fibber."*

*"Never developed the taste for lies," she replied. Her smirk slipped when she picked up a sound in the distance. One she hadn't heard in months. Fingers twitched at her sides.*

*"Don't pretend you're not curious," he teased. "If there's one thing I know about you—"*

"Wait." She stopped in realization.

"Hey, your nearest and dearest is trying to make a point here."

"There's nothing in the flatlands."

Beaming, he asked, "Sure about that now?"

**The conniving, devious twit.**

She charged toward her friend. He shuffled back several steps. "Whoa, watch the hot commodity!"

"A chamber?"

"Let it never be said that you're totally oblivious."

"Answer me!"

"A chamber," he sighed. "Took me a while to find one this far out, but yeah."

"Are you deranged?"

He shrugged. "We haven't opened one in ages."

**Two years, but who's counting?**

"Thought it was about time we remedied that," he added.

"Just like that?" Taking a menacing step toward him, she leveled her gaze with his. "How many times must I say it?"

"It's a risk, yes. I'm aware of this fact. But this—" Motioning to their surroundings, he said, "What we're doing, it isn't right."

"It's always the same argument with you."

"We were put here for a reason."

"Precisely," she replied. "It is that very reason those—those nuisances want us in the first place, you ridiculous man! Have you forgotten all you've already lost?"

"Watch it."

"Why risk exposure? The two of us are all that's left."

He watched her pace. "We can't hide forever. And, even if we do, what kind of life is this? Why not make ourselves useful?"

"Useful?"

"Don't play dumb." He stepped toward her. "The urge, the

*calling stirs in you too. That's why we can't sleep. It's why we continue to move. Don't we owe it to ourselves to stop avoiding our purpose?"*

*"And what is that? What should we be doing? Saving the world?" She indicated the town kilometers away. "Helping people?"*

*"Yes."*

*"By putting them in danger?"*

*"They're already in danger."*

*"So?"*

*"The least we can—so?"*

*"Humanity went willingly. If they choose to—" Jingling stopped her argument. She scanned the area for its source but saw nothing. "What is that?" When he didn't respond, she returned her eyes to him. But he'd disappeared.*

*"Ten!"*

*Her breaths became uneven.*

**No... that's not what happened next. This isn't right. Wake up!**

Eleven sprang up. She forced herself to inhale deeply. Blinking offered no relief to her stinging eyes.

She remembered the dry heat from that day. How dehydrated the pair of them had been just minutes into their journey. Then Eleven smiled. Recalling how most referred to Ten as "Handsome" amused her. It suited him more than anything he came up with in their time together.

Eleven hadn't been asleep long. It hardly felt like morning without Vera tinkering in one of the laboratories. Felix had no trouble sleeping the day away. The shipyard hideout was quieter than ever.

Her ears perked at a weak rattling.

*There it is again.*

Unwrapping herself from the sheets, Eleven moved to the

center of her room. Her teeth clenched to the point of breaking. The noise had returned louder than ever.

Something rolled out from under Eleven's cot. The forgotten green stone progressed toward her, stopping short of her bare feet. Resting on her knees, she warily picked it up.

*Once more, you get your way, Handsome. Time to make myself useful.*

# 16

"CRUX?"

Eleven wasted no time in preparing for the day. She ran to the usual meeting spot to find herself alone. The locator noticed all evidence surrounding yesterday's heated exercise was absent. Much like her instructor.

*I'm on time. Early even.*

Looking upward to the Dusslorean's office, Eleven called again, "Crux, I need to talk to you."

No answer. The grueling sun, mixed with the familiar but lethal aromas, added to Eleven's growing agitation. A hum emanated from her pocket. Her hand lingered over the fabric, keeping the small green item hidden.

*Wait.*

Straining her ears, the locator listened for frequencies. Dissatisfied, Eleven hurried to the ground level shipping container underneath Crux's office. She pressed a palm against the ridged wall. Her pulse quickened.

*Where's the frequency?*

Eleven opened both doors without the need of her picking tools. Her heart thumped against her ribcage as she took in the sight of an empty container. The bevy of jars had vanished.

*What are you playing at now, Dusslorean?*

In the far distance, a whisper called. Eleven's hands dropped to her sides. She stretched out her fingers and closed her eyes. The sound emitted again, louder this time.

*The complex.*

· · · · · · · · · · ·

OUT OF ALL THE WORKSHOPS AND LABORATORIES, just one container held a vehicle. Eleven kicked at dry tread-shaped muck in the center of the fortress's garage.

*Vera must've taken the car.*

Pinpointing the sound's location had not proved simple. Eleven had gone from level to level, being careful not to rouse Felix. The locator's momentum had slowed in her pursuit. Forcibly accelerating her breaths, Eleven's heartbeat picked up. She wiggled her fingers.

*Come on.*

Eleven's pulse jumped at loud clangs to her left. Another harsh crash pushed the door of a tall metal cabinet open. The sound rippled as the unbarred latch settled.

Eleven reached forward. A wooden block leapt from the cabinet. She captured it with both hands. Numerous faint knocks from the interior had Eleven hurrying to find a crease. Not one of its six sides showed a hint of an opening.

*Kindling it is then.*

Hurling the curiosity to the ground, it splintered apart. Multicolored fragments danced among pieces of fractured timber. However, as the wood settled, the fragments hurled themselves at Eleven's feet.

Eleven picked up the nearest bit. She pinched it between her right thumb and forefinger. Though plentiful in quantity, Eleven counted only seven colors. The one she held was devoid of any hue. A small hole drilled into its center gave her pause. After scooping up several more, Eleven noticed the same gap.

*That's... something.*

The day came and went. Eleven spent the hours sitting between the tread marks, testing her newfound skill. She threw the strange fragments, as well as the green mineral, across the garage. No matter where she scattered them, they always returned to her. She allowed herself not to think of where Crux was. Nor did she wonder why Felix hadn't bothered with his standard eight questions per day.

The garage's large metal door loudly retracted. Eleven retreated to the shadows of a loaded shelf near the doorway. She watched as a sleek dark vehicle with two bright beams pulled into the space.

Windows rolled down in unison after the garage door closed. A helmeted figure sat behind the steering wheel.

"Waiting for little ol' me?" Vera asked as she exited the vehicle. She grabbed two bags from the trunk. Removing her helmet, she ran a gloved hand through her hair. "Guessing he hasn't gone over stealth with you just yet."

Vera's cavalier tone appeared not to be at full strength. Eleven pocketed the chamber remnant and box fragments. With little sleep and a small reserve of energy from Felix's late-night grilled cheese, the locator didn't have it in her to keep up the charade of hiding. She revealed herself as Vera peeled off a baggy smock. The modern cut and fabric dyes of her tailored outfit differed from her standard thrift store clearance with vintage military flair.

"Unger around?"

Eleven crossed her arms. "I'm not his keeper."

"Sure about that?" Vera chuckled. A splintering underfoot gave her pause. She grimaced at seeing what remained of the wooden box. "See you've made yourself at home." Eleven noticed a large bruise had just begun to take shape along Vera's left cheek. The tech expert hovered a hand over it. "There's one hell of a story attached, believe me."

"I'm sure Crux will be happy to hear it." Walking backward, Eleven approached the threshold.

Vera chucked her gloves onto the vehicle's hood. "Don't like me much, huh?"

"Does it matter?"

"No." Vera dropped the heavy bags to the side of her. "Funny enough, I don't like anybody."

*Lies.*

"Guess we have that in common," she added.

Eleven faced the door. "I'll give you your space."

"You hungry?"

"Pardon?" Eleven glanced over her shoulder.

Vera patted her closed lips with her left hand. "Hunger. It's kind of a thing." She snatched a large brown sack from the passenger side window. "Interested?"

The smell triggered Eleven's stomach to chime in. "Isn't that for Felix?"

Shrugging, Vera said, "He'll cook up something all by his lonesome. I mean, unless lurking in the garage is an all-night sort of thing."

• • • • • • • • • • •

THE WOMEN SAT OPPOSITE ONE ANOTHER ON THE floor of Lab 1. A barrier consisting of nachos and burritos separated them. Neither allowed more than murmurs between chews for the first few minutes.

"What's with the bracelet?"

Meeting Vera's eyes, Eleven asked, "Bracelet?"

"The box you were so keen on destroying. It had a bracelet

inside."

"It belonged to you?"

"Long time ago." Vera shrugged. "Crux's better half fashioned it for me. Wore it all of twice before busting it. Wasn't really my style anyway."

The locator lowered her food. Still chewing, she said, "Did Helot tell you anything about it?"

"Don't think so. Why?"

"No reason," Eleven replied.

"Aren't you gonna ask about my trip?"

*Hadn't planned on it.*

Eleven noticed a bullet hole at the front of Vera's jacket. She had missed it during her earlier inspection. "Thrilling, I'm sure."

"How fucking right you are." Tossing a wrapper, Vera brushed at specks of food. She stretched out her legs while leaning back on her palms.

*The bullet was fired at close range. No blood around the entry. Layer underneath must have a synthetic coating.*

Vera motioned to the bag closest to Eleven. "Top of the heap."

"I'm quite all right."

"Just look, will ya?" Vera pressed. "It is free of trickery, scout's honor. Well, *activated* trickery anyway."

Swallowing, Eleven investigated the bag. It was covered in dust and filth.

"Blue box," Vera said.

Several weapons pushed forward as Eleven unzipped the duffel. She sifted through a second layer of guns when the aforementioned box presented itself. Dents and scratches hinted that the stone ring box itself had seen better days.

*I've had my fill of trinkets today.*

"Go on."

"Vera."

"You'll want to see it."

Eleven flipped the top. Baffled, she removed the box's lone item: a metallic tube the size of a gun shell with perforations along the sides. The locator allowed it to slide back and forth in her palm.

"Recognize it?"

*No.*

"Because you should." Vera snagged the peculiar component from Eleven. She displayed the casing between her fingers. "Give it a second. It'll come to you."

*No wonder she gets along with Crux so well.*

"Taken years to finesse this kind of artillery. All worth it."

"Why?" Eleven asked.

"You know that better than anyone else," Vera answered. "Anyone still breathing, that is."

*The grooves and near-microscopic gaps aren't like anything else currently on the market. Clearly underground. Guns. They're a fool's weapon. Anything at a distance is. What game are you playing at—?* That night.

Vera pointed at Eleven. "*There* it is."

"You killed me with one of these?"

"This exact one if you can believe it," Vera said. She cupped the casing in her hand. "Recycling as much as possible is downright necessity. These babies aren't easy to come by."

Immediate regret permeated every fiber of Eleven's being. Death, or *deaths*, and guns had a well-versed history. She recalled the vicious whistle. Her recollection of the grating sound had made concentration near impossible and overloaded the senses.

*The shrilling blare must have accounted for its speed.*

"What about this qualifies as something I had to see?"

Vera tossed the shell back to Eleven. "What do you make of it?"

Eleven stress tested the metal. It didn't show the slightest hint of use or wear. The high caliber make was atypical. Just what one would expect from a creation of Vera's.

"Silicon?"

"Someone kept up with her reading. Good eye. What else?"

Eleven snapped the package shut. Placing it back atop the heap of weaponry, she asked, "Why not save me the trouble?"

"Where's the fun in that?" Vera pulled her own bag to the side of her leg. Keeping her eyes fixed to Eleven's, she opened the half-filled sack.

"Jewels," Eleven observed.

"*Diamonds*," Vera corrected. "Also known as component number 2. Took years to sort through what did and didn't work. Turns out, even my weapons are finicky bitches." She chuckled to herself. "Being that they're fucking diamonds, I've tried alternatives. Nothing else does the trick."

"You stole them?"

"I prefer the term 'liberated,' it has a better ring to it." Laughing, Vera said, "There are only so many wedding rings and brooches one can lift from beyond the grave. Not ideal, but I work with what I got." She picked at the plate in front of her. Tossing a stale tortilla chip back, Vera added, "It's all about being resourceful."

*Is this the longest Vera has ever spoken to me?*

"Why are you telling me this?"

"Consolation prize. I mean, you worked so hard. Least I could do is explain the reason behind it."

Vera had been adamant on the locator learning "real world" skills. The tech expert's forcefulness had confused Eleven on numerous occasions. Thinking back to the constant study of locks and so on, Eleven fought the urge to laugh.

*He meant for me to help her?*

Vera chewed at callouses to the side of her left thumbnail. "Fared fine all by my lonesome."

"Why did the plan change?"

"Plans got a way of doing that," Vera replied.

"How?"

Vera shrugged. "Crux wouldn't say. He never gives up much when it comes to seekers, or locators, or whatever the fuck you want to call yourselves." She stood and went to a corner of the lab. When Vera returned, she carried a very familiar piece of apparel. "I know how important this is."

"It's just a jacket."

Vera tossed it onto Eleven's head. "I didn't say who it was important to. He'd have killed me for tearing it up anyhow."

Dragging it from her hair, Eleven examined Lani's jacket. She ran her fingers along the drawstring and hood. "Thank you."

*That smile of his has faded. Maybe this will bring it back.*

A loud beeping emitted from the opposite end of the laboratory. "The hell?" Vera hurried to the sound. She swiped open the nearest portable and clicked away.

Eleven followed. "Vera?"

"Shit," Vera said under her breath. "Shit fuck. Fuck shit."

"What is it?"

Ignoring the query, Vera pounded in commands. Pressing a button on the nearest wall, a dim tone proceeded flashing red. A hail from one of several computers at a workstation signaled. Vera ran to it. Pressing in a passcode, she said, "Hey, old man?"

No response.

Vera tried again on the portable she held. "Come on, Crux. We've got problems."

"I don't think he's here," Eleven said.

"Motherfucker," Vera said more to herself than to Eleven. She entered another code. "Unger?" Her patience wearing thin, Vera tugged at the back of her scalp. "For fuck's sake, Felix!"

A window on her portable opened. Sound waves could be seen. Some grumbling anteceded a fatigued Felix. "V? Is that you?"

"Who the fuck else would it be? Listen, we don't got a lot of time. Is Crux with you?"

"Of course not," Felix replied. The odd timbre of his voice didn't go unnoticed. "Why?"

Vera frowned as she met Eleven's gaze. "Sensors are picking up multiple unknowns skimming the perimeter. They're closing in fast."

"You were followed?" Eleven asked Vera.

"Not possible."

"Arm the barriers," Felix growled. His talk box window closed.

"Vera, it *is* possible," Eleven said.

"Anybody that could've followed is flat-lined, okay?" Vera snapped. She multitasked between the portable and the computer. Not finding what she wanted, Vera punched the nearest surface. "Where the fuck are you when I need you, you big red bastard?"

*That portable picks up heat signatures. There's us, and Felix is still in his quarters, but I don't see Crux.*

Frustrated, Vera pushed away from the workstation. A series of explosions went off in the distance. Handing the portable to Eleven, she said, "Barely slowed them down. Tell Felix they're inside."

Eleven strained to remember the code Vera had entered. After a few tries, she punched in the correct sequence. "South entrance has just been breached, Felix."

"Ain't that peachy?" Vera began to gather any pertinent material in the immediate vicinity.

"Looters, maybe?" Felix asked through a cough.

Vera forced a laugh. "Cause we're that fucking lucky. Those signatures aren't human and I couldn't get a count."

*The difference is subtle, but she's right. We could very well be dealing with Banaedrut.*

"We—" Felix started. "We've got to—"

Vera stopped mid-panic. "What's going on, Unger?"

"We've got to—this—I—" His feed cut out again.

Eleven tried to reconnect. "Repeat." When Felix didn't hail them back, she reexamined the heat signatures. "No movement from his location."

"They've infiltrated?" Vera asked as she signed into a bulky laptop.

"No, we're still clear."

"You think this is your fan club?"

"We can't rule anything out."

Furiously, Vera typed in several lines of code into what appeared to be a basic program. "Security feeds are streaming. Wherever Crux is, he'll think better of showing up now. He'll be okay. Just wish I could say the same for us."

"What are you doing?" Eleven asked. She retrieved Lani's jacket.

"Setting the charges. Fuck diamonds. Detonators are a girl's best friend."

*She's going to level the place.*

Vera finished up her work before throwing the laptop against a wall. A swift boot to what remained destroyed the potential of salvaging it. The other computers went dark. Vera tucked a thick stack of papers under her arm as she returned to the bags storing diamonds and weapons.

"There's a panic room underground. If we leave now, fat chance of them following." This response didn't satisfy Eleven. Vera considered the jacket Eleven held. "If Unger is functional, he'll meet us there."

"And if he isn't?"

Vera's shifty yet widened eyes did nothing to satisfy the locator. Without another word, Eleven ran for the door. "The fuck are you doing?"

"What you won't," Eleven said. She hastily threw on Lani's

jacket.

"Eleven!"

The locator was half a floor up the ladder when she heard commotion from below. Moments later, Vera joined in her ascent.

Arriving on Felix's level, Eleven found his bedroom door open. The guardian convulsed on the ground beneath his computer monitors. Dumbfounded at the sight, Eleven hesitated. Vera pushed past her.

Pulling Felix into her lap, Vera said, "Unger? Get up, Felix. We have to go." He continued to shake. His teeth chattered as he strained to respond.

Eleven rushed to Felix. She blanched when checking his accelerating pulse. Peering into his eyes, she noticed an oddity. A thick ring of black circled both irises. Eleven glanced around Felix's room.

"Is this withdrawal?" Vera asked.

*I FOUND HIM AFTER I PROMISED MY BELOVED I WOULD STOP SEARCHING. THE DEBT OWED BY OPHIDIAN RUNS DEEPER THAN WORDS TO THE ONE I CHERISH MOST.*

*Helot tracked a Banaedrut after lacing their drink with something.*

Felix convulsed. Vera struggled to gain control of his limbs. "Eleven!"

*The dose.*

Eleven steadied Felix's head. "Where do you keep the doses? Felix, this is important." His eyes wouldn't focus. Biting down on his lip, blood filled his mouth.

"We're running out of time," Vera said in a rush.

Unwilling to relent, the locator slapped Felix hard across the face. "If it's in here, show me."

Felix's gaze shot to his cot. Eleven went to it. Tearing it apart, she found a vial hiding between the cushion and frame. Large chunks of sediment rested at the bottom.

Vera choked back a sob. "Whatever you're gonna do, do it fast!"

Just as Eleven noticed the vial bubbling over, it combusted. The concoction scalded her skin. She chucked what remained against a wall.

Examining her healing hand, Eleven muttered, "No."

*How could I have missed this?*

"Eleven."

*Felix.*

"Eleven?"

*They used him.*

"God damn it, Eleven!"

The locator turned to find a limp body in Vera's arms. She took a step forward. "We have to go."

"Why isn't he waking up?" Vera asked.

"His doses were tampered with. There's nothing—" Eleven stopped herself. Lowering her voice, she said, "He's lost."

Vera cupped Felix's face. His eyes, still crazed, had lost life.

Eleven's lower lip trembled. "I'm sorry."

Vera pushed Felix off of her as if he were nothing but a burden. "We're playing fast and loose with extraction protocols."

"Vera—"

"Don't."

*I should've seen it before.*

Vera went to the bags she'd dumped near the door. Arming herself, she asked, "These banana dudes bulletproof?"

"No one is bulletproof," Eleven replied.

"Heard the fuckers are wicked fast."

"Banaedrut can be."

"Then we better get going, yeah?" Vera left the room.

The locator hesitated for a brief moment. Keeping her back

to Felix, she closed her eyes. Eleven was unsure of all but one thing.

*This isn't Banaedrut.*

# 17

*"BE NICE."*

*"What?"*

*"Be nice to them. We're their guests."*

*"I am nice."*

*"To me. Most of the time, anyway."*

*"Hosting us doesn't mean we owe them."*

*"They're not like that and you know it, gloomy girl. Would it be so horrible to try and make friends?"*

An unseen crack broke Eleven's stride. She shook away the distracting memory and resumed her pacing behind a stoic Vera. A dank yet humid corridor at the bottom of a long staircase offered no light. Holding the lone lantern, Vera led the way.

*What good is a locator if their being comes at the expense of others?*

A change in pressure, paired with the fact that the refugees were several feet underground, left both women unsettled.

With two choices in direction, Vera hesitated. Tensing as Eleven closed the gap between them, she turned to the right.

Overhead explosions agitated the walls of the undisclosed tunnel. Dust and debris peppered them. Eleven listened carefully for the door they had used in their escape to open. Her assigned task was to alert Vera when or if that happened. The air raised goosebumps on Eleven's arms. She rolled down the sleeves of Lani's jacket.

"Copacetic?" Vera whispered.

Eleven nodded. When she realized the stupidity of such a gesture given the murkiness, she said, "Of course." Their environment intrigued the locator. The lantern's limited illumination left much to the imagination. Atypical smells and sounds furthered Eleven's curiosity as to what surrounded them.

"What is this place?"

Just when Eleven didn't think she would get a response, Vera said, "Old railways." She kept her eyes on the unseen ahead. "Quakes fucked these up some time ago. Makes for good hiding places."

"Is that why you chose it?"

"What makes you think I chose?"

Eleven didn't pose a follow-up. Nor did she allow herself to voice the numerous concerns regarding their attackers. The locator took notice of the cracked brick and concrete that had shifted over time.

Everything of substance went unsaid. Broken walls paled in comparison to the dramatizations plaguing Eleven's imagination. A rusted creak echoed off calcified stonework.

"We're not alone."

Vera's lantern further deepened the lines of her face. "Pick up the pace."

*Please let me be wrong.*

"How much farther?" Eleven asked. When Vera didn't answer, she pressed the issue. "Vera?"

"I don't know," Vera admitted. The pair moved fast through the passageway's permeated murk.

*If it came down to a battle, we'd be at a disadvantage.*

"Vera?"

"I've been here all the once—give me a second." Vera stopped. The gravel pushed her forward as her footing ceased. Eleven bumped into her. Vera approached a large mass. Placing the lantern against a matted flat surface revealed metallic lettering. "Voi-fucking-la."

This *is the panic room?*

Eleven tried to recall the offworld six-sided behemoth towering before her. Its walls absorbed most of the light shone on it. Veering a corner, Vera left Eleven standing in the dark.

The locator examined the unusual crate. "What is this, Vera?"

"Our way out." Vera circled the object, testing the surfaces as she went.

*It's hollow inside.*

When she reached the opposite side, color had left Vera's face. "There's no door."

"Should there be?"

"If you want to stay out of third-kind clutches." Vera scratched the top of her scalp.

"What can I do?"

"I—I don't know."

*Don't fall apart now.*

"Vera," Eleven started again. "What can I do?"

"Fuck, I don't know." Eleven could hear Vera's heartbeat quicken. "I helped him load the fucking thing for shit's sake." Vera tugged on a fistful of hair. Panicked, she grazed a hand near the golden writing. Dissatisfied with the outcome, Vera smacked the wall. "There was a goddamn door right here."

"I believe you," Eleven said.

"Everything is in there. Fucking everything!"

*Crux… his involvement should've been an indication that this would not be a simple undertaking.*

Sounds in the distance caused both women to look back. Vera drew her gun, turning off the safety with a flick of her thumb. Eleven gripped a metal bat Vera referred to as "Peacemaker."

"Vera."

"I know."

Eleven stepped toward their supposed means of escape. She examined the ebony cube as best she could through the darkness. The glint of writing caught her attention. Snagging Vera's lamp, the locator went to the curious typography.

*No creases. If not for Vera's conviction, I'd say this never had an opening… just like the bracelet's wooden box.*

All closing in, both literally and figuratively, mounted the pressure. Though Eleven prided herself on interpretation, no translation for the nonsensical wording came forth.

"We're fucked," Vera said. "We're fucked, we are so viciously fucked."

*A new language, maybe?*

"When the final charges go off, there's a damn good chance anything underground is gonna cave in. If we're not out of here—"

"I understand what's at stake."

Eleven ran her fingers across the letters with her free hand. The words smeared. She examined her fingertips and watched the powdered smudges soak into the skin. Adrenaline played merry with her heart rate. A subtle fluctuation from inside caught Eleven's ears. Fragments still resting in her pockets began to hum. The inner workings of the large mass became clear.

*Not Felix or even Vera were meant to open this.*

Their escape relied on Eleven's ability to manipulate chamber contents and remnants. She wished now more than ever that she had been a quick study like the Dusslorean had hoped. Pressing an ear to the wall, the locator listened.

"What the fuck are you doing?" Vera swept her eyes from left to right. She walked backward to meet the locator, never forgetting the abyss ahead of them.

"I can open it."

"Then hop to."

Eleven rubbed her thumb against the fingers that had absorbed the inscription. She had yet to master the complicated dance of emotions and chambers with only a day of intense training under her belt. Forcing down the dread bubbling to the surface, Eleven closed her eyes. Her digits twitched as pulsations increased.

*It's just another lock... created by an offworlder with recycled chamber elements. Simple.*

"Come on."

*Chambers tied to* you.

"Come on, come on."

*Keep breathing.*

"What's the hold up?" Vera asked.

"Hovering over my shoulder won't make me figure this out any faster."

"Yeah? How about a full lobotomy? Because that's what you're getting if you don't haul ass."

"These aren't—" Eleven's running theory was cut off when a slug hit the backside of her kneecap. Vera caught Eleven as she collapsed.

"Lower your weapons."

*That elocution.*

Vera aimed toward the firearm's source. "Right. That's gonna happen." She kept Eleven close, but readjusted to stabilize her gun-wielding hand. Vera extended her left arm as she scanned the perimeter.

"How many?" Eleven whispered.

"Two," Vera answered.

"You're certain?"

Vera nodded. "Might be able to keep them busy while you chip away."

"Final warning," said the other assailant. "Lower your weapons."

*Two here... but they're not alone. A full offense requires more than a pair.*

Steadying Eleven to the flattest section of the cube, Vera raised her arm. An arrow struck her trigger hand. Torn metacarpals and tendons forced Vera to drop her gun.

"Do not move," ordered the first voice.

Darkness evaporated with the discharge of a foreign green flare. Drifting several feet above them, the light illuminated their aggressors. Two cloaked men stood armed at the ready. One had a longbow, while his partner held a revolver the women had left behind in the scramble to escape.

*Definitely not Banaedrut.*

Vera broke apart the arrow lodged in her hand. She tossed the bulk of it aside, keeping only what remained firmly in place. Vera's eyes then fell to her discarded gun.

"If you wish to continue this course," the archer started. "The next shot will be to the head of your partner."

*Body type, posturing, speech pattern... it's them.*

"See if I care." Vera shrugged.

Eleven considered the unremitting archer. "Vera."

"Sorry, did you miss the part where they shot you in the fucking leg?"

"It wasn't a kill shot."

Vera gave into the pain of her hand. Blood continued to fall from the wound. "This ain't either, but I'm pissed all the same."

"They're not Banaedrut."

"What?"

"They're not Banaedrut. Do as they say."

"You're beyond cracked if you think that's happening," Vera said as she turned to the shrouded men. The gunman quirked his head. His stride slowed as Vera pulled a blade from her belt with her uninjured hand. "Back off, asshole."

Eleven addressed their attackers. "Drop your arms and we'll follow suit."

The duo glanced at one another as they lowered their weaponry. Eleven noticed a saw-like blade at the side of the pistol carrier's hip. They glared at Vera.

"Vera."

Shaking her head, Vera said, "Fat fucking chance."

"You have to trust me." Eleven reached forward. She placed a hand over Vera's shaky grip.

"If they're not Banaedrut, then what the fuck are they?"

Eleven inhaled. "Let's find out together."

"Felix wouldn't go for this."

"Felix isn't here."

Vera shrugged out of Eleven's grasp. She then lowered the knife. "We're totally fucked."

"Maybe not."

"What's the plan?"

*That is an excellent question.*

Eleven braced herself against the cube. "Who are you?"

The men acknowledged one another. They removed their hoods, then did the same with their visors. Their appearance cut off Vera's breath.

*Dussloreans.*

"They do not fear us," said the second to the first. The observant archer hadn't spoken in anything resembling the English language.

*They have no interest in a locator. At least not a human one.*

"We're not the target," Eleven whispered.

Vera leaned in. "You understand them?"

"We mean you no harm," said the first.

The archer appraised the cube behind Vera and Eleven. He zeroed in on the now-sullied amalgamated message near Eleven's head. He then took a whiff of the air. "Scorched ozone here as well," he told his partner in the offworld dialect.

Advancing further, the Dussloreans stopped at a glimmer of light from Vera's blade. She clenched the weapon at her side. The gunman shot her an intense look.

"Am I supposed to pretend like you talking third-kind is a good sign?" Vera looked to the Dussloreans. "Fluent in bastard if you're keen."

"Do not try my patience, female," warned the gunman.

Eleven took a deep breath. "Vera, please."

With hesitation, Vera loosened her grip. Eleven spotted scorched brandings underneath the gunman's right eye.

*The leader.*

Vera's acquiescence intrigued the Dusslorean leader. He then noticed Eleven's healed leg. The gunman slanted toward the archer on his right. "The information spoke of one drudge. She makes two."

*He thinks I'm a guardian—that settles it. Crux is their prize, not me.*

Dussloreans had a habit of implanting trackers in fluids. They had tampered Felix's doses all for the sake of finding Crux.

Vera spoke from a corner of her mouth. "How's that exit strategy coming along?"

Out of the two main Dusslorean dialects, Oudesloy proved to be the more difficult. The shape of Eleven's tongue would limit her to rudimentary speech, but she assumed it would be enough. Both crimson raiders gazed at her with piqued curiosity.

*I've never tried to speak Oudesloy. No time like the present.*

"How?" Eleven spoke in their native tongue. She huddled

closer to Vera.

The opposition shifted to the presence of someone who spoke their language. They whispered low enough that Eleven couldn't discern their words. Shadows made lip reading near impossible.

"No harm, you said." Oudesloy caused Eleven's tongue to tire quickly. "Someone *was* harmed." She pushed off from the cube. Monstrous thumping in her ribcage fed her nervousness. The insides of her pocket and the ebony box rattled. "I deserve answers."

"You are owed nothing," the archer replied.

*These are nothing like the people I've studied. These Dussloreans have never known peace.*

Channeling all the might she could muster, Eleven threw Peacemaker to the ground as a sign of good faith. Vera gave her a telling glance.

"Nothing?" Eleven asked. She advanced toward the Dussloreans. "You invade… attack unprovoked." Eleven stopped less than a meter from them. "Much is warranted."

A wide grin transformed the leader's face. The amused man handed his gun to his Dusslorean lesser. He approached Eleven. "What are you called?"

"Names are of little consequence at this stage," Eleven replied in English. The neighboring racket still beckoned.

"Perhaps." Stopping at an arm's length in front of the stalwart woman before him, the Dusslorean leader scrutinized every viewable bit of her.

Eleven widened her stance. "You lead this mission?"

The gunman continued to speak in Oudesloy. "I am Oliab."

"You killed a good man, Oliab."

"My clan had no intention to eradicate your friend. We seek another like us."

*One whose absence is anything but coincidental.*

Disgust tightened Eleven's throat. Had Crux warned them,

Felix may not have died. The locator's mixed feelings toward her Dusslorean kin became less so. The longer she thought on the possibilities, the more Eleven cursed Crux's cowardice.

"Reveal his location and we shall conclude this call," Oliab said.

Eleven shrugged. "Your guess is as good as mine."

"Not all his people are so brave."

*"These aren't regulation. Others have been feeling the difference too."*

*We're not the only ones being paid a visit.*

"Smy?" Oliab called. The archer went to his leader's side. "Is this the daughter?"

"Her blood is wrong. Different than the other." Smy fixated on Eleven's fingertips. He then examined her "injured" leg. "She is kindred."

Oliab leered at Eleven's fingernails. "The deceiver would leave one of his own behind?"

Though too late, Eleven folded her fingers into her palms. Dussloreans loathed locators more than any human ever could. Helot and Crux had made that much clear in their chronicles.

*I foresee more bloodshed.*

"What the fuck is happening?" Vera interjected.

"They want Crux."

Uttering that name appeared to be in bad taste. Oliab grabbed Eleven by the collar, throwing her against a wall of exposed brick. Falling onto her stomach, Eleven landed on coarse bits of debris.

"Shit!" Vera rushed to her gun. She took the shot she had longed for, hitting Oliab below the neck.

Oliab turned to Smy. "If she does it again, end her."

Vera readied herself to take another shot.

"Don't, Vera. They won't hesitate next time." Eleven motioned to Smy. The archer had a clear shot of Vera.

Oliab leaned down until his gaze met Eleven's. The green light painted him sinister. "You wish to protect this one?"

"Yes."

"The deceiver must answer for his atrocities."

The Dusslorean continued speaking. Eleven's heartbeat drowned all sound with one exception. The cube had become a large music box, its melody heard by her alone.

*Turn the key. We can still make it out of here.* Both *of us.*

A swift jab to Eleven's side triggered a reaction inside the cube. Oliab leaned in close. "Where is he?"

*Three moves left. Maybe four… I* will *open it.*

Vera's hold on the knife slipped against a blood-drenched palm while her other hand kept aim on Oliab. Eleven halted Vera.

"How many…? How many have you killed, Oliab?"

Oliab dipped his head to the side. "Your kind feigns affection for the lives of others. I have not forgotten the stories of how convincing this act can be."

*Another… come on.*

"How many?" Eleven asked again.

"Like the one you lost? Dozens." Oliab motioned to Vera. "Like her? Much more."

Eleven clenched her fist. A tick after she pulled back signified the interior lock was quite responsive to her movements. "And those like me?"

"Seekers?" Oliab gripped Eleven's chin. Smiling, he added, "Too few."

Dussloreans once lived in harmony with the land and all else that surrounded them. That changed when the chambers took residence on their planet. Tranquility and balance soon gave way to retribution.

Eleven's heartbeat slowed. Inspecting the damage Vera's bullet had inflicted on Oliab's left collarbone, she watched a thick dark pool of blood form before her. He hadn't addressed the wound in the slightest. Oliab offered Eleven his assistance. The locator sought guidance in the face of her comrade. Vera shook her head. Another flare flashed in the distance. A Dusslorean horde headed in their direction.

Against Vera's wishes, Eleven took Oliab's extended hand. More of the cube's inner workings shifted. Oliab tentatively helped Eleven up before gripping the small of her wrist hard enough to fracture it.

*Focus... please.*

More movement.

Oliab spoke in English. "You will divulge the location of the one you call Crux."

Eleven wrenched out of Oliab's hold. She massaged her now-healed wrist. Taking the saw-like blade from its sheath, Oliab laid it flat against Eleven's cheek.

*One more.*

"Thought you knew my kind." Eleven smirked to the blade.

Oliab leered as he turned the edge in. "What do you know of despair?"

Eleven lifted her hand a little. Nothing happened. She tried again with the same result.

*Anything else will be too obvious.*

"Worthless," Eleven said. "This entire undertaking is a waste of *all* our energies."

"I disagree, seeker." Stepping into her, Oliab's breath warmed Eleven's skin. He slid the blade down to her torso. "Your deaths will pain him. For now, that will satisfy us." He looked to the archer. "Smy."

*To hell with it.*

Vera, who had been studying closely, kicked Peacemaker toward Eleven without delay. She shot at Smy as he drew an arrow.

A booming barrage from above collapsed the walls. Large chunks of debris fell between them and the Dusslorean reinforcements. Taking advantage of the distraction, Eleven head-butted Oliab hard as she pushed aside his blade.

He fought to regain his footing by retreating several paces. The raining concrete made it impossible for Eleven to see Vera. Short on time and options, the locator faced the black cube.

*Open, damn you!*

Eleven jettisoned both arms forward. The panic room began to open. A faint purple glow pierced the dwindling green light.

*Yes!*

"Vera!"

Cracks formed along what remained of the brickwork. Vera could no longer be seen. Grunts and gunfire ricocheted. Eleven started to run toward the barrage when a thick arm wrapped around her neck. Oliab cut off Eleven's circulation as he plunged his serrated blade deep into her back.

"May you know only despair," Oliab snarled against Eleven's earlobe. He followed his fervent words with a knee to her thigh. Eleven fell face-first onto rubble. A blood-curdling cry in the distance kept her conscious. Numerous shots rang out.

*Vera.*

Disoriented, Eleven blinked. Warmth spread across her back, numbing the pain. Her thigh healed slower than usual. The locator saw Peacemaker buried under fallen concrete.

With some difficulty, Eleven returned to the cube. Its door now wide open, the locator found everything neatly shelved in their respective spots. But still no sign of Vera.

*Listen… where are you?*

A sputtered exhale had Eleven moving in seconds. She found a wounded Vera propped atop a pile of bricks. An arrow was lodged deep in her ribcage. Breaking off the arrow's shaft, Vera reloaded with a clip from her side as Eleven approached.

"Vera—"

"You're lucky this isn't my first melee," Vera interrupted. She coughed as she sat upright.

Eleven swallowed hard. "Did you get them?"

"Just Robin Hood." Vera motioned to the dead Dusslorean meters from them. Eleven tucked her head underneath Vera's arm. The wounded woman stiffened. "What the fuck are you doing?"

"We have to get out of here."

"Go without me." Vera pushed Eleven away. She kept her injured hand raised while clutching the arrow in her chest. "I'll just slow you down."

"Vera, get up now!"

Oliab shoved them apart.

Landing hard against a corner of the cube, Eleven searched for Vera. The Dusslorean twisted the arrow in Vera's ribs. Vera stifled her cries. "That the best you got, motherfucker?"

Eleven sprinted to Peacemaker, subsequently running toward Vera. She toppled Oliab with all the momentum she could muster. The locator put her weight onto both ends of the bat, crushing Oliab's windpipe. Oliab dug fingers into the wound in Eleven's back and pulled. He used the diversion to throw her off him.

The agitated leader ran toward the caved-in stonework dividing him and his brethren. Oliab turned at the sound of Vera's gunshot to find Eleven rebounding with renewed purpose. Peacemaker's first blow fractured Oliab's jaw. Knowing of a Dusslorean's unworldly speed, the enraged locator followed with a hit to the opposite side. Eleven's now frenzy-like state resulted in her lunging for the Dusslorean. Again and again, from all angles, Eleven inflicted pain. She cracked limbs, making it difficult for Oliab to defend himself.

*Another home taken.*

*"Just don't know how good you got it until you're pulled from the thick of it."*

*Another friend lost.*

Before long, a gentle but shaky hand on her shoulder snapped Eleven back to reality. Drenched in cooling blood, she saw Oliab's distorted head. It resembled a puzzle, give or take a few key pieces being reduced to mush.

Standing proved difficult for Vera. She steadied herself with a punctured palm on her waist. Her good hand covered the arrow lodged in her chest.

Neither said anything as they approached the panic room. The lilac lighting, not unlike that of Crux's office and irises, brightened as the two passed the threshold.

Eleven winced as the cube fortified itself. Her dry throat strained her words. "What now?"

"Now," Vera started. The wounded woman leaned against a cool, white wall. "We get the fuck out of Dodge."

Both struggled to gather their bearings as they observed one another. Keeping a hand on the broken bit of arrow, Vera surveyed the items on a cold metal slab in front of them.

With an exhausted grunt, she tried to pull one of two packed bags from the lone shelf above. Blood sprayed onto the table. Eleven stopped her, taking the initiative to bring the bags to the slab. She made no mention of Vera's situation. Or her own.

"Unger showed you how, right?" Vera motioned to the shelf's back corner.

*A teleporter.*

"Yes." Eleven ached with the memory of Felix.

"The cube is protected or some shit. Anything inside comes with us." Vera's breathing slowed. She regarded her oozing fist. "That was Crux's plan anyway."

"Where?"

"All the coordinates are stowed away somewhere in here. Nearest camp should do."

Eleven's forehead creased. "No."

"Sorry?"

"We may not be the only camp affected, Vera."

"Well, we can't fucking stay here."

Picking up more movement outside, Eleven said, "Agreed."

"Can't make it far in this kind of shape, but I might know a place... just hope nobody's torn it down."

The locator offered Vera the teleporter. When the techie refused, Eleven retracted her arm. She had used a device much like it when leaving Onward Betty's with Felix. "Is this different from the other?"

"That one had presets. This is purely mental." Vera gave Eleven the coordinates. She made Eleven repeat them back until she could recite them verbatim. "Keep those numbers at the front of your mind. Whatever you do, don't stop thinking of those coordinates."

Eleven nodded. She secured each of the five guards around her left hand. Splaying her hand wide, the recognizable croon didn't have the same effect as last time.

"Fuck this place." Vera closed her eyes. She struggled to stay upright.

Following her example, Eleven allowed her eyelids to fall. A spark of light soon turned into a full burst.

In an instant, the two were covered in darkness.

# 18

"I'LL BE DAMNED," VERA SAID IN A SHAKY VOICE. "It's all still here."

Standing amongst long-expired sundries and withered countertops, Eleven and Vera had been transported to a dilapidated storefront. Nailed bits of wood blocked the outside world. Mildew-crusted glass windows further prevented viewing in either direction.

The rising sun peeked through in narrow streaks. Aged advertisements and promotions riddled the crumbling sheetrock. Multiple pungent aromas near the retired fridges and freezers threatened to turn Eleven's stomach.

Vera surveyed every conceivable exit with a noticeable limp. Blood trailed her steps. Her breathing was shallow. When content, she rested against the sturdiest shelf across from Eleven.

*Keep her active.*

"You've been here before?"

"Lifetime ago." Vera dropped the hand shielding the broken arrow. Her shredded metacarpals were miniscule in comparison to the damage of her upper torso. She cautiously slid her left arm from a jacket sleeve. Blood soaked every inch of her clothing. "Some fucking day, huh?"

"You need a physician."

Motioning to the pile at their feet, Vera said, "Who needs a doctor when one has poorly put together med supplies at their disposal?" Pressing around the frayed shaft, she knelt down to the nearest duffel.

Lightheadedness compelled Eleven to rest fully on the counter to her back. Vera doubled in the locator's vision for a moment. Eleven leaned with discretion as Vera searched through the plethora of provisions.

"Could use your help."

*I have to replenish.*

"Eleven?"

Eleven blinked. "Sorry."

Neither woman said more than necessary as they searched pack after pack. The medical kit consisted of gauze, a few bandages, and aspirin.

"Well, fuck."

"This won't do," Eleven said.

"It'll have to." Vera removed her drenched blouse at a glacial pace. Wary of the foreign object residing between her ribs, she disrobed. Heavy crimson droplets fell to the checkerboard linoleum as she stood.

*Her heart rate is too fast, she's sweating too much, her eyes won't focus… she doesn't have long.*

Goosebumps rose as Eleven snatched the bandages from Vera. Contemplating how best to dress the wound, she asked, "Why here?"

Vera flinched after a throttled groan. "Good a place as any."

*Damn it. Her lips are turning blue.*

"It's so cracked," Vera continued. "Can you believe this place used to sell fossil fuel? What, we didn't learn our lesson the first time?"

Using t-shirt cloth, Eleven dabbed around the half-clotted section above Vera's breast. The patient withheld curses throughout the entire cleaning process.

"Got something to say, just say it, Eleven."

"What are you going to do?" Eleven asked, pointing at the fixed broadhead.

"Taking it out isn't an option just yet. Trust me, the bleeding could be a lot worse. I'll take care of it good and proper-like when we get to the next camp."

"What if there is no next camp, Vera?"

Eleven hadn't intended to vocalize the question, but the words escaped her. Pushing through the awkwardness, she continued to dress Vera's wound. Multiple bandages were applied to the outer edges of the rupture. Blood saturated the amateur dressings immediately.

"Your hand—"

"Don't worry about it," Vera said.

Another vertigo spell stopped Eleven from pressing the issue of Vera's other injury. Fisting her hands, the locator fought the whirling sensation threatening to break her.

*Snap out of this. You've had worse.*

Vera retrieved a spare shirt from their supplies. The dark tee was two sizes too big. She struggled putting it on. Vera then tore the shirt in an effort not to agitate her wound.

Staring at the teleporter on the counter behind Eleven, Vera said, "This teleporter is short-range. Has to charge for a few hours after each go."

"Hours?"

*She doesn't have hours.*

"Got somewhere to be?" Vera asked.

*Is she stalling? Waiting for something... or someone?*

Eleven stumbled between two shelves across from the counter to create distance between her and Vera. The locator centered herself in a wide aisle. The position did little to restore her balance.

"There's no reason to freak out. Nobody comes here, okay? We're fine."

*We are most certainly not fine. Not at all.*

A sharp pain shot through Eleven's spine, halting Vera's additional assurances. The locator's hold on a shelf behind her slipped. Eleven landed on her tailbone.

Vera took Eleven's pulse. "Jesus, you're burning up."

"That's impossible." Eleven tuned out Vera's prying. When she attempted to stand, Vera pushed her down.

*I'm anxious, scared even, but the fragments… why can't I hear them? Feel them? My pulse is slowing.*

"Despair," Eleven said.

*Oliab knew I couldn't be killed.*

The locator closed her eyes. "Alipo."

"Eleven?"

*It can't be.*

Vera cupped the back of Eleven's neck. "You stroking out on me?"

The ailing locator checked where Oliab's knife had ruined Lani's jacket. Eleven presented a bloody palm to Vera.

"Why the fuck are you bleeding?" Forcing Eleven against her, Vera examined the wound. "Yeah, that's the opposite of healed."

Waning adrenaline and her own injuries caused Vera to lose her balance. The shelves skidded as she swayed. Ignoring the growing blotch on her shirt, the tech expert sat beside Eleven. "The blade was coated?"

"Appears so." Eleven rested the back of her head on the grooved shelf's steel ledge. "Consolation is knowing this wasn't meant for me."

"But Crux is like you."

Eleven turned to Vera. "Precisely."

"Y'all are all superhuman and whatnot last time I checked. When we get out of here—"

Eleven stifled a chuckle. "You don't actually believe we're getting out of here, do you?"

"I've got to."

"Severe blood loss brings out the optimist in you, Vera?" A loaded, genuine smile brightened Vera's face.

*I'm losing feeling in my feet and back. How long before the rest of me succumbs?*

"When the teleporter is ready, continue without me."

Exhaling, Vera said, "Not happening. Squash that shit right now."

"You tried," Eleven responded. "No one would dispute that."

"Couple people spring to mind."

*That's just it, isn't it? A daughter expecting her father to return.*

"You're waiting for him," the locator said.

Vera licked her lips, ready to protest, but a harsh cough stopped her. Her entire face contorted in pain. All the while she covered the arrow. "Fuck," she choked.

"Don't delay for Crux."

"Oh, fuck it." Wriggling, Vera slid to the ground. As her back hit the grime-covered tile, she placed an outer ankle against the opposite knee with counterfeit vigor.

"What are you doing?"

"Getting comfortable."

Numbness reached Eleven's right arm, halting her disapproval. Her unease became apparent through a shaky exhale. Vera took the locator's fingers and intertwined them with hers.

"Guess you're one of us after all," Vera teased. She turned from Eleven. "Still a pain in the ass though."

*There are worse things to be called.*

"Got a tendency to surround myself with pains in the ass,"

Vera continued.

"As do I."

*I finally decide to act and here I am—poisoned in a convenient store with Vera Ross-Dao. Ten wouldn't have made such a mess of things.*

"I have an utterly pathetic question," Vera said after minutes of silence.

Eleven gazed at the ceiling. "Planning to keep me in suspense?"

Excessive blood loss began to take its toll on Vera. Her eyes looked worse against her now sallow skin.

"Ever had somebody? Like, really had someone to call your own?" Vera asked. She rambled on. "Boy, girl, bot? No judgments." Smirking at Eleven's crinkled brow, she said, "I'll take that as a *no*."

Talking about death bordered on blasé with the likes of a locator. Choosing to speak in detail about what came next piqued both their interests, yet neither were keen on discussing the topic. Love, on the other hand, served as a welcome distraction.

Eleven choked back pooling saliva. "Is it worth anything?"

A short laugh morphed into an unpleasant hacking. Eleven surveyed blood gushing through Vera's right middle and ring fingers.

Clearing her throat, Vera asked, "Where was I?"

"Conserve your energy," Eleven said.

"Why delay the inevitable?"

Normalcy and locators never went hand-in-hand. Whatever the outcome, Eleven couldn't be bothered by her body's sudden revolt. Not when another comrade lay at death's door.

"One of my first assignments was this shitty off-the-grid setup. Head to toe bohemian bullshit. Fucking miserable." Vera grinned at the memory. "But Crux, with his stiff upper lip, kept waxing philosophical, talking about the *greater good*, blah, blah, blah."

"But something changed."

Vera's smile turned sad as tears fell. "The good got great."
*Felix.*

"Didn't last... but what does these days?"

"Love is that fickle?" Eleven asked.

"Never stopped loving him." Closing her eyes, Vera lost herself in the memory of a better time. Then, just like that, she returned to the harsh light of now. "Love isn't everything."

*It takes dying to have a real conversation. The irony is not lost on me.*

All feeling had gone from Eleven's arm. She willed her right set of fingers to no avail. The locator adjusted accordingly. In doing so, she noticed Vera's grip around the arrow had loosened. Eleven's legs gave in. She collapsed to the floor.

*You need the distraction just as much as she.*

"How long before he changed?" When no answer came, Eleven faced Vera. Her barely opened eyes showed just a sliver of white. "Vera?"

Eleven squirmed, trying to make her right hand cooperate with no success. She shot her left arm over as fast as possible to check vitals. Vera's pulse, now only a shadow of the thrum from earlier, grew weaker as Eleven hovered.

Tears ran down both cheeks. "Please."

*Open your eyes.*

"I promised."

*"I'll watch her."*

*Yes, that's a perfect description of what I did.* Watched *Vera bottle raw emotion from the death of Felix for my sake. I* watched *her take, not one, but two arrows because of me and my hesitance to act... me, pointless being that I am.*

Over her many years, every flash of extrinsic hope had soon given into bloodied realities. This often resulted in death, though never her own. Not fully. The eleventh locator fought doubt.

*Stay.*

Chambers had an affinity for elixirs and tonics. Unlike the occasional kazoo, tonics were collected just as often as any weapon or scroll—or more so, some might argue. As she recalled their related frequencies, her left hand twitched.

Putting her last pliable limb to her face caused Eleven to slide down to a flat back. She concentrated on the etchings under her cuticles and thought again of reverberations. Her knuckles spasmed as the pocketed chamber contents stirred.

*I call, they come. That's the ability Crux wanted to awaken… but to what end?*

The question looped in her mind. Its volume increased as Eleven's mental query went unanswered. Her hidden remnants did the same.

*Call.*

A hypothesis formed. "Ridiculous."

*"Do not confuse the impossible for what one is simply unable to achieve without effort."*

*Can I do it?*

Absurdity or not, Eleven couldn't will away the idea. The more she pondered it, the stronger the urge to try became. It wouldn't be long before her left arm suffered the same fate as the rest of her. Tears came in streams.

*I've never opened a chamber with my left hand, I don't know—stop questioning yourself and try. Try before you're too late to do even that.*

With an inkling of valor gathered, Eleven raised her hand. She steadied her arm by locking it at the elbow. The locator clenched her eyes shut. "Let me do something right."

*Remedies. What was the frequency for remedies?*

Nerve endings where her left arm socket and shoulder met

anaesthetized. Each inhale proved more difficult than the last. Eleven's resolve somehow did not waver. Her nostrils flared from the effort. Still, her arm stayed above her.

*Let me be useful just this once.*

A change in the atmosphere squeezed at Eleven's temples, causing veins to audibly throb. The area had changed. All went quiet. All but the hovering croon floating overhead.

*A cure-all from... Hynlai.*

Eleven opened her eyes. She was cautious at the frailty of the chamber humming near the tips of her outstretched fingers. Eleven swirled her hand in a measured, spiral motion. Another turn. Then another. Stop.

Hope and fear rose to the back of her throat. Eleven thrust her hand into the void. Keeping her composure with a shaky arm, she retracted it to reveal an amber-like flask.

For reasons unknown, Eleven inherently knew what to do with the alien concoction. She would pour medicine directly onto the arrow wound. If Vera's heart kept beating, it would travel through the bloodstream and heal her throughout.

The amber vial lowered, as did Eleven's arm. She saw the remedy in her hand but couldn't feel it. Summoning and opening a chamber seemed to have sped up the paralytic process overtaking Eleven. Though she couldn't sense the item in her palm, her grip had yet to falter.

Angling her left hand onto Vera's chest, Eleven knew she didn't have long. The locator clasped the arrowhead. She managed to keep hold of the Hynlai potion. She maneuvered the arrow and Vera toward her with a hard pull. No longer impeded, blood gushed from the wound.

Eleven bit at the top of the flask in a last-ditch effort to open it. Underestimating the strength of her bite, the trim surrounding the opening splintered. The locator spit shards out as she poured the contents onto Vera's fatal lesion. Every last ounce of Eleven's energy went into depleting the healing supply. The container shattered between the floor and the weight of Eleven's heavy hand.

The locator strained to listen for a change in Vera's breathing. It had slowed but hadn't stopped completely. Not yet.

For all her internalization, what Eleven longed for most was the ability to scream once more. Inner turmoil served to be more hellacious than anything Dr. Isaac Kepler or Crux could dream up. Shadows shortened as the daylight grew stronger. The brightness would have stung had Eleven been capable of wincing.

A deep, desperate gasp proceeded a wild spasm of Vera's leg. After a short bout of hyperventilation, her breathing normalized. Though Vera didn't wake immediately, vindication seeped through Eleven's body. Fingers wiggled at Vera's sides, testing her dexterity. Her entire body relaxed in the minutes that followed.

Vera sucked in air as she jolted upright. She clutched her chest, choking on dust that'd gathered around her. "How long was I out?"

*Too long.*

Vera leaned onto what remained of the Hynlai vial. She hissed. Picking at the embedded bits, she watched as the cuts in her palm healed.

"The fuck—?"

Vera's confusion turned to fury. She took in the state of her left hand, inspecting the vestige of former damage. Grazing her ribcage, dried blood could be found. Nothing more.

"What'd you do?" Vera leaned over Eleven. Looking deep into her eyes, her bottom lip sagged. "Why the hell would you—? God damn it… God fucking damn it!"

Vera brought down Eleven's eyelids before standing. Her footwork carried purpose. She mustered stuttered breaths. Her silhouette disappeared and reappeared. Her rapid heartbeat solidified the locator's suspicion.

"I'm sorry."

With a blinding light teasing the backs of Eleven's eyes, Vera was gone.

*At least I was able to keep my word.*

# 19

TWO INDIVIDUALS WITH VARYING GAITS ARRIVED. Meticulous bustling told Eleven these newcomers sought something. The more buoyant of the two drew closer.

"Found something," said a young male voice. The boy bent down next to Eleven. Heavy steps scurried and stopped behind him. "She's gone."

"Preposterous."

*Crux.*

"She's cold to the touch, man."

"No," Crux said under his breath.

"What about Vera?" the boy asked.

"No one else knew of this place. She must have moved to a safer location."

"Wishful thinking."

"That is enough, Abraham."

The moonlight painted the two in silhouette. Profiles of both Crux and the gangly, red-haired Abraham became clearer as the Dusslorean forced the paralyzed woman's eyes open.

Hopping to the other side of Eleven, Crux checked her pulse.

"See?" Abraham said to Crux.

"Why would Vera leave Eleven behind?"

Adjusting his jacket collar, the boy grumbled, "Probably couldn't afford dead weight."

"Do not be crude, Mr. Porter. It is unbecoming." Producing a flashlight, Crux shined it into Eleven's unresponsive eyes. He grimaced. "Gather the materials."

The teenager nodded as he moved out of sight. Crux pulled up Eleven by her arm. A stiffening akin to rigor mortis had long set in. With difficulty, the belated Dusslorean delicately sat Eleven upright. He kept her in place.

Crux tucked a blood-drenched curl behind Eleven's ear. "I will make this right."

His gaze fell to the pooled blood next to her and the foreign glass at Eleven's thigh. The Dusslorean examined what he could with the small light in his hand.

Abraham groaned. "Can't carry this all by myself."

"You can and you will," Crux replied. Pocketing his light, he scooped Eleven into his thick arms.

"Hey, I know she's your friend—"

"This is not up for discussion."

A sigh rife with attitude escaped the boy's lips. Meeting at the front counter, Crux waited for Abraham to collect the few items Vera had left behind. The teenager overdramatically slung bags over both shoulders.

"Aren't you gonna close her eyes?" Abraham asked.

"Abraham."

"Yeah, yeah, I know the drill."

Crux's heavy palm covered Eleven's eyes for what felt like seconds. Eleven found herself in a strange new environment when the Dusslorean lifted his hand. Strategically placed lamps warmed a carpeted room with a blue accent wall. Knickknacks and framed amateur photographs busied a stone fireplace's ledge across from them.

Continuing to hold the inflexible locator, Crux adjusted to the abrupt change in scenery. Loud thuds accompanied Abraham's hasty drop of the panic room surplus.

"Abe?" called an aged female voice.

"Living room," Abraham replied.

Bustled strides bounced off multiple surfaces. A lean blonde girl with dark brown eyes descended down a nearby wooden staircase. She followed a middle-aged couple as they met Crux and Abraham.

"What happened?" asked the salt-and-pepper haired man.

"Hell by the look of it," Abraham replied. The woman smacked him on the back of his head. "Just guessing they ran into a few kinks is all, dang."

"I miscalculated," Crux admitted.

The matron turned to the girl. "Get me the kit."

"That will not be necessary, Judith."

Inching forward, the man noticed Eleven's state. "Is she dead?"

Abe rubbed his chin. "Yeah."

"No," Crux refuted. Four sets of eyes zeroed in on the dead-eyed damsel.

The young girl approached. "That's her, right?"

"Yes," Crux said.

"I thought—"

The man interrupted. "What about the others?"

When the Dusslorean didn't answer, Abraham did. "Found what was left of Felix. Can't figure how they poisoned a guardian."

"It is irrelevant," Crux said.

"Vera?" the man pried.

"No sign of her." Abe scratched at the back of his head. "But she made it out."

"We've gone silent on all channels," Judith told Crux. She

met her male counterpart's concern. "Just give us the word."

"Clearly, I have more pressing concerns than the where-abouts of Vera."

The room fell silent in the aftermath of Crux's harsh delivery. Nothing in their expressions signified a shred of anger or annoyance. Only sympathy.

Abraham clapped his hands together. "Dinner ready? I'm starving." The people, presumably his family, shot him dirty looks. "What?"

"Has been for some time now." Judith gave Crux a sad smile. First signaling to Abraham and the older gentleman, she then motioned to the cargo. "Help Dave get these squared. I'll fix you a plate."

Both men took equal share of the panic room findings. The young girl started to follow Judith out.

"Margaret?"

The girl stopped. "Yeah, Crux?"

"I am in need of your services," Crux said.

Margaret glanced at Judith for approval. With a squeeze of her toned bicep, her matriarch continued exiting the room. The girl crossed her arms. "What can I do?"

Crux waited for the rest of this strange camp to finish leaving. "I require access to your greenhouse."

"Why?"

"There is no time for explanations."

Margaret frowned. "I just—"

"*Please*," Crux interrupted.

Reservation clouded Margaret's eyes. Despite this, she led Crux down a hallway. Using her limited peripheral vision, Eleven concluded she had been brought to a home in the suburbs. The locator had read of provincial living in stories and seen the numerous advertisements. In any other circumstance, she would be tempted to let her mind wander. Instead, Eleven focused on what awaited her in the greenhouse.

Crux proceeded down each step of the dwelling's third level with discretion, always mindful of the frozen woman in his arms. Margaret's greenhouse appeared to be in a converted basement. Eleven noticed warped wood panels. Condensation built on glassware, plastic, and metal throughout.

A sea of assorted greenery awaited the three as they reached ground level. Artificial lights reflected vibrant foliage, tinting the occupants in various shades of forest. Mist curled Margaret's dampening hair and sprinkled Crux's forehead.

Both stopped when reaching the apparent center of the cellar turned arboretum. Miscellaneous potters occupied workstations with one exception. Crux carefully placed Eleven over the framework of a flatbed. Her limbs awkwardly dangled from all sides.

"I'm pretty sure Dad didn't have body stashing in mind when he built me this place," Margaret said.

The Dusslorean considered Margaret. "I have no intention of defiling your sanctum."

"Crux?"

"Trust, young one."

With noticeable hesitance, Margaret moved several benches and larger plants that obstructed wide wooden planks. The lifted lumber revealed loose soil below. With Crux's help, a large pile of panels soon formed. This limited Eleven's view.

Crux grabbed one of three shovels resting against a table parallel with Eleven. He thrust the spade into the earth. Margaret watched him. After creating a decent dent, Crux stopped. "This still troubles you?"

"You could say that."

Crux wiped a sleeve across his face. "Your help would be useful."

"Don't you care?"

"Margaret."

Staring at her feet, Margaret kept on. "I'm not talking about the greenhouse, Crux. Felix is dead. Vera's missing. All you seem to be worried about is planting that poor woman in my garden."

"All will be made clear in due time."

"That's a crock. It's never the right time with you, Crux. For crying out loud, does anything phase you?"

"Yes."

"I'm not sure that's true," Margaret replied. "Would *our* deaths even register or is this kind of thing just par for the course?"

"I do not understand that reference." Crux put aside the tools. "Your family means a great deal to me. As do Vera and Mr. Unger… and Eleven." His tone turned stern. "But there are more pressing issues at hand than the matter of your apprehensions, Margaret. If you are to stay here, assist me as I requested." Without waiting for a response, he reclaimed his shovel.

Margaret exhaled, worry falling from her face. "How deep?"

"A meter. Give or take."

Margaret snagged her own trowel. The hole took shape in minutes. Eleven unwillingly stared as the two readied her final resting place. Staying conscious shouldn't have been possible without heartbeat or air filling her lungs.

*Suspended between life and death—Oliab's wish comes to fruition.*

The diggers arose from the would-be grave soaked in sweat. After catching their breaths, the two approached Eleven's dormant body.

"Do you recall the antiquity I placed in your possession?" Crux asked Margaret.

"Of course."

"Where is it now?"

"Right where you left it," Margaret answered with a nod to an unseen corner. The Dusslorean peered down at Eleven.

"Why?"

Moving to Eleven's head, Crux said, "Take her feet."

As instructed, Margaret picked up Eleven by the ankles while Crux took her shoulders. Rigidity made transporting Eleven complicated. Hopping in first, Margaret let go of Eleven's feet and wrapped her arms around the torso. Crux released his hold on Eleven, entered the plot himself, and assisted Margaret in easing the remainder of Eleven's body to the ground. He repositioned her head to align, forcing her vision straightforward.

Margaret pulled herself out of the hole. Glancing back at Crux, she asked, "You ready?"

The Dusslorean didn't take an offered shovel. Ignoring Margaret, he brushed Eleven's cheek with the back of his grimy, swollen fingers.

"Crux?" Margaret lowered the shovel until it rested along the grave's edge. "We don't have to do this." Shaking his head to regain a speck of sanity, Crux brought himself to standing. He moved to Eleven's feet. "Or, if it'd be easier, me and Abe could do it for you."

"No," Crux replied. "I will proceed alone from here."

"How's that?"

"Your services are no longer required," he said. Crux turned to Margaret. "I very much appreciate all you have done for my kin."

"Really, it's—"

"Goodnight, Margaret."

Dirt covered every inch of Margaret's body with the exception of her blonde locks. She strode toward the stairs. "Yeah. Night."

"Margaret?"

She stopped, but refused to face him. "What?"

"Regardless of what you may hear, do not return to this place unless instructed otherwise."

Margaret nodded as she resumed her exit from the basement-turned-greenhouse. Crux waited for the door to shut before proceeding. He hopped to a seated position at the edge of the freshly dug hole.

"All we have is time. My beloved used to say it when worry outdid me." Crux twisted away from Eleven. "The declaration is the epitome of arrogance."

In the absence of witness, the Dusslorean locator allowed himself to come undone. A single tear descended. Dirt crumpled as he gripped the uneven edges of Eleven's plot. A small amount fell onto Eleven.

"It was an error on my part. In defiance of the evidence, I had every intention of returning before their arrival. My mistakes before now pale in comparison, and that—"

Crux halted. For him to display grief of this magnitude solidified the disabled locator's deep-seated fear.

*Please don't do this.*

"Mardeuint." Crux shot his gaze to the beams above him. "Loosely translated from Oudesloy, it means to forgive... something I do not deserve. Fitting words do not exist."

*He knows I can hear him. He has to.*

"We continue to fall while oppositions triumph unscathed." Crux's eyes returned to Eleven's. Red overtook the white surrounding his deep plum irises. "You once questioned my regret in what I had done. I told you I did not and that was the truth. Then. Now, seeing another flaunt a fate intended for her lesser." Crux fisted his hands with such force skin threatened to crack from the pressure. "Contrition stirs."

*Restitution. That's what this is... for the world he and Helot couldn't save. For placing his trust in Ophidian. We're supposed to be salvation? Would any of this have happened if he'd chosen a different locator?*

The misery in Crux's admission labored his breaths. Strengthening his resolve, the Dusslorean got to his feet. He disappeared into the man-made underground forest surrounding them.

"As you may know, the Alipo is native to Dusslore. I have encountered few toxins more powerful in all my years."

Leaves rustled and tools clanged as he searched through a metallic cupboard. Eleven spied the shovel Margaret had left planted at the foot of her grave as best she could. The locator grew to hate the very presence of it, wanting to throw it far from her. A normally insignificant tool possessed a finality.

"Alipo is just a garden variety weed in its plant form. Concentrated—well, I am certain a ventured guess is not necessary."

Crux gripped a thick burgundy glass cylinder when he returned to Eleven, jumping into her grave. He placed the rod-shaped piece atop Eleven's breastplate. Her rigorous digits kept the object in place.

"Take comfort in a light only darkness provides." Trailing his cryptic phrasing, Crux's coarse fingers closed Eleven's eyes.

The shadow of his palms faded away. Eleven took consolation in what she couldn't see. Large scoops of loose earth fell onto her.

*There is no light.*

More dirt.

*No comfort.*

Brightness dwindled.

*Only despair.*

Filling the hole took far less time than what went into creating it. Crux muttered seven syllables as he finished the burial. The earth at Eleven's ears made a detailed discernment impossible. Faint murmurs turned inaudible.

*Gone.*

The sense of accomplishment in regards to saving Vera's life had lost its luster. Eleven agonized over the guilt in contemplating her choice. If given the opportunity again, now knowing what awaited her, she might have saved herself instead.

*No. I've lived long enough. Maybe too long.*

Her newest constants, maddening silence and uninterrupted thought, would drive away sanity before too long. A fleeting cerebral chortle at the thought of spending an eternity under a family's floorboards gave way to memories she'd tried so hard to suppress.

•••••••••••

A SATURATED SHATTER ACCOMPANIED DENSE cracking. The foreign phonic wonder broke the monotony surrounding Eleven. Rustling dirt pestered the locator's ears.

*An aberration. Already?*

The locator hadn't expected to lose herself so early on. Relativity played merry with the passage of time.

*"All we have is time."*

*Is it arrogant if it's true? Even in "death," I'm still here. Still alone… still.*

Damage to a locator's brain resulted in a fugue-like state. One where they trusted those like themselves, no one else. The importance of such a thing as time had no meaning to those unfettered by endings. Consistent beginnings. Reticence deranged Eleven's mind.

*"You know what I'd call you if I had my way?"*
*"Do I want to know?"*
*"Oh, I think you do… 'Selene.'"*
*"No."*
*"But you haven't even heard my reason."*
*"Do tell."*
*"Means 'moon.'"*

*"Yes, I know."*

*"Waited hours for you that night. My one companion was the moon. It was almost full, but not quite. Whenever I see it, I think of you."*

The cool ground surrounding Eleven sent a shiver down her spine.

*So cold.*

A heavy pulsation chased Eleven's sudden awareness. Both lungs inflated as her heart fluttered awake. The sensation of pain returned to her back but dissipated moments later. Circulation hinted at a dull ache encapsulating her entire body.

*It's wearing off?*

Eleven moved her closed eyes from side to side. The action surprised her. Taking in a mouthful of dirt, soil caught in the back of her throat. Trying to cover her mouth, Eleven found her arms bound and movement restricted. Unyielding trappings impeded any attempt to free herself.

*No.*

One curbed grunt issued forth, nothing more. A weighty arm snatched the hood of Eleven's jacket. She emerged from her grave.

Landing on secured wood panels, Eleven struggled to catch her breath. She coughed up what she could of the dirt she had inhaled.

"Do not attempt to remove them," Crux instructed. The weary Dusslorean exhibited an aberrant severity. He took Eleven's face in his hands. "The task is not yet done."

A steadying constriction drew Eleven's gaze to her restrained limbs. Spiraled crystalline roots enveloped her. They molded to the curves of the locator's body. All but her head had been overtaken.

"Interrupting the process is ill-advised, Eleven."

Pushing her flat against the floor, the Dusslorean held Eleven down with level arms. Flustered, she hurried to respond. Groans and wheezes passed her lips. Stinging stopped any further attempts to speak. Senses rejuvenated with synchronicity. Popping eardrums overwhelmed her clearing vision. The aroma of fertilizer turned her stomach. Reignited pain settled in her veins.

Eleven looked at her chest to find the origin of the sharp panging. The offworld webbing covering her body originated from a five-petaled exotic blossom deep-rooted in her chest plate. Its reach exceeded that of the surface. The worst of the hurt centered at her ribcage. Her trapped hands circled a large puncture wound tightening around the plant.

*What is this?*

The plant's hold on the locator loosened. As the pain in her chest tapered, Eleven relaxed. Bit by bit her lungs allowed fuller breaths.

*Let it be over.*

The plant's multiple extensions started wilting. Only then did Crux tug at them. The transparent branches ensnaring Eleven broke apart without difficulty. Succumbing to the shock of all she had been exposed to, Eleven willed her eyes shut. Crux plucked the substance slower than to her liking. He reached for the bud entrenched between Eleven's breasts.

Stilling his hands with hers, Eleven sputtered, "Don't."

"It must be done."

Crux gripped the bloom at its base, placing his free arm across Eleven's collarbones. The insistent Dusslorean wrenched the flower from Eleven's bosom. Drenched in blood, it sprayed plants in the immediate vicinity.

Eleven gave a cry of exquisite suffering. Her shriek shredded the inner linings of her gullet. Crux endeavored to still Eleven's convulsing body with one arm while picking at remaining bits of floweret with the other. The damage it left behind rapidly mended.

Her howls waned as Crux released Eleven. Coagulated crimson bunched at the ragged roots hanging from the bud in Crux's hand. It shriveled further. Deterioration accelerated until reaching a petrified state. Crux threw the bud to the side of them.

"Water. You need water."

Crux flicked the cap off of a nearby water jug. He scooped Eleven into his arms. She lifted her head as he brought the brim to her mouth. She hadn't realized the extent of her dehydration until the first drop of water hit her tongue. She choked on rushed gulps but continued to empty the container.

Exhaustion riddled her face as well as the Dusslorean's. Though her throat had healed, Eleven's words were hoarse. "What was it?"

"Save your strength."

Crux wiped at the sides of Eleven's face with the inside of a sleeve. He ran a hand through her tousled locks. Another passage of Helot's came to mind.

DUSSLORE WAS A WORLD OF BALANCE. WITH DARKNESS CAME LIGHT, TO PUT IT SIMPLY. ERVASSÉ IS SISTER TO ALIPO. ON THE VERGE OF EXTINCTION BECAUSE OF ITS CAPABILITY.

"Ervassé?"

Crux smiled. "Ever the quick study."

"When Dusslore was destroyed—"

"A gifted seedling." Brushing Eleven's cheek, Crux added, "I had hoped to never have use for it."

SEEKS OUT CONTAMINANTS IN ORGANISMS... ABSORBS THEM INTO ITSELF.

"There isn't another," Eleven realized.

"Yet the sister thrives."

*I won't be as fortunate next time… and there will be a next time.*

"Can you move your extremities?" Eleven nodded, but only displayed subtle twitches. "How do you feel?"

"In a word," Eleven started. Crux quirked his head. "Shitty."

Her uncommon use of vulgarity amused Crux. "That is an acceptable rejoinder."

*Vera… where are you?*

# 20

*"WHAT IF THIS IS IT?"*

*"Yeah, I'm gonna need you to elaborate."*

*"What if we're all that's left?"*

*"I've got to believe we're stronger than that. Maybe you should try optimism on for size."*

*"That* is *optimism."*

Rough fingertips to the underside of Eleven's neck pulled her from another memory of Ten. Eleven snatched at the unknown's soft wrist and dragged them to the ground. She rolled on top of the stranger. Eleven kept them in place with a firm grip on their throat.

"Lights," said a strained female voice. Fluorescent tubes sputtered on in full at the command. Margaret lay beneath the frenzied locator. She showed Eleven both her hands, indicating she meant no harm. "I am so sorry."

The girl's panic mirrored Eleven's. She retreated from Margaret, backing against the nearest wall. Eleven took in her surroundings. Dizziness threatened to bring her back to the filth-covered wood paneling.

*When did I fall asleep?*

Margaret held her throat. "Holy crap."

"Where is he?"

"Crux? Errands." The young woman sat up. Not a shred of fear etched her face. "Don't worry, you're safe here. I'm—"

"Margaret," Eleven interrupted. "Yes, I know."

*Back to life all of five minutes and he's abandoned me again. Should I be so surprised?*

The girl raised an eyebrow. "Maggie, actually." Bringing herself to standing, the girl waltzed over to Eleven. Extending a hand, Maggie said, "Pleased to meet you, Eleven."

*Her youth might explain such naiveté.*

Eleven looked at Maggie's palm. The teenager waited, armed with a wary smile. Eleven took the curious girl's hand against her better judgment, before releasing it quickly.

"I'm supposed to get you settled."

"Settled?"

"Whenever you're ready. Guest room upstairs is yours if you want it. Unless you prefer the ground." Again, Maggie smiled. Her grin wavered at Eleven's melancholy. "But my parents would kill both of us if you walk around the house like that." She stopped and thought about the statement. Chuckling, Maggie added, "Well, they'd try their darndest anyway. Come on."

Eleven kept her distance from the girl but followed her up the stairs. Maggie didn't appear to notice the locator's reservation.

"Abe and Dad are already asleep, but Judy, my stepmom, she's kind of a night owl," Maggie whispered. "I'm sure I could get her to fix you something if you're wanting to eat. Something tells me you've worked up one heck of an appetite."

*Suburbia. And here I thought the grave was bad.*

"The water pressure can be finicky at night. That's solar power for you." Flipping on switches, Maggie leaned against the doorframe of a fragrant lavatory at the end of a long hallway. Eleven scrutinized the bountiful space. Folded clothes rested in the center of a Jack and Jill countertop. "Not a fan, but Dad says it's worth it. We're actually considering demoing the whole thing and starting from scratch."

Eleven entered the bathroom. She patted down the bright-colored, lightweight attire on the sink. "Are these for me?"

"All I could rustle up on short notice," Maggie said. "Probably not what you're used to."

"It's fine."

"I'll salvage what I can tomorrow."

Eleven's blank expression combatted Maggie's far friendlier one. Eventually, the girl dropped her gaze and rubbed her nervous palms along her hipbones.

"Guess I'll leave you to it."

Eleven locked the door the second Maggie crossed over the threshold. Turning to the mirror, the locator froze. Her reflection exposed the scope of what she had experienced—it brought a small pool of tears to her eyes. Eleven leaned in. Thick clumps of soot stuck to her cheeks and jawline. Dried blood painted her an unflattering dark crimson with splashes of tar-colored mud. Her nails and cuticles housed well-rooted grime.

A faint clatter broke Eleven's concentration. She turned to the door, zeroing in on the sliver of visible latch. Frustration led her to slam both palms against the door. The resulting sound reverberated off the tiled walls. Delicate footsteps from the other side scurried and faded.

*Teenagers.*

Eleven pushed away from the door and hurried to the tub's

faucet. Turning it to full blast, the loud rush of water drowned out everything. She then returned to the mirror.

Lani's jacket peeled off with some difficulty. Eleven cursed herself at the state of it, wishing she could salvage anything that would remind her of Felix. A wrinkling sound gave the locator pause. Eleven pulled a folded scrap of paper from an interior pocket. Opening it revealed blue handwriting barely legible thanks to the blood.

NEED TIME TO THINK.

WE'RE NOT OKAY. NOT BY A FUCKING LONG SHOT.

DO NOT COME LOOKING. I'M BETTER AT HIDING THAN YOU ARE.

- V

P.S. DON'T GO TRYING TO SAVE THE WORLD W/O ME.

*Would she still hide if she knew I was back? Part of me prays she would.*

"Vera."

*Does she have it in her to forgive Crux? Hell, do I? Do we stand a chance without her?*

Refolding the paper at its previous creases, Eleven tossed Vera's note into the sink. She dismissed inquiries rising to the surface. Layer after grungy layer gathered around her feet. Eleven examined her lower back in the mirror, searching every centimeter. Her skin carried the memory of a scar seen by no one.

*Is there still a "we" after this?*

Clumps of dirt trailed Eleven as she approached the off-white acrylic bathtub. Halfway full by the time she entered, the rising water relieved Eleven's aching toes. Switching the flow to the showerhead, she allowed her chest to be scalded by the rain-like onslaught. Twitches and muscle spasms made it difficult to balance at first.

Getting lost in the routine of showering with the audible downpour as her soundtrack, Eleven kept mental minutiae at bay. Droplets soon went from scalding to tepid. She welcomed the noticeable temperature change. Much like the tips of her fingers, numbness overrode emotion.

Maggie's vibrant wardrobe clung to Eleven in areas missed during her toweling off. She hid Vera's note to her right hip with the pants' waistband.

Steam accompanied Eleven as she left the bathroom. The faux hardwood floors had been cleaned since her shower. She meandered through the photo-riddled hall. Nonsensical bric-a-brac strewn about and shelving filled most surfaces of a den she hadn't noticed earlier. Noise, presumably music, emanated from a refurbished radio in the corner.

*Not a soul in sight.*

Without realizing it, the locator had stopped in front of the basement door. She tried the knob but found it locked.

Eleven halfheartedly searched for metal to manipulate into picks. She then stared at her hands. They were unsteady. Fisting them into her palms did nothing to sway the tremors.

*I can feel the Ervassé even now.*

• • • • • • • • • • •

JUDY APPEARED TO HAVE FALLEN VICTIM TO THE late hour, but not before leaving a lukewarm plate for the locator. Eleven exited the kitchen, grateful she didn't have to interact with others. Rather than return to the basement, Eleven retreated to the study across from the kitchen.

*Mysteries, thrillers, romance—ugh.*

Eleven grazed fingertips across the spines as she continued to peruse the home library of the Porters. She chuckled to herself at book jackets and browsed through some of the more grounded works. Eleven found four blank covers on the bottom shelf's furthest corner. She snagged the thickest volume within reach.

*Photos albums? People still have these?*

The very idea of a scrapbook baffled the mind. Eleven made allowances for commonplace things that weren't her kind of normal, yet something about this particular quirk bothered her the longer she gripped the textured cover. Taking inventory of her surroundings, she realized the Porters had spared many modern advances.

*Solar and wind.*

Page upon page showcased road trips, projects, parties, holidays, and milestones. Their genuine happiness further puzzled Eleven. She grinned while examining images of better lives lived.

Until the fourth page.

A younger Judy and Dave held a baby Abe in their arms with a pigtailed Maggie hugging her father's leg. The disenchanted teenager standing to the side of them reeked of peculiarity. Arms crossed, with a line where most would find a smile, the ebony-haired girl had no interest in anything or anyone around her.

*Vera.*

History once hinted at became clear. Crux had a long-standing relationship with the Porters. As did Vera Ross-Dao. Eleven fought a laugh at the realization.

"She was never fond of being photographed." Eleven dropped the album, turning to find Crux peeking over her shoulder.

*I have to get this man a bell.*

"I interrupted you," Crux said. "Shall I return later?"

"No." Without forethought, Eleven added, "I don't want—" She stopped herself from finishing the statement.

*—to be alone.*

"Is my company deserving of an audience?" Taking a step toward Eleven, Crux paused when detecting her reluctance. He retreated to a recliner behind him.

"Where were you, Crux?"

"Seeing to survivors. And, in all honesty, seeking rationale."

"*Before*," Eleven pressed. "When we needed you."

Crux focused on the hardwood floor. "Another camp."

*And how did they fare, I wonder.*

"You knew they were here."

A huffed exhale escaped Crux's nostrils. "I did."

"A *miscalculation*, Crux? Is that all it was?" Eleven's referral to his graveside discourse earned her an intense gaze. "Given your history, I find that hard to believe."

"It is the truth." Crux's lids sagged just as they had before burying her. Eleven saw the hurt in his eyes.

*This is far from his first setback or loss.*

Nothing of importance came without some kind of risk. When underground, Crux had Eleven's forgiveness.

But that had changed.

Eleven hated herself for not noticing the alterations to Felix's doses. She cursed Felix for making no mention of just how different the treatments truly were. But the bulk of the blame rested on Crux.

*"Earthquakes are uncommon in this district, are they not?"*

*He had to have known then.*

WE'RE NOT OKAY. NOT BY A FUCKING LONG SHOT.

*Couldn't have said it better myself, Vera.*

"The lesson adjustment," Eleven started. "That impromptu training session had less to do with the chambers and more with fighting people that want you dead."

"Such fire in you," Crux said.

"It's what you wanted."

"Not like this," Crux snapped. "*This* is not what I wanted." His torment became palpable. Helot's chronicles came to
mind.

*There's more at work here than he'll admit even to himself.*

"Tough," Eleven countered. "There are consequences for
your actions, Crux. Perhaps one of these days you'll pay the
price instead of someone less deserving."

"She said she had lost it." Crux went to the inner lining of
his jacket. He revealed what remained of Vera's bracelet. "I
fail to see the motive in lying."

*As long as there's reason for it, lies are justifiable?*

"Vera can be very withholding. You taught her well in that
regard."

*Was Crux trying to find her earlier?*

"She'll come back when she's ready." Eleven watched as
her words registered.

Crux gripped the small stones in his crimson palm. "The
death of Mr. Unger rouses uncertainty."

Felix and Vera belonged to one another regardless of complications. Instead of questioning her own grief, the locator
pondered how Vera was dealing with it all.

"Will you tell me what happened?" Crux asked.

Eleven shook her head. "Maybe I'll write it down one of
these days. You do enjoy a good journal entry."

"Please?"

"No."

Defeated, Crux said, "She is alive. That is more than enough.
More than I deserve."

Emotion threatened to drown Eleven's eyes. She blinked
tears away, instead focusing on a matter of immediate importance. "How long have they been here?"

"Understand—"

Eleven cut off his disapproval. "They knew who to dose, Crux. How many camps did they hit?"

Crux's gaze shot downward. "Seventeen."

"Survivors?" Attempting to reign in her temper, Eleven's whole body constricted.

"Few."

"You told no one. Not even someone you regard as *precious*."

"It would have caused alarm."

"And what do you call this?" Eleven gestured to their new surroundings. "Feeling safe is a luxury none of us can afford. Everyone needs to be prepared, Crux. Not just you. It was selfish of you to think it then, and it is borderline homicidal to think it now."

"*Us?*"

"What?" Eleven asked. She forced herself to take a calming breath.

Crux's face carried raw hopefulness. "You would stay on course?"

*Not this. Not right now.*

"That depends on you."

Crux looked down in deep contemplation. "They want those responsible... me."

*What of Helot or Ophidian? Is this man incapable of a straight answer even now?*

"I was working on a truce," Crux continued. "My life for theirs. Yours."

Eleven scowled. "You'd leave us to fend for ourselves?"

"I intended for you to be my successor."

"And now, Crux? Who's to say they'd stop?"

The Dusslorean sighed. "We are people of our word."

*We'll see about that.*

"But you are not ready. And we have not the numbers for

such a risk."

"Never forget why that is, Dusslorean." Crux's eyes widened. Before he could respond, Eleven pressed on. "I think I've had my fill of civility for tonight."

Eleven pulled the folded sheet of paper from her waistband. She tossed Vera's note at Crux's feet.

"You may want to read this before running any more *errands*. Last thing either of us needs is another miscalculation."

• • • • • • • • • • •

ELEVEN WITNESSED HER FIRST CLEAR SUNRISE since being liberated. The view from the Porters' upstairs guest room soothed her. Few buildings obstructed the sight.

*"Those pages you hold so dear got nothing on this view, gloomy girl."*

*You'd know what to do, wouldn't you? Not the slightest bit of hesitation in your decision either.*

Eleven's ears perked as the door latch moved then righted itself. She strained to identify who or what awaited her on the other side. A loud knock tore her away from the window. Hesitant to respond, the locator stared at the knob.

Crinkled paper slid beneath the door. A freckled teenager on bended knee fell backward when Eleven swung the door open.

"Sweet mother of sanity," Abe said to himself.

"What do you want?"

"Nothing, just—" The young man pushed himself up. Abe grabbed a folded set of clothes lying to the side of him. He presented them to Eleven. "For you, My Lady."

The locator frowned at his choice of moniker. He added insult to injury by curtseying. Eleven took the folded clothes but kept her eyes on Abe.

"Mags says introductions aren't necessary."

"Abraham Porter."

Abe saluted the locator. "At your service. Well, not like a butler or anything."

"Is that all?"

"Think so," the boy said with a shrug. Abe showed no sign of leaving. "Ever been this far out?"

Eleven listened for distinctions. No hint at their current position presented itself. "And where is that?"

"D18."

"There is no District 18," Eleven replied.

"Yeah, in 5. That's where you're from, right?"

*I've crossed borders?*

"Where are we?"

"Welcome to Region 2." Abe leaned against the doorframe. "Not all it's cracked up to be. The parental units bought this place a little after they got engaged. My stepdad's idea, not Mom's. She never takes much stock in paperwork." The teenage boy allowed himself to get carried away by a memory for a moment. His cheeks flushed upon realizing his faux pas. "Anyway, border districts like this one tend to be easier for people like us."

*People like us?*

Abe smirked. "Think you got a monopoly on hiding?"

*Wishful thinking.*

"Pancakes downstairs if you're interested."

"Thank you," Eleven replied. "I'm not hungry."

"Yeah, right."

Bored with the interaction, Eleven nodded as she began to shut the door. Abe's foot stopped it from closing. "Thought you couldn't die."

"What business is it of yours?" Eleven asked.

The teenager shrugged. "Big lady with a number for a name. You're supposed to be this big deal, but I've got to say, not really impressed."

*Don't try me right now, boy.*

Abe chuckled while pointing at Eleven. "You should see your face. Geez, lighten up. I'm just fucking with you."

"What?" Eleven blinked.

Abe waved off her inquiry. "Seriously, you should get down there before Mom cleans up. Take my word for it, the last thing you want is Maggie trying to cook."

"Abe?" called Judy from the ground level.

"Coming." He scanned the locator from head to toe. "Oh, please don't tell anyone I said 'fuck.' I'll never hear the end of it." Abe exited the room, securing the door behind him.

The offered clothes were similar to the ones Eleven had shed before her shower. The most obvious carried a resemblance to something Felix had gifted her. Putting all but that to the side, she inspected it.

*Amazing.*

The cleaned and pressed jacket was Lani's. Lopsided stitching along the hood connected patterns of fabric close in color to the original coat. Eleven ran fingers down the brim.

*Felix.*

As Eleven tugged at the bottom of her shirt, a hard pound of her heart stopped her from undressing. Forcing her arms to her sides, she clenched her fists. Blood ran hot underneath her nails.

A familiar sensation teased.

*Ervassé.*

# 21

CHANGING IN A HURRY, ELEVEN LEFT GREETINGS unacknowledged as she made her way downstairs. Intangible coercion rooted her. Something beckoned, willing the locator's body forward. A semblance of sense came when she reached the ground level of the greenhouse.

"Haven't had your fill of Dungeon de Mags?"

Abe stood at the top of the stairway. Ignoring him, Eleven walked into the heart of the fecund greenery.

*Was it always this small?*

A nagging thought surfaced, one she couldn't disregard. "The night you found me. When was that?"

Abe descended the stairs. "A week ago tomorrow."

*Days? Felt like mere hours.*

"For what it's worth," Abe continued, "Crux was plenty scared. Spent the whole time down here. Didn't even come up to eat."

Abe joined Eleven in the open center space. Eleven searched what remained of her final resting place. Few planks had yet to be returned to the floor. She knelt and picked up several, tossing them with no regard toward the curious boy beside her.

"Eleven?"

*Where is it?*

"Care to share with the rest of the class?"

Disappointed, Eleven turned to Abe. "I'm looking for something."

"No kidding."

"A flower."

Abe rolled his eyes. "After everything you've been through, you want to have a go at floristry? There's a joke in there somewhe—" A slight rattle brought Eleven to her feet. Both assessed a tall, rusted set of drawers. "The hell?"

"You heard that?"

Abe shrugged. "Kind of hard to miss."

*Even someone like him could hear it?*

Eleven approached the antique tool chest with a quirked brow and anxious fingers. A vertical padlock stacked along the nine pale blue rows gave her pause.

*Simple enough.*

Taking in her surroundings, Eleven zeroed in on two pieces of scrap metal. She manipulated the pliable alloys into a make-shift tensioner and rake.

"That's my stepsister's."

"Quiet."

Abe watched as Eleven undid the padlock. The teenager didn't hide his astonishment as she searched drawers. "Fancy that."

*Seeds… soil samples… pods.*

Yanking the fourth drawer open, a petrified bud rolled to the front. Dried edges brushed against Eleven's knuckles. With care, she placed it in her palm.

"This is the toy prize?" Abe asked Eleven. Keeping her eyes glued to the meager Ervassé remnants, she nodded. "Don't seem like much."

"Never appraise something at face value."

Abe chuckled. "Aren't pearls of wisdom Crux's gig?"

The door at the top of the stairs swung wide open. Abe and Eleven paused as shoes descended. As soon as he laid eyes on his stepsister, Abe relaxed.

Maggie reached the end of the staircase. "What are you doing?"

"Minding our own business," Abe replied. Inching closer to Eleven, he continued. "Try it sometime, Mags."

Maggie walked further into the underground garden when noticing the open tool chest. She grimaced at the fossilized flower resting in Eleven's hand. "Who said you could take that?"

Abe swaggered toward Maggie. "Isn't there a djembe you should be restringing or some other kind of beatnik bunk?"

With flaring nostrils, Maggie said, "Plants are not *bunk*, Abe. Not all of us are interested in being a gofer. And stop acting like you own the place."

"Or what?" Abe asked. "You'll jab me with a spear you made yourself?"

"You can't just bust in—"

"Enough." Eleven looked to the shelves in front of her. Sibling rivalries wouldn't help the locator figure out why the Ervassé called to her. It crinkled in Eleven's grasp. "You're interested in botany."

"What?" the siblings asked in unison.

Eleven faced Maggie. "Botany."

"What was your first clue?" Abe asked with both palms showcasing the underground garden.

Maggie sighed. "Why?"

Eleven considered the numerous violations surrounding her. Licenses and permits imposed on most growing operations. The majority of Maggie's plants, though relatively harmless, were unauthorized and carried hefty repercussions should she be found out.

"What do you make of it?" Eleven presented the Ervassé to Maggie.

"Not sure I understand."

"Crux wouldn't have let just anyone have access to this. Why you?"

Taking the plant, Maggie asked, "Is this from 5?"

"No."

*How much do these children really know?*

"Most other regions don't have a lot of flora."

Eleven stepped forward. "He hasn't told you."

*Play it safe.*

"Unknown origin."

"Sexy," Maggie said.

Abe groaned at the eagerness in her response. Maggie hurried to the chest Eleven had broken into. She took out a scratched magnifying glass. The small bit of stem left appeared to be of great interest. Maggie wiped at a dark, thick substance. It flaked to the touch as if dry, but her fingers pulled back dampness.

"Can't make heads or tails of this," Maggie said to herself.

Eleven's eyes shifted from side to side. "Blood."

The Porter children turned to her.

"You sure?" Abe asked.

"Quite."

"Well," Maggie started. "That's one mystery solved. Just a billion or so to go." She flicked a nearby light on but was careful not to place the Ervassé too close. "Does the coagulation matter or—?"

"I don't care about the blood," Eleven told the would-be botanist. Her lips twisted. "What can you tell me about the plant?"

"Nothing based off this specimen." Eleven folded both arms

to her chest. Maggie's all-knowing smile fell. "The flora's deterioration is too severe."

"Is there anything similar?" Eleven asked.

Maggie shrugged. "Off this sample, your guess is as good as mine."

*There has to be more.*

"Without further analysis that is," Maggie added. Her face softened as she took a step toward Eleven. "Get me a live sample."

"What you're holding is the last of its kind."

Frowning, Maggie said, "Crux didn't tell me that."

"What's the big deal?" Abe asked. "It's just a plant."

"No, it isn't." Eleven toyed with what to reveal. The teenagers looked from Eleven to the Ervassé. Maggie and Abe had questions itching at their lips, yet neither said anything.

*To hell with finesse.*

"It's Dusslorean."

"Dusslorean? As in Dusslore?" Maggie asked Eleven.

"None other than."

Abe tilted his head. "I thought everything was destroyed."

"Apparently not," Maggie mumbled.

*Has Crux divulged anything useful?*

"Okay," Abe said. "I'm tapping out. I don't follow."

"Whatever incapacitated her is still out there, lamoid." Maggie assessed the Ervassé with renewed interest. "I'm guessing this can happen again, and only about ten other people on this planet have her kind of resolve."

"Even guardians?" Abe asked Eleven. "Is that what got Felix?"

Eleven flinched. "No."

"Smooth," Maggie said to her stepbrother. Pulling several vials labeled "glycerin" and a wooden box from the bottom drawer of her tool chest, she spread the contents out on the table next to the lamp. Using a fine point blade from the box, she cut at the base of a withered petal. "Things are never easy with you people."

"What is all that shit, Mags?"

"Preserving what I can. If I'd been told beforehand, there might've been more to save." Maggie dropped the blade. Wiping her forehead, she said, "I have no idea what I'm looking for, and there's no telling how long something like this is gonna take."

"Something like what?" Abe asked.

Maggie sighed. "The density of your skull continues to baffle me."

The Ervassé was gone, but Eleven held out hope. Her anxiety over the looming threat of another Alipo encounter dissipated as she watched Maggie dissect the plant.

*The fate of us all may very well rest in the hands of Margaret Porter.*

· · · · · · · · · · ·

WEARING THE REPAIRED HOODED JACKET, ELEVEN hugged her knees as she sat on the Porters' flattop roof. She relished hiding amongst the plethora of solar panels and windmills. A taller neighborhood to the west blocked a full view of the sunset, yet the locator kept her eyes on the horizon.

"Trying your hand at voyeurism?" she asked.

"Were this a month ago, you would not have sensed me." Lurking in the shadows, Crux forced a laugh. "Discerning my movements at this stage is impressive."

*Took brutality and the closest I've come to real death to factor in Dusslore's gravity versus ours.*

"You'll find other ways to amuse yourself," Eleven said.

Crux joined his pupil in witnessing the last shreds of daylight. Rose faded to purple, then to blue and black. A crescent moon amidst scattered stars offered faint lighting. Limited exterior lanterns made landmarks difficult to see.

"Margaret has become quite determined," Crux said.

"Just giving you what you want."

"Why are you refusing food?"

"Doubt I'll have much of an appetite for a while." Eleven exhaled. Lifting her chin, she said, "The Ervassé wasn't mine to take."

"No." Crux watched the darkening skyline.

The eleventh locator did the same. "I never thought about it. The healing. It just happened. My body worked as it should. I can feel it traveling in my veins. Soaking through me, moving—" Eleven searched for the right word. "Cataloging."

"Do you believe the Ervassé can be replicated?"

"We have to try." Eleven turned to Crux.

"They admire you, Eleven."

"The children?"

"Very much so. Margaret and Abraham are—"

"Gullible," Eleven finished.

"We are constant, they are not, yes. But it does not lessen them or their potential."

"These are good people?"

"Yes," Crux answered without hesitation.

Eleven watched him. "You know better than I do how easily *good people* die."

"I do."

"What significance does their admiration hold?"

"You may not like the answer."

• • • • • • • • • • •

FOLLOWING CRUX WITH CAUTION, ELEVEN DE-scended to the first floor. The Porter household was darker than it had been in all of her time there. The fireplace in the den roared. Judy and Dave sat close together, watching the dancing flames.

"Please sit," Judy said.

Neither she nor her husband looked at the locators. Crux motioned to the couch as he sat in a recliner opposite. Eleven lowered to sitting.

"What do you hear?" Dave asked.

Eleven's nose wrinkled. "Sorry?"

"Listen," he pressed.

Eleven narrowed her gaze on Dave. No one moved to clarify the request. Falling back into a snug groove of his seat, Crux covered his mouth. Eleven released a breath as she strained to listen.

*Nothing.*

For the first time, Eleven fully assessed the peculiar dwelling. Architecture suggested the Porters' home had been built approximately fifty years ago. The partial pier and beam foundation deviated from the standard full slab. Aesthetics notwithstanding, few things of the original layout had been preserved.

*Soundproof.*

Not a single noise was heard outside the immediate space. What transpired behind the myriad of closed doors stayed secret. A rural layout of the neighborhood didn't warrant the multiple layers in the floors or walls. Internal structure had been updated repeatedly over the years. Even archways and halls were devoid of distinguishable resonance.

*Years of alterations. This could be for my benefit... but Abe heard the Ervassé just as I did.*

"Abe."

"Not just Abraham," Crux said.

"*Both* of them?" Eleven asked the Porters. When Dave didn't answer, she implored Judy to respond. The mother's eyes returned to the fire.

*Maggie too... but neither of them have the telltale signs of dosing. I would've noticed immediately.*

"Legacies," Eleven realized.

Humans born with the traits of a guardian. Dissimilar to Felix, legacies like Maggie and Abe did not require medicinal assistance. This often stemmed from one or both parents having some level of dosage in their system prior to fertilization.

Dave cleared his throat. "My first wife and I tried to start a family." He gripped Judy's hand. "But we couldn't... and adoption was damn near impossible."

*One can assume due to earning class.*

Eleven said, "Health services."

"If you can call them that," Crux replied.

*Human desperation... it's what Cerulemans rely on to replenish their ranks.*

Judy wiped at her nose, shrugging off her husband's concern. The sniffling woman kept her eyes on the fire.

"My wife died in childbirth," Dave continued.

*But Maggie survived.*

Nothing is without price. These miraculous children are born with their fate all but set. Cerulemans, as always, provided families with the illusion of choice. For sympathizers, the decision is simple. For people like Dave, however, it is anything but.

*With her aptitude for science, Maggie would be an asset. They'd assign Abe to active duty... he might even make a locator's detail.*

"Have they come for them?" Eleven asked Crux.

"Helot and I robbed them of the opportunity."

Eleven regarded the Porters. "You've been in hiding."

"Me and Abe had similar circumstances, more or less," Judy admitted. She brushed an anxious palm against Dave's. "Funny how things have a way of working out."

"Funny?" Eleven repeated, the humor lost on her.

Crux grinned. "It would appear I am a matchmaker."

The lighthearted remark tugged at the couple. Eleven's

thoughts momentarily drifted to Felix and Vera.

Judy met Eleven's cynical gaze. "Do you have family?" Eleven didn't respond. Mrs. Porter shrugged, not letting the issue drop. "Parents? Aunts? Uncles?"

Dave pressed. "Siblings?"

*Ten is more than enough family.*

"*We* are her family," Crux said.

"But—what I mean is—she—*you* can't give us any sort of guarantee, can you?" Judy shifted in her seat.

"Baby," Dave said. His hoarse voice strained with the plea.

"What is this?" Eleven's tone betrayed emotion. She searched Crux's eyes for answers and found none. "What am I missing?"

"Eleven."

"*Crux.*" Eleven spoke his name like a curse.

Noticing her displeasure, the Dusslorean locator raised a hand. "We have suffered setbacks. With Mr. Unger gone, the departure of Vera, and the change in numbers—"

*Was Felix family?*

"—adjustments have to be made."

*Is Vera...?* Wait.

"Adjustments?" Eleven repeated.

"There are those like Abraham and Margaret who have been waiting to be called upon. Now is a time for action. Their time."

Eleven sat with mouth agape when she realized Crux's intentions. She had stopped breathing altogether while glaring at the Porters.

"You require a new crew," the Dusslorean added.

*"They admire you, Eleven."*

*He baited me with that forsaken Ervassé.*

His matter-of-factly dissection of Eleven's needs disturbed her. Neither Vera nor Felix was easy to replace. Crux knew that better than she did. This came off as a last-ditch effort to fill complex positions. Eleven couldn't help but feel insulted.

"They're children."

"Margaret and Abraham know the risks."

Shaking her head in disbelief, Eleven fumbled for a response. "You're prepared to add them to the growing list of bodies? To have them end up like Felix? Like Vera, had I not intervened?"

*Like Dusslore?*

Crux's expression said it all. Eleven looked to the Porters. "And you?"

"The Porters have discussed this at length," Crux answered. He motioned to Judy and Dave. The couple nodded. "Margaret and Abraham have made their decision."

"Neither of them truly know what they're agreeing to. I'll work on my own before I—"

"They are no different from us," Crux said.

"*We* don't have a choice!"

"Neither do they," Judy confessed.

"We know you can't promise they'll come back," Dave told Eleven. "You'd be lying if you did."

Eleven stared at the parents. "Keep them here."

"They want to help," Dave replied. "To make a difference."

*Give them something. Anything to see reason.*

The eleventh locator bit her cheek. "How many died in these attacks, Crux?"

"72."

"And when Dusslore was destroyed?"

"Eleven—"

"It's a simple question," she interrupted.

"14,543,832,614… approximately."

*Some approximation.*

"And those are just the ones *he* is responsible for," Eleven said to Judy and Dave. "Where we go, death follows."

"That is an oversimplification, Eleven."

"It's the way it is, Crux!"

"Crux has his faults," Dave started. "So do we. So do you. Rattle off numbers all you like—death shadows anyone trying to swim upstream these days. At least with you, our children stand a chance."

*Is he right?*

"Will you try for us? For them?" Judy pressed.

*Yes. They're in danger no matter their location.*

Looking to Crux, Dave asked, "Is she okay?"

*Just like me.*

"Eleven?" Crux said.

*Like* us.

The locator closed her eyes while saying, "You have my word."

# 22

*Seven Months Later*

ELEVEN'S EYES SHOT OPEN IN THE WAKE OF MUTED madness. Darkness surrounded her.

"Abe...? Maggie?"

No answer. Not even a reflection of the call. The locator couldn't make sense of location or position.

"Crux?"

Locked in place, Eleven's extremities twitched. When she cried out, no sound passed her lips. Cardiac thumping quickened with her breath. Closing her eyes offered more light than the exterior world. This allowed Eleven to discern darkness from the backs of her eyes.

A slow piercing sound presented itself. Coarse writhing started at her feet, then broke out into several points. Tightening around Eleven's limbs cut off her circulation. Her body began to swell. Slithering vines continued on all sides. A rush of light pierced the top of Eleven's insulated torture cell. She examined herself. The blocked blood flow resulted in atrophy. Her swollen, delicate skin tore. Eleven watched as her hands and feet fell away from her.

Horrified, she tried to scream, to call out for help, but the disintegrating locator couldn't make a sound. Worse, Eleven failed to heal. Blood oozed from multiple points and pooled around her. Midnight walls advanced inward, drowning Eleven in an inordinate amount of deep, warm crimson. She choked, knowing full well that she couldn't sustain herself for long. A thick coat of red blinded her.

"No!"

Eleven woke with tense limbs and a strained neck. Sheets clung to her as she sat up. Wiping tears from her cheeks, Eleven's lips trembled.

*It was just a dream.*

Light knocking startled her. "Eleven?"

"What?" Eleven asked as she caressed her nape.

"Are you all right?"

"Of course, Maggie."

"I—I heard screaming."

"It's nothing. Just leave me be."

"Have it your way," Maggie mumbled as she left the threshold. "I'm headed to the lobby if you need anything."

Rubbing her temples, Eleven groaned. "I'm fine."

*"You have a tendency to say as much when circumstances are anything but."*

The locator dragged both hands down her face. Eleven stopped when detecting the pressure change in her room. "Thought we established your days of hiding from me are over."

*Right around the time of this new arrangement.*

A shadowed Dusslorean kept still. "Not a sliver of what I see before me could be categorized as *fine*."

*Away for weeks without a word, and he berates me at the earliest opportunity. Who needs parents when I've got Crux?*

"Been lurking long?"

"Long enough to see your lies have not improved," Crux said. "You assured me these hallucinations were under control."

"Dreams," Eleven corrected. "They're just dreams."

*Nightmares that have only gotten worse since Ervassé... 227 days, but who's counting?*

"I witnessed nothing just."

"Why are you here?" Eleven asked with an edge to her voice.

Crux leaned forward. "It has been weeks since our last meeting. A visitation was overdue."

*The timing can't be coincidental.*

"Abe," Eleven said to herself. She wiped at the corners of her mouth. "When did he call you?"

"Upon your return."

*Didn't I tell him to leave it alone? That boy's concern is the very definition of stifling.*

Crux said, "If what he says is the truth, Abraham was right to worry, Eleven."

After pushing herself off the bed, Eleven rushed to the light switch. An overhanging light wobbled in its socket, flickering as it adjusted. Yellow paint peeled and cracked from all four walls. Stacks upon stacks of books towered throughout the majority of the room.

Keeping her back to him, Eleven sighed. "He's overreacting."

"My preference is a personal assessment."

"It's late. Can you—"

Crux finished Eleven's statement for her. "Allow hallucinations and insomnia to best you again?"

*Don't sleep for 57 hours once,* once, *and suddenly everyone has "a right to worry."*

Shaking her head, Eleven said, "Third column to your left, tenth book from the top."

The Dusslorean followed her line of sight. He approached the desired literary pylon. Crux snatched the first nine books with one hand and the tenth with the other. His curiosity became evident with his clumsy re-stacking of the books.

"I see you took my suggestion."

"I'm more of a reader than a writer. Abe's been doing his best to remember everything." Eleven shrugged. "I'd go as far as to say he has a knack for it."

"Then what is this?"

"Just open the forsaken book, Crux."

Opening it revealed pages cut in the same place over and over. Resting at the bottom of the makeshift hiding spot was an aged metal resembling a charm or pendant. "Explain."

Eleven slumped back onto her bed. She stared at the sliver of darkness underneath her door. "I started with objects I was familiar with. Documents, mostly. Trinkets or something, anything that might prove useful in the right circumstance."

"Yes," Crux said. He sat in the room's only chair. "I have been informed of your progress. It pleases me."

*Maggie's keeping him updated too. Fantastic.*

"Neither you nor Helot had encountered a concoction like the one I used on Vera. I'd never studied Hynlai, let alone anything a chamber might've held."

"I am afraid I do not understand." Crux fidgeted.

*Not sure I do either.*

"What has Abe told you?"

"There was an issue with an outpost?"

Nodding, Eleven looked in every direction Crux wasn't. "I'm beginning to get recognized… actively pursued."

It had been almost a year since Felix and Vera had plucked Eleven from Ceruleman clutches. In that time, Cerulemans had searched for the locator to no avail. The longer she stayed away, the more Eleven saw her face.

**ANYONE WITH INFORMATION ON THE WHEREABOUTS OF JANE DOE IS ASKED TO INFORM THE NEAREST AUTHORITY. ALL WILL REMAIN ANONYMOUS AND BE ELIGIBLE FOR A MONETARY REWARD.**

"The bounty on me increased again."

"To an obscene amount if I recall correctly."

"The outpost meeting was a trap," Eleven told Crux. "Abe and I were outnumbered and—and then—" She stopped herself.

"Eleven?"

"And then we weren't," she finished.

"You killed them? These bounty hunters?"

*Civilians at best.*

Eleven scratched her neck. "Afterward... we had to."

*Keep telling yourself that.*

The locator focused on her bedroom door. She took note of the concerned Dusslorean in her right side peripheral vision. "Chambers are coming to me as I need them."

"I see no indication of purpose or origin."

"That metal you're holding—it emits a pulse which targets living tissue. Dissolves the bulk of anything it comes into contact with," Eleven said in a flattened tone. "The Loezi people haven't a name for it."

*If Abe hadn't been a legacy—*

"How did you arrive at this?" Crux asked.

"I just know."

"Since your initial introduction to Margaret and Abraham, have you felt anything out of the ordinary? Other than the obvious, that is." Eleven thought hard on the question. Crux continued. "There are several theories to support logic where

267

a legacy could benefit a locator as much as one of their own. Given the current state of affairs, we cannot rule out the possibility that having them near you may play a factor."

"Nothing is ever easy, is it?"

"No. Not for us."

*He ventures guesses in the absence of answers and accepts them as gospel. I, on the other hand, only have more questions.*

• • • • • • • • • • •

"ABE?"

Eleven pressed an ear to Abe's bedroom door. When she heard no stirrings, she tried the knob. Whining from inside stopped the locator as she pulled lock-picking tools from her back pocket.

"Five more minutes," Abe mumbled.

"Abraham."

"It's too early for the *Abraham* shtick, boss lady."

*To hell with the lock.*

Eleven pocketed her instruments. Agitated, she backed away from the entrance to give herself just enough space then kicked open the door on her first attempt.

Abe bolted upright. "What the actual hell, woman?"

Miscellaneous comics, clothes, and a slew of questionable textures cluttered a room shrouded in darkness, save for the light from the hall. Plywood and sheets covered Abe's window, often making it difficult to gauge the true time of day. The hall light painted a harsh silhouette as Eleven glared at the less than cooperative teenager. "This what you call being ready?"

"Anyone ever tell you that your manners could use a little work?"

Abe fell back onto his pillow and threw blankets over his face. Eleven heard labored snuffles underneath a crumpled comforter in the center of an ancient mattress. When she yanked back the sheets, Abe balled up in a fetal position. He covered his eyes with a lazy arm.

"Get up. Get dressed. Now. Have you forgotten—?"

"How could I forget anything with you nagging me every chance you get?"

"I'm serious," Eleven said.

"I know, I know. Grave importance, end all, be all." Abe mumbled obscenities. Eleven flicked a switch at the side of his door. "*Why*? Come on, Eleven. I don't need to tell you how crucial it is that I get my beauty sleep."

"Your protests carry no weight. Ready yourself."

"*Ready myself?*" Abe mocked. He leaned against the bed's unsecured headboard. "Can you please talk like someone born in the last millennium?"

"I'm not your mother, Abraham."

Laughing, he said, "Oh, trust me, I am aware of that. Thanks for the clarification all the same."

"So don't assume I won't resort to bloodshed."

Abe staggered off the bed. When Eleven didn't move, he stopped sifting through the clothes cluttering his bedroom floor. "Plan on watching me get dressed? No offense, but you're not really my type."

Eleven held back her own brand of derision. Abe slammed the misaligned door shut when she exited.

*Don't stab him… least not until after we return.*

The locator hurried down a wrecked hallway with grimy, yellowing walls. Dislocated foundation and problematic stairs caused Eleven to take time in her descent. Four flights later, she reached the lowest level of a long-forgotten office building the eleventh locator now called home.

"Let me guess."

"Don't bother," Eleven said as she met Maggie near what remained of a circular desk in the lobby. "How's it coming along?"

"Good." Maggie stayed on task. "May have literally pat myself on the back earlier, but, lucky for me, no one was around to witness it."

A surplus of inventory cluttered the former reception area. Eleven leaned an elbow against one of the few unencumbered spots on the limited counter space.

"Tired?" Maggie asked. The locator gave a curt nod. "Doubt you would be if we repaired that elevator."

"We've been over this."

"A girl can dream." Maggie shrugged. She began bagging essential items. "Quakes are supposed to pick up later today."

"Worried about structural integrity?"

"Wouldn't you be?" Maggie motioned to the open space.

Zeroing in on the cracks and broken plaster, Eleven surveyed their surroundings. The abandoned IT building occupied a district wrought with earthquakes. Being near an active fault line limited Ceruleman interaction. It also increased the probability of one or all being trapped under fallen debris.

"You worry for nothing."

"Well, *obviously*. I'm a textbook worrywart." Maggie glanced over to the stairs. Groaning, she said, "It's not just that. The longer the less attractive Porter takes, the likelier it is that you're gonna have to deal with the aforementioned quakes out in the open."

"Tremors are standard, Maggie."

"Be careful, okay?" The worried teenage girl handed Eleven a list of supplies. She then took a swig from a large thermal cup.

"Maggie."

"What?"

"You're staring."

Maggie pursed her lips. "It's just—please explain to me again why you can't just call for it?"

"Chambers aren't always that simple."

"Then just leave it," Maggie replied. "It isn't worth the risk."

"Maggie—"

The teenager waved away Eleven's rebuttal. "I get that it's *calling* to you or whatever, but after what just happened—" Maggie stopped herself.

"Abe will be fine."

"He's not the one I'm worried about."

*She's scared... of what I'll do, or who might find me?*

Changing the subject, Eleven asked, "When's the last time you slept?"

"What's the expression? 'No rest for the wicked'?" Maggie took a big gulp of her caffeine. Leaning against the counter, she continued. "Besides, those genotypes aren't gonna sequence themselves."

"Beautiful girl refusing to rest? Sounds familiar."

Both women turned to the direction of the cordial voice. Crux, ever quiet, stood at the foot of the stairs.

Maggie closed the distance, hopping over the counter to embrace the Dusslorean. "Where the heck have you been?"

"You look well, Margaret."

"I do, don't I?" Maggie stuck her tongue out. She took in the sight of the Dusslorean before her. "You too."

"You are becoming a skilled deceiver, Margaret."

Maggie nudged Crux in his ribs. Turning to Eleven, she asked, "Did you know he was here?"

"I only just arrived," Crux lied.

Eleven motioned to the inventory. "You're certain of the coordinates?"

"Yep." Maggie returned to the desk. She answered Crux's curiosity. "Fixed chamber. Kind of crunchy."

"Crunchy?"

"Time sensitive," she clarified for the Dusslorean.

Crux smiled. "Where is your brother?"

"My *step*brother is still asleep. Shocking no one."

"May I offer my assistance?" Crux turned to Eleven.

Eleven's brow hinted at her reservation. "That's not necessary."

"Young Margaret said it best. Time is sensitive." Crux approached Eleven. She handed the list back to Maggie. "It would afford us the opportunity to speak at length."

*Abe has no idea how much carnage he's in store for.*

"Fair point," Eleven said to Crux.

"I mean," Maggie started, "unless you want to postpone."

*She's almost as stubborn as I am.*

"No more delays," Eleven replied.

Maggie rolled her eyes. "You're the boss." She motioned to the bags and reviewed her portable device. "So... according to the last census, the chamber is smack-dab in the middle of what was supposed to be an indoor waterpark."

"Waterpark?" Crux asked. Eleven shook her head.

"Seriously?" Maggie asked. Her incredulous countenance left both locators baffled. "Aquatic amusement? Waterslides, wave pools, overpriced everythi—? Forget it. This bout of dandy is wasted on the pair of you."

"Why multiple signal disruptors?" Eleven asked.

"Since we couldn't canvas beforehand, there's no telling what might be in the neighborhood. Jammers can only override tech for so long. Figured better safe than sorry."

*Safe? Yes. But it'll be harder for me to hear the chamber's frequency.*

Crux snagged both bags before making his way to Eleven's side. "Shall we?"

# 23

PROCEEDING INTO THE BUILDING TOOK LONGER than Maggie's estimation. Eleven and Crux had difficulty navigating through the countless obscure attractions, some of which had fallen apart. Both locators adjusted to the disruptor's audible density.

"I harbored discontent for this invention," Crux said. "Until now."

"Vera's work?"

"Mine."

Crux's breath quickened at the mention of Vera. Eleven distracted herself with the grand structure of attractions filling the space. "Amusement is the purpose of all this?"

*Wasting a precious resource is amusing, I suppose.*

"My apparatuses are more effective than I realized." Crux strained for an indication of a chamber. "Can you tell me of the contents?"

"The signal's too weak," Eleven said.

"Excusable price for the sake of secrecy."

Coming to a stop, Eleven pulled back her hood. Peeling off her gloves, she gauged her ability.

*Not south… nor west.*

Her right middle finger twitched when pointed north. "This way."

Crux followed close behind his determined comrade. "There is a matter I wish to discuss."

"Now?"

"It is regarding Four."

Eleven stopped. "What about him?"

"A team is being put in place. They believe an extraction is possible."

"You want to discuss something like that here? Right this very second?"

"The situation is… *crunchy*."

"Crux."

He ceased her hesitation. "An unforeseen opportunity has come to our attention, and we cannot afford to ignore it."

"We haven't the resources."

"A rather notable resource comes to mind."

Eleven didn't miss a beat. "Vera."

"Her specifications are vital," Crux justified.

"When you say this is an opportunity, do you mean for Four's sake, or do you just want your daughter back?"

"My incentives have nothing to do with ego."

"It appears Four is stuck for the time being. Vera said it best, Crux. If she doesn't want to be found, she won't be."

"It is my belief that she will return," Crux started, "upon your request, that is. How soon you forget the impact you have made in a short amount of time. Reiteration may be called for here. Truly, it is not greed that motivates me, but I will not argue that I—*we*—are all better when she is among our numbers. Her work is pivotal to future success. Do not deprave a locator of their freedom to prove some belabored point."

*Saving another so soon?*

The eleventh locator chewed on her lip. "I'll think about it."

"When might you reach a decision?"

"Crunchy!" Eleven continued north.

Three attractions into their new surroundings, Crux grew quiet. The Dusslorean's unease had become downright infectious. Eleven dismissed the idea that it was only about Vera. Something else toyed at the back of her mind but refused to come forward. Warped construction and discolored kitsch oddities lost their appeal. Settling kept both on edge. Eleven's walk turned brisk, almost into a full run.

"Eleven?"

The two stopped in an open space underneath a large series of multi-colored tubing. Nuts and bolts had long since rusted. Certain areas were ready to crumble. Crux and Eleven shared a look after a flock of birds flew by a neighboring row of windows. Eleven searched for the chamber's exact location.

*Where are you…? Finally.*

"*This* called to you?"

*So all locators eavesdrop.*

"Yes," Eleven exhaled.

"Do other chambers?"

"Those within range."

Looking to the Dusslorean, Eleven saw his gears turning. "Better in our hands than the opposition's," Crux said. "What does it harbor?"

Eleven rubbed her clammy palms against her hips. Moving closer, she listened for the chamber's song. "Stone." The locator closed her eyes. "Unknown attributes. No categorized planet of origin. Neighboring galaxy, likely an asteroid belt."

"I am nearing obsolescence," Crux joked.

Since Eleven's initial assessment, the environment had shifted. She could not brush off her apprehension. Both locators recoiled at a rush of frequencies.

*The disruptors.*

A low rumble brewed below their feet. Eleven and Crux withdrew as a crack in thick molding above them widened.

"Tremors," Eleven deduced. "They're ahead of schedule."

"No, Eleven. Not tremors."

"The area isn't stable. Theoretically, a chamber could modify the foundation."

"This upheaval was deliberate." An unnerving screech solidified what she feared. The two were no longer alone. Crux took the teleporter from his pocket. "I have traveled too much. It requires time to charge."

"How long?"

"Only minutes."

"We might not have that." Eleven reached for a gun holstered inside her jacket. Taking the arm from her side, she checked ammunition.

"Has your aim improved?"

"Still abysmal," Eleven admitted. "But they don't know that."

"Let us retreat on foot."

"The disruptors were taken out simultaneously, Crux. Safe to say we're surrounded."

Taking a short sword from the bag Maggie had prepared, Crux checked the balance with a light grip. He threw a military issue baton to Eleven. She returned the gun to its hidden location. Steady heartbeats circled from multiple directions. Eleven and Crux narrowed the space between them, standing side by side.

"The years have been kind to you, seeker," said a booming voice.

*Oudesloy.*

Both readied themselves as a group of Dusslorean soldiers entered the space's lone exit. Eleven pressed her back against Crux's as the group enclosed them. Their overall appearance was similar to that of Oliab and Smy. The three females had broader shoulders and longer necks than their male counterparts.

*Keep mobile. Anticipate moves through their footwork. Avoid anything that can penetrate the skin.*

"They often are to my kind," Crux said in English.

Eight in total, the Dussloreans calculated each movement toward their prey. All stopped concurrently less than two meters from Crux and Eleven. Neither locator gave an indication of panic or fright.

"*Your kind,*" the presumed leader repeated. Branded skin under his right eye confirmed his status. Amethyst irises stuck to their targets. Weapons from all angles took aim at Eleven and Crux. "Do you wish for slaughter?"

Facing the hooded leader, Eleven kept her eyes on the assorted weaponry at play. The threat of Alipo-laced arms could not be overlooked.

"What do they call you?" Crux asked. The leader pulled a blade from his side, toying with the grip. Nothing hinted at a motive. "We are entitled to know our murderers."

"We are after your time, deceiver."

"Yet here I stand."

"Prwoyn," said the leader. "Offspring of the fallen. Bound by blood and honor—"

Crux finished the statement. "To seek and destroy all who oppose you… remarkable how little changes." Eleven's forehead wrinkled at Crux's audacious response. "I do wonder how you found me."

"Not you, seeker." Prwoyn looked from Crux to Eleven. The Dusslorean stepped forward. "This one."

*They know you. Use it to your advantage.*

"Then you're fools to come here." In a fit of bravery or stupidity, Eleven pushed away from Crux.

Prwoyn's fingers itched at the blade on his side. His knife

bared a likeness to Oliab's. With full sneer in place, Prwoyn took notice of the locator's distinguishable fingertips and flawless skin. "You do not frighten us, girl."

"And Banaedrut?" Eleven approached the intimidating leader. Quite the bluff, one she had to make. Despite Crux's skill and her own, she questioned their ability to match those fueled by vengeance. "You might take him or me, but what of them?" She advanced further. "That's why you hide, isn't it? Stick to the shadows? Because your numbers can't match theirs and they terrify you."

Drawing out his blade, Prwoyn said, "Deliberate your next words."

"And the noise you must've made," Eleven continued. "The exposure... how long before they arrive?"

"This is a deception," Prwoyn replied.

"Is it?" Crux asked. He evaluated those surrounding them. "I have partnered with a Ceruleman or two in the past."

Prwoyn peered deep into Eleven's hazel eyes. Glancing from side to side, he signaled to his soldiers. They lowered their weapons. "There were three of you that night, yes? Your companion keeps his groups small. One of many things he learned from us." Cocking his head to the side, Prwoyn asked, "Where are they now?" The Dusslorean chuckled. "How soon until your guilt matches his?"

"Banaedrut are inbound."

"Are all your kind abhorrent in falsehoods?" Prwoyn asked Eleven.

Eleven lifted her chin as she stared hard at him. "You're only solidifying your fate by staying here."

Turning his back, Prwoyn returned to Oudesloy. "Take them both. Contaminate the blood. Their kind was made to suffer."

Crux intertwined his arms with Eleven's and used his weight to flip the locator over. He pushed Eleven to the ground as arrows and blades approached at great speed. Weapons from all angles narrowly missed the pair thanks to Crux's maneuverability.

"Run!"

Before Eleven could argue, Prwoyn progressed toward her. Readying his blade, Crux stopped the attack by engaging the leader himself. Both men, equally matched, tensed as they fought one another.

Prwoyn waved off those rushing to his aide. Eleven dodged several darts only for thrown thick blades to follow. She avoided the last of the projectiles with just enough time to duck multiple swings. Landing blows on a Dusslorean proved difficult. Eleven countered with the baton, but missed time after time.

A woman thrust her blade at Eleven. Eleven dodged, which left the woman wide open. Eleven knocked the knife out of the Dusslorean female's hand. She caught the handle before it fell, following the save with a heavy swing which slit her adversary's throat. Eleven pushed the dying woman in the direction of the other Dussloreans.

The path to the door no longer obstructed, Eleven turned to Crux. Every move seemed choreographed. Both Dussloreans shifted constantly to anticipate the other's next strike.

Crux shoved Prwoyn. "Now is not the time for heroics, Eleven!"

*He'd leave you.*

Three Dussloreans closed in behind him. Hearing their advances, Crux stepped into their attacks. Blow to the temple, slice of the neck, and blade to the eye.

"Crux—"

"Kin of mine," Crux bellowed. Prwoyn stalked him. "Do as you are told!"

Eleven was tackled to the ground as she reached for the gun in her jacket. A male attacker pressed a baton against Eleven's neck. Pressing down on both ends, the Dusslorean's weight caused blood vessels to burst. The sheen of a knife secured on the raider's leg caught her eye.

Wasting no time, Eleven took the blade and drove it deep into his upper thigh. His grip on the baton loosened. Eleven pulled the knife toward her, widening the gash. Thick drops of blood splattered as the Dusslorean bled out. As he panicked, Eleven cracked his skull with the knife's pommel.

Turning to Crux, she found others advancing. Eleven bolted to the unguarded door.

*I can't take them all... not all at once.*

Swerving in and out of slides, Eleven scrambled to reach the outside. An attack from behind pushed her into a spiked chunk of hardened plastic. Eleven's face spilt open. A heavy boot to the abdomen knocked the wind out of her.

"Trash," said the latest assailant.

He snagged the blade Eleven had dropped. With great force, the Dusslorean threw the locator against a thick wall of tubing. Eleven spewed a combination of blood and teeth into his eyes, temporarily blinding him. She elbowed his jaw. Her vision blurred as her wounds mended.

*Run. I still have the gun, but I can't aim even when my target is stationary.*

A new set of opponents matched Eleven's speed. She summoned all the strength she could muster as she dashed away. Resisting the impulse to look back, Eleven jumped through hurdles and oversized attractions.

*Concentrate. What do you need?*

Eleven became lightheaded. The locator stifled a groan while forcing her legs to continue on.

*A weapon.* Anything. *You've done this before. Just do it again.*

Then she realized Dussloreans weren't the only thing following her. Eleven had summoned another chamber on her own. Unlike the one she and Crux had traveled to find, this chamber kept in step.

*From the planet Gove. Should be more than sufficient.*

Unwilling to question the sudden edge this marvel offered, Eleven opened the chamber with unsteady hands. The locator pulled a metallic ball of strands from it. Unwinding the peculiar item while running revealed serrated chain links that resembled a whip without a stem.

*They're not cutting me.*

Examining the object slowed the locator. Her two foes now had her in their sights. Eleven scrutinized the path ahead as she resumed her earlier pace. Factoring trajectory to the best of her ability, she threw the heavy end of the chain at decorative piping ahead. It wrapped itself in a tangled knot around the rusted work.

*Nope. It never does get easier.*

The closer of the two Dussloreans gained an edge when Eleven stumbled. Just as he reached out, she maneuvered to the side and yanked the serrated rope's excess. Momentum carried him forward, resulting in his body slicing into halves. Legs continued for several seconds before tumbling past his twitching upper body. The Dusslorean's partner stopped a meter short of the jagged finish line.

Eleven panicked to readjust. She flicked the rope, but it stayed in place. As the Dusslorean approached, Eleven moved toward the chain, making full use of the give. Using the opposite end, she whipped the soldier's weapon from his hand.

Bleeding heavily, the Dusslorean thrust Eleven into exposed pipework. She bound her attacker's neck with the rope's slack. The soldier's blood warmed Eleven as his skin shredded and tore. She didn't let go until all manner of life left his distinctly purple eyes.

*Crux.*

Still recovering from her injuries, Eleven had trouble catching her breath. Short bursts of energy resulted in short-lived sprints with staggered walking in-between. She stood on shaky feet as she observed Prwoyn and Crux still at odds.

*I can't call for another… I'm too weak.*

Eleven patted her inner pocket. Taking out the gun from her jacket, she failed to aim when the tremors finally hit. Just as Maggie had predicted.

The sparring Dussloreans took notice of the quakes as well. Uneven terrain left Prwoyn open. Crux kicked in the side of his knee, following with a palm to Prwoyn's chest.

"Let's go," Eleven called.

Distressed nuts and bolts fell to Crux's feet. He gazed up as multi-colored chunks of tubing came down hard.

A hunk of concrete hit Eleven on the top of her skull. The blow dropped her to the floor. Through her doubling eyesight, Eleven found wreckage where Crux had stood only moments ago.

"Crux!"

Eleven wobbled over to free him from the growing pile of rubble. A thrown ax halted her approach. She glowered at Prwoyn. Worse for wear, the pair watched as the quake tore at the waterpark. Sunlight ripped through the roof, the bright beams contrasting with the crudeness of the scene before them.

Multiple obstacles prevented Prwoyn from advancing. Keeping his eyes on Eleven, he drew back in pursuit of cover. Eleven hustled to the now wide opening of the roof. Her gaze alternated between the pile trapping Crux and Prwoyn waiting in the wings.

*He's okay. I just have to get to him before Prwoyn.*

Upheaval lasted minutes. Destruction worsened an already dismal location, making it unrecognizable from its appearance just an hour earlier. Prwoyn glared at the eleventh locator as he cooled his belly on forgotten pipes. He listened to the ground, unfettered by the seismic activity.

When the tremors came to an end, Eleven hurried to Crux. Prwoyn left his shelter. Limping, he pointed his blade toward Eleven. "Ready yourself."

An odd facial tick from the Dusslorean trailed a fleeting glint. Prwoyn's eyes grew wide as his weapon fell from spasming fingers. His legs buckled as he struggled to form a vocal response. He choked on the beginnings of words. As his kneecaps hit cracked concrete, the Dusslorean's head popped off like a champagne cork. Prwoyn's collapse revealed a posed slender figure with slick black hair and deep blue eyes wielding a sword.

*Banaedrut... they found me.*

"No," Eleven said under her breath.

Two other figures came into focus.

*Guardians.*

The Ceruleman conqueror stood and returned his blade to its scabbard. The three soldiers inspected the location, searching for other potential threats.

*Just one Banaedrut... there's still a chance.*

"Exemplary work, Xolin. Trah-Ul will be pleased."

*No.*

Dr. Isaac Kepler emerged from the shadows. "Locator Eleven."

***NO!***

The shocked locator clenched the gun in her left hand. She balled the right to stop it from shaking.

"Let me assure you," Isaac started, "finding you has been quite the undertaking."

Eleven cursed her inability to sense him. She clamped her eyes shut, willing herself to wake.

"You're not here," she mouthed.

*It's just a hallucination.*

The Banaedrut spoke. "She's armed."

*All of it.*

"I see that." Isaac stopped next to the Ceruleman. "Is her memory intact?"

"Which memory would that be, *sir*?" Xolin's smirk deepened with the doctor's disapproval. The Banaedrut turned his attention to Eleven. "We can't know for certain until examination."

Isaac took a step toward Eleven. "Do you know who I am?"

*A bad dream. Worse than any night terror.*

Ignoring the question, Eleven called for another chamber. Anything that would help in her escape. As she feared, nothing presented itself.

"Be cautious," the Banaedrut warned.

Sneering, Isaac advanced. "She won't harm me."

Eleven's knuckles whitened around the gun.

Responding to her discernible hostility, Isaac said, "Designation EH93." On cue, the guardian on his left took aim.

*They carry firearms now?*

The doctor nodded. "Where are we right now?"

*A circle of hell. Question is: which one?*

"Locator Eleven?" Isaac pressed.

The placid Banaedrut mere meters behind Isaac stole her focus. Xolin assessed the locator shrouded in blood and surrounded by bodies of fallen Dussloreans.

"Fascinating, isn't he?" Isaac asked, motioning to the Banaedrut. "Xolin specializes in recovery. He assisted in pinpointing your location."

Xolin quirked his head. "Why isn't she speaking?"

"Leave this to me," Isaac replied.

*Xolin isn't leading this "rescue," Isaac is. That does not soothe me.*

"Drop your weapon. *Now*, Locator Eleven."

Eleven tossed the gun at her feet. Her eyes turned red, yet she kept threatening tears from surfacing.

"Good girl." Isaac stopped within arm's reach.

That's when Eleven saw Crux hiding in a discarded tube to the left.

*The teleporter. It's charged.*

Any hope she had upon that realization was dashed with a closer look at Crux. Both his hands shook around the teleporter. His eyes stuck to Xolin. It wasn't hard for Eleven to read the Dusslorean's lips. He repeated only one word: "No."

When Crux finally looked to Eleven, his expression elicited what she already knew but didn't want to accept.

*I'm going back.*

She stepped forward when Xolin's gaze began following hers.

The doctor dipped his head down. "You're alone?"

*Again.*

Eleven nodded.

"Poor lost girl nearly of heaven." Isaac closed the distance between them. Caressing Eleven's cheek, he continued. "Surrounded by dangers unkno—"

Pulling the nearest lock pick tool from her back pocket, Eleven jabbed the metal hard into Isaac's right eye. "I'm well-versed in the dangers."

She shoved him away.

Isaac wailed as he tumbled to the ground. Writhing in pain, he managed two words. "Take her!"

Designation EH93 shot her right leg. As Eleven fell, the guardians advanced.

"Stand down!"

The guardians looked to Xolin. He held them back with splayed arms.

"Sir?" Designation EH93 asked.

"I said stand down." When neither did as commanded, Xolin announced, "I'm assuming authority."

"What about Dr. Kepler?"

All eyes went to Isaac. His cries had stopped. The locator could still hear the fitful beating of his heart.

"Let him bleed," Xolin commanded. With reservation, the

guardians lowered weapons to their sides.

*I should've killed him.*

"This resembles stories."

Xolin's eyes were set wider than most Cerulemans. His jawline was more prominent. Unlike the Banaedrut Eleven had encountered before, he had an ease to him. As if he didn't have a care in the world.

"Stories of you. The troublesome eleventh locator. I wonder how many are true."

"I'm more than stories."

"Evidently." He kicked Prwoyn's headless corpse. Xolin then considered the Dusslorean bodies. "Tenacious thing, aren't you?"

*He's more talkative than other Banaedrut.*

The Ceruleman soldier approached Eleven. Towering over her, Xolin extended a hand. "Come."

Eleven fixated on his gloved Banaedrut palm.

*"Xolin specializes in recovery."*

*The guardian could've easily shot to kill, yet she didn't.*

"Or do you wish to delay what's inevitable?"

*They don't just need me back.*

Keeping her face emotionless, Eleven reclaimed the gun she had thrown. Her fingers slid against the weapon's grooved grip.

*They want to read me.*

"Locator Eleven?"

*Know who took me. How. Why.*

"Should I refuse?"

Xolin dropped his hand. "I'd advise against it."

"We're not opposed to carrying you, Princess." Designation EH93 stepped forward.

"Hold," Xolin commanded. He looked to the guardian. "And do not threaten her again."

*"Easy decisions are a fallacy."*

Eleven shuffled away from the Banaedrut. Her grip on the gun halted a shiver.

"I take comfort in a light only darkness provides."

Xolin's eyes widened. "What did you say?"

*Maybe they'll have better luck with Four.*

Raising the gun, the three in front of her stiffened. Xolin inched forward. "This is foolish, Eleven."

The locator chuckled.

*This happens my way.*

"What do you hope to accomplish with this—this display, Eleven?"

*My terms.*

Placing the gun underneath her chin, Eleven said, "Absolutely nothing."

"Wait—"

"You're fast," Eleven interrupted. She locked the hammer into place. "But a bullet is still faster."

"I implore you. Trust when I say—you don't want to suffer the consequences."

"Want is irrelevant," she told Xolin. The locator looked to Designation EH93. "Seems you'll have to carry me after all."

Closing her eyes, three pairs of boots crunched under the ground. Eleven pulled the trigger just as the scent of Xolin reached her. As the world around her dimmed, she felt secure in his trembling embrace.

Darkness.

# 24

AN ALARM CLOCK BLARED. A FIST SILENCED IT. THE cool air soothed her pale, exhausted limb. She was secure beneath crisp bedding and pillows. Shades from a window pulled back to reveal morning. Sunshine bounced off the stark walls devoid of personality. A muffled groan emitted from the bed as rhythmic knocking echoed throughout the space.

"Special delivery," said a man from the other side of a door. His cheerfulness did nothing to improve her mood.

The tired woman sighed. "Go away."

Breaching her bedspread surface, the eleventh locator wiped at her face with a heavy palm and worked a hand through knotted hair. Another knock. "It is quite clear I heard you."

*More nightmares.*

Eleven glanced at the barren shelves opposite her. Something teased in her psyche. Images of blood and light flickered.

*Medical will have plenty to say about that.*

Throwing her legs to the side, she stretched upward. Her clock attempted to function despite the damage she had inflicted upon it. Sparks flew from the device. She noticed a bit of blood around the initial crack. The locator grazed fingers over a blank notepad on the table but found no hint of previous scribbles. Her nose crinkled.

"Okay, open up. I'm starting to think you're avoiding me. You wouldn't want me to get a complex, would you?"

Eleven stomped toward the door. The slow undoing of locks added to her aggravation. She opened the door armed with little in way of a wardrobe. "Satisfied?"

"Ah! Christ! You—I—for crying—what are—" Ten stammered. When his words failed him, he presented a covered food tray with a portable resting above it. He averted his gaze. "Breakfast plus today's itinerary, mademoiselle."

His cordiality mitigated her irritation. In a move completely out of character, Eleven pulled him close and wrapped her arms around Ten's neck.

"Uh—"

Eleven sniffled as tears pooled. She buried her head underneath Ten's jaw. His surprise soon gave way to concern. He clumsily balanced the food tray and portable.

"Eleven?"

"Yeah?"

Ten chuckled to himself. "I don't want to alarm you, but… you're hugging me."

"Stranger things have happened," she said through a sad smile.

"True," he replied. "Like the eleventh locator clinging to a ruggedly handsome man while practically naked in full view of passersby."

Eleven avoided his eyes as she released him. She snagged her itinerary. "Must be something in the air."

"Right." Ten wiped at her cheeks. "Those allergies we don't have can be a real bitch."

"You're an idiot."

"And you associate with the likes of said idiot." Ten pinched Eleven's nose. The tenth locator pushed past her. "What's that say about you?"

"Are you joining me?"

"Depends," Ten replied. He scanned Eleven's sparse bookshelves.

"On?"

He blushed. "Whether or not you're gonna put some damn clothes on."

Throbbing temples caused Eleven to hastily drop the portable. She cupped the top of her head.

*This isn't—what's missing—? How can this—breathe!*

Overanalyzing led to a skull-penetrating migraine. Eleven ran her fingertips along her pulsating scalp.

"Come on, talk to me." Ten came back into focus. He watched her closely. "Are all of them like this?"

"All of what?"

"The headaches."

Leaning toward her, Ten placed the back of his hand on Eleven's forehead. Then to the side of her neck. Eleven pushed aside his concern. Tilting her head down, she kicked at the portable near her feet.

"Something's up with you."

"Just headache," Eleven dismissed. "As you said."

"Are the nightmares getting worse?" Ten pocketed his hands.

*You just had to tell him, didn't you?*

Now fully awake, she couldn't look away from him. The hunger begging for consideration didn't matter. Nor the need to review the day's agenda.

"Do I have something on my face?"

Ten's question broke Eleven's trance. "What?"

"I'm being ogled and it's not even noon." Ten's very presence dumbfounded Eleven. She fought back more tears.

"Okay, what's wrong, Eleven?"

"Nothing. I—it's just—" Eleven stopped.

Wiping her cheek with his thumb, Ten asked, "Did something happen?"

"No."

*Right?*

"I'm taking you to the doc. Get dressed."

Eleven stopped Ten's determined footsteps. "You're overreacting."

"Yeah, well you're... *under*reacting. Wait, is that a word?"

"Ten," Eleven started. She plopped onto her bed. "I'm just—"

*Choose your words carefully. You know how he worries.*

"—*tired*. I didn't sleep well, and I was roused by a very nosy but thoughtful friend at an ungodly hour."

Ten motioned to Eleven's broken clock. "It's past ten."

*Are you trying to convince him you're all right . . . or yourself?*

"I'll walk down with you," he added.

"I've got a mission tomorrow. Safe to say I'm already on the books today."

"But that's just the standard bologna."

*Unlike the others, this isn't just an act for him. He cares.*

"I'll tell them."

"Promise?" Ten asked with an arched brow.

"I promise."

His tone lightened. "Few things are as thrilling as being poked and prodded, I know. Hell, I'm starting to think I've got a thing for lab coats."

"I needn't know the particulars of your nether region stimuli."

An overhead alert cut off the beginnings of Ten's no doubt witty reply. "Damn it." He walked toward the door. "I forgot I've got a briefing with the Great and Powerful after training.

I should go."

The feeling of unease resurfaced in full force.

"When do you leave tomorrow?" Ten asked.

"In the afternoon, I think."

"You think?" Ten moved several strands of curls from Eleven's face. His touch eased the looming tension. "What happened to that steel trap memory of yours?"

"Apparently still asleep."

Ten frowned but released Eleven. "Dinner tonight?"

"Yes."

"It's a date," Ten said. He stopped before opening the door. "You better tell the doctor. I have ways of finding out if you didn't."

"Pleading and bribery?"

"Hey, can't knock it if it works, right?"

Eleven sighed. "It's unlikely they could do anything."

"They've got all those fancy degrees. Several, in fact. Doctors are the first ones to say as much." Ten shifted. "They could surprise you and come up with a solution." He opened the door. Strumming his fingers along the doorframe, Ten said, "You promised, remember? That's on the record."

"You're behind schedule," Eleven replied. She waved Ten off. "Get out of here."

"Yeah, yeah. Later, gloomy girl."

• • • • • • • • • • •

MAYBE THERE WON'T BE TIME TO TELL THEM ABOUT *the drea—No, Eleven. Don't back down.*

After inhaling the breakfast Ten had brought her, Eleven spent the remainder of her morning going over checklists for the mission ahead. Everything seemed standard.

The locator waited until the last possible moment to leave for her appointment. No matter the day or the reason, the medical facilities always unsettled Eleven.

With wet hair, she walked briskly down one of many identical hallways. She ignored the unsubtle glares and whispers directed toward her. Eleven was more than accustomed to being ogled at this point in her career.

*Philistines.*

Distracted, Eleven ran into a tall figure as she made a sharp corner turn. She backed away, blinking in the aftermath of her negligence.

"Watch where you're going," Eleven snapped. "Is that so difficult?"

"Apologies, I—"

"Just move."

Tilting her head down, Eleven began to pass. A hand gripped the top of her shoulder, stopping her movement.

*This is what abrasiveness earns you: confrontation.*

"You."

The surprise in the man's voice and gentle touch forced Eleven to face him. A Ceruleman in civilian clothes peered down at her. The hallway's lighting made his sapphire eyes almost black.

Seeing her puzzlement, he said, "A hit-and-run can lead to the death penalty, even on base. Are you willing to take the risk?"

"That ordinance is exclusive to vehicular collisions."

His grin grew wide. He combed his black hair back with confidence. "Yes. That would be the joke, Locator Eleven."

"Do we know one another?"

"Strictly by reputation."

"Well," Eleven started.

His friendliness seemed genuine. Nothing in his mannerisms or speech suggested otherwise. Still, Eleven scowled.

"Well?" he pressed.

"What?"

"You were saying?"

*What was I saying?*

"I—I really must be going."

"I'm keeping you," he said. The Ceruleman stepped away from Eleven. "My apologies." Before Eleven could respond, he continued down the hall.

His brisk steps had him disappearing into the crowd in a matter of seconds. Eleven's stoicism returned as she again took notice of those evaluating her.

*Forget him.*

• • • • • • • • • • •

ELEVEN SAT IN THE MIDDLE OF A COLORLESS LABO-ratory. She stared at her etched cuticles, twiddling her thumbs now and again.

"Good afternoon," said a soft, female voice. The petite blonde woman approached Eleven. "So sorry I'm late. Pleasure to see you, as always, Locator Eleven."

The doctor flicked a switch behind Eleven's headrest. The routine required little in way of instruction.

"How are we feeling?"

"Fine, Dr. Edwards."

The physician nodded. "Happy to hear it. Still having head-aches?"

"Yes."

"That's no fun," Dr. Edwards said through a pout. "Is there anything I should know before we kick things off today? Changes in vision? Memory lapses? Loss of sleep?"

*Tell her.*

Her mouth agape, Eleven stopped for what felt like an eter-nity. Eleven couldn't bring herself to mention the nightmares. The fever dreams that often woke her in a cold sweat.

*You promised Ten.*

"No," Eleven answered. "Fortunately."

"Excellent."

Eleven's seat reclined fully. The lab's one exit locked as overhead lights faded to black. A familiar blue illuminated both of them.

*Promises can be broken.*

"Okay. We have some lost time to make up for, don't we?" Dr. Edwards flicked a switch before looking down into Eleven's hesitant hazel eyes. "Let's get started."

## THE END

# ACKNOWLEDGEMENTS

One of Few started out as a reoccurring dream. A dream that plagued me as a teenager and didn't truly leave my subconscious until I started this journey.

Whether you had your hands in the creation, read a draft, or simply showed your support, I owe you. Big time.

Let's be honest, some of you are just wondering if you're going to see your name. Well, those brave enough to read the afterword.

Acknowledgements are a lot like wedding invitations. You don't want to leave anyone out! I apologize in advance if you're not mentioned.

Don't take it personally—I see you there, taking it personally, girl who kept my coffee fresh at the café that one day my internet was down.

Readers are important. Why? Well, you know, books. They need people willing to jump into their little worlds. That you spent time in my little pocket universe is pretty damn cool. Hopefully, we'll meet again down the road.

I had given up on the idea of writing outside the world of scripts. I hate to think where I'd be if you hadn't needed a narrator for The Thunderbird Legacy, Erin. You've shown me that a good support system and tenacity can get you far. I'll always be grateful to you.

Ellie Ann, you took a chance on a first-time writer by tackling the creative. Thank you for helping steer this baby in the right direction.

Sara, you were so much more than a tech editor on this fine-looking baby. You were my soundboard. And, often, the human equivalent of a straightjacket. Which is a good thing.

I looked at all the different ways to thank you, Stephen. No matter how I phrased it, the words still came up short. You make me want to be the best version of myself while remaining true. This story wouldn't exist without you.

# ABOUT THE AUTHOR

Terri Doty is a graduate of Tarrant County College. Her degree in Radio/Television Broadcasting and Film led her to a career in voiceover. She currently lives in the Lone Star State with her husband and their chocolate lab mix overlord Zoey.